UNMASKING THE SILVER HEIRESS

THE SILVER LEAF SEDUCTIONS - BOOK 1

AVA DEVLIN

Unmasking the Silver Heiress

The Silver Leaf Seductions - Book 1

Ava Devlin

Printed in the United States of America

First Printing, 2020

http://avadevlin.com

Contact the author at ava@avadevlin.com

Cover art by BZN Studio Designs

http://covers.bzndesignstudios.com

Copyediting by Claudette Cruz

https://www.theeditingsweetheart.com/

Flip to the end of the book for FREE bonus material

 Created with Vellum

PROLOGUE

My Dearest Brother,

Please read the entirety of this letter before you leave your quarters this morning. For my sake and yours, it is best that you get all of the relevant information directly from me, ahead of speaking to anyone else.

Firstly, and most importantly, you should know that I have left Somerton with Nathaniel Atlas. By the time you read this letter, we will already be thoroughly entrenched in our journey north toward Newcastle-on-Tyne. The purpose of this flight was not to elope, but of course an elopement must now occur to maintain propriety.

I have told you more than once that you sleep far too heavily and that you ought to mention it to a doctor. I know this might not be the appropriate time to nag you about it, but for God's sake, Peter. I intend to slip this message directly into your hands tonight and I know for a certainty that you will not stir. It concerns me!

No matter.

Last night you slept through a great deal of chaos. An intruder broke into Somerton and waited in the shadows of Lord Alex's bedroom. His search of that room turned up just as little as mine did (and yours and Nathaniel's, for that matter). So, he waited for Alex's return, threatened him for the location of what he brought home from Oxford, and then clubbed him on the head.

Alex Somers is perfectly well. I know you will have shot up onto your feet at this, but I implore you, Brother, please sit back down. There is more you must know before you leave your bedchamber.

I am certain that I know who took the valise from Somerton and what route he is taking to deliver it to his employer. I considered waking you to come with me, but I realized that I did not wish to leave Mr. Atlas behind lest he confront Alex Somers about the whole affair. I know you were just as startled as I when Atlas suggested having Somers injured, and since he seems to have no qualms with such measures, I thought it best to remove him entirely while we attempt to resolve the situation.

Further, I do not wish to see my friend Gloriana married to a possible murderer. I am far better equipped to manage a dangerous spouse than she is, whether you believe it or not. I remind you that I have been an agent of the Silver Leaf for far longer than you, and have never been caught, despite turning quite a lot of sensitive information over to concerned parties.

Atlas has seemed frantic about the failure of his first mission, and rightfully so. A recruit who cannot complete his initial task is rarely retained. Why he is so determined to participate in a minor operation like ours remains a mystery, but I have leveraged this knowledge to remove both Alex and Gloriana from any danger he might present.

Perhaps least relevant of all, I did not wish to die a spinster nor settle for the type of man who might have begrudgingly accepted me. I do not expect to have a fairy tale life of romance with the spouse I have chosen, but it will set me up nicely for a position in Society to be respected, not pitied. Our parents will be thrilled, of course, and Aunt Zelda will come to see the logic in it, in time.

I know you too well to request your immediate forgiveness, for I know you will be too angry to give it. I only ask that your frustrations with me be short-lived. I ask that sense and reason, which I know you possess in spades, lead you to realize that what I've done is already done, and cannot be improved by discontent. It is what I want. Beyond that, and perhaps more importantly, it will make life better (and safer) for a great many people for whom we both care deeply.

I beseech you to manage the events following my departure with care. There is no use in attempting to come after me, as I have already penned a letter to Lady Somers alerting her to what I've done. You cannot fix or undo this, Peter, and so please accept it, and trust me.

Once we have retrieved the parcel, I will insist we return immediately to London. If I do not find you there, I will leave another letter for you. Do not worry, please. I am well.

Your devoted sister,

Nell

CHAPTER 1

*E*leanor Applegate was in over her head.

Perhaps such a thing was less than shocking for a woman of such modest stature. All the same, it was not a feeling she enjoyed. Nell had never felt quite so small in her life as she did in this particular moment, and she had spent a lifetime feeling small.

When this had begun, she had felt ten feet tall. She had marched into a scheme of her own devising with her eyes open, heart racing, and hot blood rushing in her veins. She had been filled with the certainty that she was grasping her future with both hands, that if she embarked on this adventure, she would be taking the first step in becoming the woman she had always dreamed of being.

She should have known that such a thing was ridiculous, that on the other side of her plot, she would still be nothing more than mousy, disappointing Nell Applegate. The only thing she'd accomplished these last days was betraying one of her dearest friends and securing an unenthusiastic bride-groom in the process.

This queasy twist of regret was not how she imagined she might feel, alone in a room with the most beautiful man she'd ever laid eyes upon. But here they were, sprawled on the floor of a ramshackle inn on the Scots border, caught in a pained silence instead of a passionate embrace.

What had she been thinking?

She sighed, rubbing the exhaustion from her eyes. She knew very well what she'd been thinking. From the moment she'd pressed the first note into his hand at Almack's half a year ago and had felt herself frozen in place by those chameleon's hazel eyes, she'd been fighting an impossible, persistent obsession. Nothing she had done, no amount of reasoning with herself, had been successful at stamping out her shameful desires.

Now she had him, didn't she? So why did it feel so terrible?

The moon was hiding behind a heavy layer of clouds outside, leaving little but the sad strings of light emitting from two greasy candles on either side of the room. Even her shadow looked small, she thought, and she felt even smaller. The shadow of her companion slanted across the floor like a towering giant, ready to stomp its tiny adversary to dust.

Their mission had technically been a successful one. A valise, battered and nondescript, was currently lying open on the uneven wooden floor between them, all its contents sprawled out on the threadbare rug at the foot of the bed. It was those contents, or the lack thereof, that were the problem.

"I can't believe it," she muttered, too exhausted to even lift her head to face him, her foot nudging the mismatched stack of books and papers scattered in front of her. "After everything, we still don't have it."

Nathaniel Atlas was silent, though Nell imagined she could feel the waves of cold fury coming off him all the same. Was his anger at their failure or at being stuck with her, she wondered. Were those eyes shifting and shimmering with the colors of his rage? What sort of man would he be when he was angry? The fact that she did not know only twisted her gut tighter.

Again, technically, she had been telling the truth. The thief was indeed who she suspected, and was easily found on the road to Newcastle. They had successfully retrieved the valise before it could reach its destination, absconding from the inn where they'd taken it before its disappearance could be noted. They had the valise. The useless, useless valise, filled with nothing but the remnants of a middling student's final days at Oxford.

Technicalities were not much comfort in the grand scheme of things.

Mr. Atlas would have a choice to make now, depending on his perception of whether or not Nell had held up her end of their bargain. Whether or not he chose to actually marry her, her reputation had been utterly and irrevocably soiled by this caper. His had too, she knew. He had intended to take a different bride entirely.

"What happens now?" he finally said, pushing himself to his feet in a smooth single motion. His voice was mild, unreadable, which was somehow more unsettling than outright anger. He paced to the door and poured himself a glass of water, his movements as silent and graceful as a panther's. "We still have no idea what happened to the parcel."

"No, we don't," she replied softly, squeezing her eyes shut in an effort to stamp down the horrible roils that rose in her stomach. "I suppose the best we can do is return to London with utmost haste and report what has happened. There were three of us present for it all, so there need not be any concern of duplicity."

He gave a humorless laugh, running a hand through his glossy brown hair. She had never seen him so disheveled. While a part of seeing him thus was certainly thrilling in a base way, she could not properly enjoy it in the present circumstances.

"Duplicity is rather the point, isn't it?" he said, setting the empty glass back onto the table with a sharp clatter.

She did not disagree.

"It is too late to do anything tonight," he continued. "We can make a quick stop in the morning, have marriage papers drawn up, and then head back to London as fast as possible. I suppose I can only pray that this hasn't completely destroyed my repute and potential for further involvement in the cause."

"It hasn't," she whispered.

"How could you know that?" he snapped, a hint of fire on the edge of his voice. "How is someone like you involved in such things in the first place? It is unseemly!"

"I just know," she said, finally lifting her chin to meet his eye. "I cannot explain until we get to London. I'm sorry."

"Yes, yes, it's all secrets and subterfuge. I understand," he muttered, pacing over to the corner of the bed and plopping down on the poorly stuffed mattress. "It is too late to second-guess ourselves now."

"Peter will likely have returned ahead of us," Nell said, still watching her soon-to-be husband from the floor. "He may report that we went in pursuit of the parcel, which certainly will buy us some credence. Lady Hansen's man will be panicked at having lost the valise, likely still assuming the item of value was parceled inside. Perhaps at this juncture, we can play a bluff for the same leverage we originally hoped to attain."

"A bluff?" he repeated. "What if Alex Somers still has it?"

"He doesn't." Nell sighed, frustration evident in her voice. "You said yourself that he took the parcel by mistake. If Elizabeth had been a little more verbose in her message to you when it went missing in the first place, perhaps we would have had more success in finding it."

"Verbose." He grimaced. "Doesn't that rather defeat the purpose of coded communication?"

Nell sighed, shaking her head. "Maybe we missed something? Tell me again exactly how the item moved from place to place."

"There is little point," he said. "We might as well get some sleep. We'll bring the valise south with us, and hand it off as we found it. What harm could it do?"

She nodded, busying herself with replacing the contents of the valise, perhaps a sight more neatly than they'd found them. Her hands were steady, at the very least.

Nathaniel couldn't see how badly her nerves had come undone.

They had shared a bed for the last two nights, in the absolute loosest sense of the expression. Both had remained fully clothed with separate blankets keeping each one warm. Atlas made such a point of curling himself onto the farthest reach of the mattress that Nell felt she could have sprawled out like some sort of hedonist and never touched him.

She told herself that he was preserving decency, but deep down she suspected he was repulsed by the idea that she was to be his bedfellow for the rest of their natural lives. It was understandable, after all, wasn't it? Up until a few nights ago, he had thought his future bride was going to be Gloriana Blakely, a celebrated beauty, so stunning men often stopped dead in their tracks when she passed by.

Nell could hardly resent his disappointment, could she? Surely it was rational. She was no great beauty and had never entertained hopes of becoming one. She was, however, shrewd and smart and better connected than he could possibly imagine.

She would not be as vulnerable as Glory would have been, married to such a man. She had already seen the darkness he hid beneath his exterior of politician's charm and carefully styled beauty. There was no devastation awaiting her on the other side of the altar, when a man's true colors must eventually show themselves.

This was for the best. For everyone.

He would come to see the sense in this union, she told

herself. He would have to, even if it took a while. What did time matter anyway when marriage was such a very, very long affair?

CHAPTER 2

*I*t wasn't the wedding he'd imagined for himself. That much was certain.

Rather than a resplendent bride, glowing in fine couture and bright with elation, Nathaniel Atlas found himself standing across from an exhausted, unwashed slip of a girl, whose boxy, unfashionable dress was streaked with the muck of their journey. The dark circles under her eyes were magnified behind her spectacles, which reflected back to him just how weary he looked as well.

It had been the right choice, he told himself. It had been the sensible choice, given the circumstances. Everything he'd done over the years, all the careful planning and work and sacrifice, would have meant nothing if he'd botched his first mission with the Silver Leaf Society, thus destroying his chances of ever truly joining their ranks.

Yes, his plans had included a very different bride. He had spent most of the last Season and a fair amount of this autumn courting the exquisitely beautiful Gloriana Blakely, a woman whose reputation for rejecting eligible bachelors was overtaken only by admiration for her social graces. She would have made the ideal partner as he navigated the viper pit that was High Society.

In truth, he imagined that Glory herself had probably experienced something less than heartbreak upon learning of his departure. It had been clear to most of the guests at Somerton over the last few months that her interests had diverted, rather obviously, to Alex Somers.

It didn't bother Nathaniel. He hadn't been particularly enamored of the girl, despite her looks. He wanted a wife to assist in his plans for the future, and Miss Blakely would have done just that, regardless of her romantic predilections. They would have suited one another.

Now ... well, now he was married to a woman who would be far more at home in a stack of books than she ever would be amongst the *ton*.

He supposed he shouldn't be terribly surprised. Fate had shattered his plans many times before, after all. The important thing to remember was that he always managed to find his way back onto the path he'd intended, despite all manner of surprises and obstacles.

This particular challenge wasn't even a terrible one. He would buy his dowdy wife a cottage wherever she liked and tuck her away with her books. She would be content while he carried on with his business. If necessary, they could hash out further stipulations and details as the need arose. Surely such an arrangement would satisfy them both.

He had barely slept for the last several nights. Between the mounting panic over his failure at his first mission and the distraction of sharing a bed with a woman for the first time in eons, it had been all he could do to curl onto his side and squeeze his eyes shut in lieu of sleep.

She was hardly a temptress, of course. The poor thing had been stiff as a plank of wood on her own side of the mattress, gripping the blankets at her chin. He got the impression that she didn't sleep much either, and that her wide gray eyes spent hours affixed on the alien ceilings above them rather than closed in restful slumber. He wasn't sure if her equal state of concern was a comfort or salt in the wound.

It was a little of both, he decided.

In the haze of his fatigue, it seemed to him that he blinked and suddenly a marriage license was being proffered at him to sign, which he did with markedly less finesse than his signature usually entailed. That was appropriate, he thought. This whole damned event was the opposite of finesse.

The girl, for her part, signed in neat little letters and handed the pen over to the witnesses, two complete strangers, who would seal the legality on their union. She did not tremble or quake or shed tears at the disappointment of it all, nor did she frown at the trappings of the venue.

It occurred to him that perhaps this girl thought she was getting the better end of their bargain. Maybe she was, in the grand scheme of things. He hadn't paid her much mind prior to the necessity of a shared mission. He gathered she must be somewhat of a wallflower, who likely was not entertaining many marriage prospects.

It was a good thing, he reasoned. Much better to have a

happy bride than one with discontent. If she was satisfied merely with the status of wife, he was happy to hand over his bachelorhood.

After all, Nathaniel had spent his entire life working toward a single goal, one which he had come uncomfortably close to utterly, permanently losing access to.

Little Eleanor Applegate was going to bring him directly to his desired destination, whether she realized it or not.

MUCH OF THE first day in the carriage had been passed in mutual slumber. While their plight had not been wholly resolved, they had reached enough of a conclusion to allow for a bit of rest.

Nate's dreams were a muddle of memories related to their current situation. One moment he was slipping into a corner of Almack's to unseal a letter bound in silver wax, his hands shaking with anticipation. The next, he was approached by a veiled woman as the clocks chimed midnight in the run-down London neighborhood of Seven Dials. Before she could speak, he found himself at Somerton, digging through the belongings of Alex Somers, and then in a blink, on the road with his new wife. On and on it went, no sooner ending than it would all begin again.

It didn't make for a very restorative type of sleep. He found himself jerked awake more than once by some latent concern that was long past by now, replaced by a newer, keener, more desperate fear or ten. In those few moments when he was pulled back into the waking world, he never saw a difference in his wife's reclining posture, her hands folded under her cheek as she was embraced by some perfectly serene flavor of sleep.

Enviable.

They stopped twice that first day. The first time, neither Nate nor Eleanor could be stirred from their rest, not even by the temptation of a hot meal as the horses were changed. The second time, many hours later, they begrudgingly dragged themselves from the carriage and into a way station, partially by the promise of food and a bed, but ultimately convinced by the fact that their driver also required some sleep if they were ever to make it to London.

He had hoped to drive through that first night, as to avoid any connotations or expectations befitting what was technically their wedding night.

He had opted to bathe before sleeping, and to his relief, he found his new bride had returned deeply into her own slumber before he could join her. He had pulled a pair of fresh trousers on, though they were not ideal for sleeping, just to enhance a sense of propriety onto the evening. When he found her dead asleep instead of rabidly awaiting a ravishing, he felt rather sheepish about the whole thing.

She looked so very, very small curled on the bed, blanket trailing off her body and pooling onto the floor next to her. This wasn't some conniving social climber, entrapping him for her own ends. This was a young girl who had somehow become involved in dangerous matters that someone should have shielded her from. If not that brother of hers, then a father, surely?

Those smudged spectacles of hers were discarded on the table next to her pillow, their silver frames gleaming in the light of the candle she'd left lit, as though she had not intended to fall asleep just yet. She had pulled some pins from her hair, he assumed, judging from the little stack of gleaming needle-like objects next to her spectacles. However, her dark hair was still bundled up over her head, as though it had become permanently affixed in its lopsided bun, pins or none.

He repressed the urge to sigh, opting instead to towel off his wet hair and find a shirt to sleep in. He wished to high heaven he had requested a second room. He'd sleep much easier in a bed by himself, especially after wasting all that needless worry over what she might want from him on their wedding night.

Why was he so adverse to the idea, anyhow? He frowned, rubbing the bridge of his nose. He was thinking like a spinster aunt, not a bridegroom. Surely that was the result of pragmatism, some deep instinctual reason that had kicked itself into play through the fatigue, despite the lag in his rationale.

It wasn't that he'd made any particular choice to be celibate for so long. It had simply evolved as a matter of necessity, with women fairly low on his list of important tasks that must be conquered. In the years of establishing himself as a competent statesman, a cunning ambassador, and a charming party guest, there had scarcely been time to breathe, let alone take a mistress.

Of course, there had been dalliances here and there in his youth, and there had been more than one proposition from some of the more daring ladies he'd encountered in London ballrooms. Ultimately, the risks involved in most potential trysts had outweighed the appeal of momentary satisfaction, and so he'd somehow found himself on an embarrassingly long hiatus from the pleasures of the flesh.

Perhaps he was frigid, he thought unhappily. Could men be frigid? Surely he wasn't strictly frigid if he'd found himself tempted by sharing a bed with the likes of Eleanor Applegate, even in her state of miserable exhaustion! Still, he hadn't exactly needed his full power of will to resist her these past few nights either.

He shook his head, tugging a fresh shirt over his damp torso and turning back to look at her again.

Eventually, he would have to claim his rights as a husband. It was only that she looked so delicate. He didn't relish the idea of hurting such a tiny woman, especially if breaking the dam on his long-neglected desires drove him into an animalistic frenzy.

Had he brokered the same concerns about Miss Blakely? She was not quite so petite as Eleanor, but she was also a slender little thing. Strangely, he found that he hadn't much considered her at all in this fashion, nor had he felt concerned about losing control of his baser impulses at any juncture.

He was just tired, he decided. Unbelievably tired. Once his head had cleared of fatigue, he would be much better equipped to manage the various challenges ahead of him. Once he was thinking clearly, surely the prospect of bedding a willing wife would not even brush the top of his list of concerns.

Still, he took care when climbing into bed next to her. He pulled the blanket up from the floor and draped it over her as she took steady little breaths, her eyelashes fluttering now and then in her sleep.

He tried first to sleep on his back, then rolled onto his side, facing away from the warmth alongside him. He grimaced in embarrassment at the way his body reacted to her.

It was simply a physical reaction, he told himself, natural as the sunrise. He reminded himself again that this was simply not a problem worth his concern.

His dreams begged to differ.

CHAPTER 3

*N*ell had always been an early riser, but opening her eyes of her own accord before the sun had even crested the horizon was unnatural, even for her. She had lost all sense of time over the last days, and when she awoke, she thought for the briefest moment that she was back in her own bed, alone, and that nothing at all was amiss.

She supposed such disorientation was, at the very least, a sign of very good sleep.

Everything ached. She had been sleeping in the stiff traveling dress she'd pulled on at Somerton for several nights now, her hair coiled tightly against her scalp and secured with sharp little pins. She wanted nothing more than to shed everything and stretch out in a hot, soapy bath for several hours.

She bit her lip, glancing over at the sliver of early light that was peeking through the curtains of their room. No matter how tempting, it was best not to wet her hair, for they would have to be on the road again before it could dry, and autumn had already brought the temperature down to a brisk chill. She didn't fancy catching ill, especially for nothing more than a spot of impatience. Perhaps she could just wash from the neck down, if the innkeeper was willing to heat her some water?

Her eyes fell upon Mr. Atlas, asleep next to her with an arm thrown up over his eyes. She felt momentarily paralyzed by the sight of him.

That's your husband, said a little voice in her head. *You are Mrs. Atlas now.*

It was almost too much to believe. If she hadn't been in such a state of grime and discomfort, she'd have pinched herself just to ensure this wasn't some wild fantasy found only in her dreams.

There he was, though, dressed in a loose white shirt over plain buckskin trousers. His collarbones and the top of his well-muscled chest were on display, with no jacket, waistcoat, nor cravat obscuring the sight of his magnificent torso in naught but the thin, billowing shirt. She longed to reach over and touch the skin there, to test the texture of the light brown curls that peeked out from just above his heart.

He was nigh unrecognizable in sleep, she thought, without his careful consideration of how to present himself in a given time and place. In sleep, he was simply himself, with no artifice to shape him. He had a long, straight nose and full lips that formed a perfect cupid's bow, especially parted as they were just now while he slept. He was so beautiful, it almost hurt her to look at him. He reminded her of the rows of men gracing palace halls, each made of polished white marble and preserved through the centuries on merit of their perfection.

His hair was freshly washed, fluffy and mussed as it had dried in during the night. Any aspect of Nathaniel Atlas that had not been primed to perfection was a rare pleasure to behold. She would have never guessed that his hair was capable of frizz or had a hint of natural curl. It fell over his brow in a gentle wave of sable brown, which he must smooth into submission before appearing in public. She wanted to touch this too. It looked so very soft.

She grimaced, a sudden realization occurring to her that she did not present nearly so appealing a visage for him to awake to. She imagined if he suddenly awoke, just now, and saw her bedraggled, wide-eyed staring, he would recoil in horror.

Not wishing to test that particular hypothesis, she flung her legs over the side of the bed and into her slippers and hastened down the stairs in search of the innkeeper.

The family that owned the inn had already begun to move around downstairs, with a fire blazing in the central hearth and the beginnings of breakfast creating tempting aromas that swept in from the kitchen. Nell stopped a serving maid to request bath water be brought up and some soap leaves if they had any to spare. The maid nodded, her eyes widening a little as she took note of the wrinkled dress that Nell had slept in.

"Will you be requiring a laundress as well, miss?"

"Unfortunately, we will not have time." Nell sighed. "But thank you for the offer."

She hurried back up to their rooms before anyone else could see her in such disarray.

It wasn't vanity. Not completely, anyway. It was unlikely that she'd see anyone she knew at a coaching inn in the country, but on the off chance that she did, she did not wish to be recognized. It was essential that she and Nathaniel reach London before any word of their elopement could reach the scandal sheets.

Aunt Zelda would never forgive her if a competing printing house broke the story first. After all, Mr. Atlas was an extremely eligible bachelor, and she was ... not one of the obvious contenders for his affections, to say the very least. Perhaps bringing home a morsel of profitable gossip, even at her own expense, would soften the blow of what she had done.

In her letter to Lady Somers, Nell had explained that she wished to reach her family before they could find out about her elopement through the rumor mill. Considering Lady Somers had once been the darling of the scandal sheets herself, Nell hoped that this request was in and of itself enough to delay the news coming south ahead of their arrival.

She noted with a wry twist of her lips that all three suitcases had been brought up to their rooms from the carriage: her own, Nathaniel's, and the one they'd stolen from Alex Somers.

She had packed so hastily that she wasn't even sure what she would find in her little valise. To her relief, there were two clean shifts, two clean dresses, and a simple bonnet which she could use to cover her hair until she had time to properly wash it. She had failed to bring anything to read, however, which was an unusual oversight, even under duress. Hopefully Peter would bring the rest of her things with him to London.

As the tub was being filled, she opened Alex's suitcase again and rifled through his school things. She told herself she was just looking for something to read, and yet still felt disappointed that the parcel they were after had not miraculously appeared since the last time she had looked inside.

Most of the books were dry, academic reading, but she did find a penny novel in the back that looked reasonably entertaining. It was the sort of thing Peter would have called lowbrow rubbish.

The wooden bathtub turned out to be little more than a very large bucket, and so not nearly as relaxing as Nell had anticipated. She had to kneel inside, and the water only barely reached her chest. She pondered that if Nathaniel had used this same tub the night before, it would have only come to his waist.

She shook her head and quickly instructed herself to stop imagining him undressed and standing in the tub as a blush crept to her cheeks. It was far more sensible to occupy herself with resolving the myriad challenges in front of them as she washed the dust of the road from her skin than to moon over the man she'd just trapped in marriage.

She still wished she had time to attend to her hair. It wasn't completely awful when twisted back and pinned tight into a bun, but she wanted nothing more than to feel truly clean after the past few days. She hated the sensation of a greasy scalp and disliked how much darker her hair appeared when it was dirty. It was uninspiring hair at the best of times, and so suffered greatly from any small disadvantage.

All the same, the soapy scrubbing and clean, fresh clothes made a world of difference. Her mood felt lighter, her ideas clearer, and her confidence perhaps a little more steady. She tucked away the soiled clothing in her valise and snapped it shut, ready to continue with their journey.

As Aunt Zelda always said, the only path worth dwelling upon is the one that goes forward.

THE FIRST TWO hours on the road that morning were had in complete silence. Nathaniel seemed lost in his thoughts and, not wishing to incite a conversation she could not carry, Nell attempted to bury herself in the novel she'd found. She realized, after rereading the first page for the third time, that perhaps the reason she hadn't packed any books for this trip was because she did not currently have the capacity to enjoy them.

She contented herself for a time with watching the scenery unfold from the window. Autumn was one of the most beautiful times of the year, after all, and the foliage was truly spectacular in the midlands, with all of the forested enclaves and ivy-covered villages along the way. She had grown up just west of London, in the city of Winchester, before being sent to Bath-Spa for finishing school. Of the three cities she'd spent time in, none had been what anyone could describe as wild, all with more in the way of stone and brick than the reach of Mother Nature. The green spaces she was accustomed to were all manicured lawns and trimmed topiaries, not this wild gnarl of an untamed wood.

She had always imagined that when she was grown, she would be able to explore the whole of England, searching for the perfect home, until she found a place that suited her best. She had never considered how little choice most women have in these matters, nor that she would be tied to wherever her eventual spouse held property. For that matter, she had no idea where Nathaniel Atlas lived when he wasn't required in London or abroad on official business.

She frowned, turning toward her new husband with this sudden thought, only to find him watching her intently. His changeable eyes looked almost the color of a deep merlot in the afternoon light, and they did not dart away when she met them, but rather held her gaze as though his curiosities had not yet been satisfied.

"Something amiss?" he asked after a moment, perfectly poised and controlled with this question. He showed nothing of the man at rest she'd seen before sunrise. His hair was oiled and combed back, a cravat knotted at his throat, and waistcoat tailored to his pleasing frame. If he knew that she'd seen him without his armor this morning, then it must not have troubled him, for he had returned seamlessly to the man to whom she was accustomed.

"I was just wondering where you live, when you are not in London or abroad," she replied softly. "It has occurred to me that I know very little about you, aside from details learned by reputation."

This seemed to amuse him, the corners of his lips curling up as she spoke. "I have often thought the same of you, Miss Applegate."

"I am an Applegate no longer," she reminded him, tilting her head. "I am your wife."

"So you are," he agreed. "Shall I call you Mrs. Atlas, then? Or perhaps simply Eleanor? Using your Christian name feels improper, somehow. As you said, we are not very well acquainted."

"You may call me Nell, if you like," she answered, then added after a moment of hesitation, "Nathaniel."

His teeth flashed, his smile fully formed now. "All right, then. Nell. I haven't lived much of anywhere permanently since leaving school. I own a home in Marylebone, which I use when Parliament is in session and between the various trips I've undertaken at the behest of the Crown. While abroad, I simply rent a suitable space for the duration of my stay."

"But surely you originated somewhere other than London," she persisted.

"My parents died when I was very young," he replied easily, shrugging as though it was no matter. "After that, I was with relatives for a time and then sent to school. I'm afraid I'm quite without origin, my dear."

She did not know how to reply to such a revelation. Of course, she should have known that his parents were no longer living, else they would likely play as large a part in Society as their son. She could not imagine what childhood might have been like without her parents, flawed as they were. Living with an expansive, boisterous family, not to mention one that considered Winchester baked into their very marrow, was second nature to her. It was disturbing to think of what life might be like without a place to call home nor parents to make it so.

"I'm so very sorry to hear that," she managed, after a moment. "No one should lose their parents so young."

The smile slipped from his face, his expression turning thoughtful or perhaps even surprised. "Life is often harsh," he responded. "I imagine a woman involved in the ruthless necessity of spycraft would know that better than most."

"Spycraft! Our work is hardly so glamorous or demanding," she answered with a little smile. "In fact, I was genuinely surprised that you reacted favorably to our invitation."

He raised his well-groomed eyebrows, but did not otherwise address this confession. Instead, he leaned into the carriage wall and studied her for a moment, as though he were deliberating on the best question to ask her. Nell found such scrutiny unnerving, but did her best to sit still, hoping against hope that whatever he found while examining her was satisfactory.

"We are now man and wife," he continued. "Surely such titles allow for a greater degree of intimacy? I should like to know how you came to be involved with the Silver Leaf Society in the first place. You hardly seem old enough to have been recruited, much less to be considered a seasoned agent."

"Well, that's quite a leap from asking whence a person hails," Nell said with a frown. "I did promise you that all would become apparent once we reached London."

"We are at least two days from London, Nell," he said, her name rolling off his tongue in a way that made her shiver. "I do not like to go into situations for which I am not properly prepared."

She took a deep breath, unsure where to even begin to explain her situation to someone who knew nothing. "Do you recall when I gave you the invitation to meet with Lady Silver last spring?"

"Naturally."

"Tell me what happened after that. It will be helpful to me to know what information you already possess before I attempt to inundate you with more."

Again he flashed his teeth at her, as though this answer pleased him in some way. "All right, I will play this game. The letter you gave me instructed me to dress like a laborer, carry nothing of significant value, and appear at the Swan's Tooth Public House in Seven Dials at a given time and date. As the rumors had suggested, Lady Silver arrived wearing a veil and seemed well enough known to the patrons of this pub that they did not give her a second glance."

"A veil," Nell repeated. "She does have a fondness for dramatics. So you are saying that you were aware of the Silver Leaf Society prior to recruitment?"

"Oh yes." He nodded. "I had been seeking out an introduction for some time. I am familiar with a great deal of shadow dealings in Britain as a matter of professional necessity, of course, but yours is the only one I have ever sought to join."

Why? she wanted to demand. *What are you after?*

Instead, she asked, "Lady Silver gave you an assignation that night?"

"Indeed she did. I was given the first stage of what she called a trial mission. A courier in London had let slip the hint of an affair between General Hansen's wife and another high-ranking member of the Royal Arms. She wanted to know if it was true, and if possible, to procure proof to be leveraged accordingly. This was no difficult matter. I secured an invitation to the Hansen residence once they arrived in London for the Season and fabricated some trouble with home renovations, prompting the general to invite me to stay for a few days. During that time, it was easy enough to search through Lady Hansen's things and find a cache of rather salacious love letters."

"So you gave them to my ..." She cleared her throat, coloring. "To Lady Silver, I mean."

"I did not," he said curiously, tilting his head. "I left her a message at the Swan's Tooth, as instructed, and she contacted me a few days later, instructing me to parcel the letters and an amount of coin together and to deposit it under a couch at a private concert some days later. I was to sit on this couch until approached by another agent, in this case a married lady, who made a bit of conversation before spiriting the parcel away to wherever its next location happened to be. I was assured that my coin would be returned to me upon completion of the transfer of information."

"The married lady," Nell guessed, "was Elizabeth Corden."

He nodded, still wearing that mask of light amusement that she suspected was at her expense. "Just so. She was to hold on to the parcel until such a time as to allow the full spectrum of Lady Hansen's panic to play out and then, once the dear lady had given up on retrieving her property, she would pass it along to your brother, who would then transport it from Oxford to London to Lady Silver. That is all I know.

"She assured me that she had a very secure hiding place in her Oxford home where neither her husband nor any servants would stumble upon the parcel before it could be transported to its final destination. When that hiding place turned out to be less than secure, she panicked and found me in London to beg my aid, mentioning that my reputation was at stake as well."

Nell chewed on her bottom lip, taking in this series of events. Bess had contacted Mr. Atlas rather than the Society itself to report the loss of the parcel, then. Presumably, she had been hoping to reacquire it before anyone found out she'd let it get lost in the first place. By the time Peter arrived to collect the parcel, there was no option but to tell him that it was gone, most likely taken by Alex Somers, whose presence in her home she declined to explain in detail.

"Surely, you already had all of this information, my dear wife," Nathaniel continued, those unreadable eyes flashing in the afternoon sun.

"Some of it," Nell replied, "not all. Am I to gather that you have not uncovered Lady Silver's identity through your substantial connections?"

"Not for lack of trying," he chuckled. "Come then, it is my

turn to ask questions. I still wish to know how you became involved with Lady Silver and her scheming."

"She is my aunt," Nell replied, the words tumbling out of her mouth so quickly that they overlapped each other. She winced at the way Nathaniel's easy smile fell from his face, at the way his posture suddenly became rigid and alert.

"Your aunt," he echoed, seemingly horrified.

"Yours too, now, I suppose," Nell replied with a weak attempt at a smile. "She is my mother's elder sister. Her true name is Zelda Smith. My parents are not wealthy people, Mr. Atlas, and they could not have afforded me the education nor the debut I have enjoyed. However, there has never been much attempt to disguise the workings of my aunt's machinations in my household, and so I have always known who and what she is. When I was fourteen, I proposed that she send me away to Mrs. Arlington's School for Young Ladies in exchange for intelligence about my classmates, most of whom have very influential families. She was impressed by the idea and amenable to the exchange, to my everlasting gratitude."

She looked down at her hands, not wishing to see how he took this news, lest it be eye-popping horror. The sight of her blunt, peeling fingernails did little to soothe her anxiety.

She had hoped perhaps he would speak his rebuke, likely his horror at marrying a woman who had spied upon her peers and friends from childhood. It would be easier to only have to hear such words, and not see his beautiful face twisted in disgust.

No words came forth, however. Only a long silence, until

she could stand it no longer, and raised her head to face him.

His face was neutral, unreadable, though he was scratching at his jaw in a thoughtful way. "Zelda Smith," he said carefully, once she met his gaze. "The print shop mistress? On Bond Street?"

"The very same," Nell agreed with a little sigh. "So you see, she will not dismiss you if you wish to continue to aid her. She is my host in London during the Season, as my parents have no finances for such things nor time between my many, many siblings. We will go directly to the flat she keeps above the shop and explain what has happened."

"She paid for your brother's education as well?" he asked curiously.

Nell shook her head. "No. Peter was admitted to Oxford on merit of his academic prowess, sponsored by the administration in the hopes that he will remain on at the completion of his studies as an educator. He does not involve himself much in Aunt Zelda's affairs, but in this instance, he agreed to act as courier. It was not expected to be a complex matter."

Atlas nodded, his expression unchanged. "This is unexpected," he confessed, lacing his fingers together. "I have many questions, as you can imagine, but none are pertinent to the matter of the lost parcel. You are a very curious creature, Miss Applegate."

"Nell," she corrected, her voice little more than a whisper.

"Nell," he amended in a voice that could have meant a great many different things.

CHAPTER 4

*N*ate had never put much stock in the concept of fate. That type of whimsical diversion was much more the domain of his cousin, Kit. After all, surely if there were some divine accountant of destiny, the world would be a much fairer place overall.

Still, he had to marvel at his luck in recent days. It wasn't just the business with Alex Somers, though that certainly pushed the limits of serendipity. He had just married into the family of the most mysterious woman in England. He might have served as an agent for Lady Silver for several years and still come no closer to learning her identity, if not for the slapdash marriage he'd fallen into with her niece.

Kit would have seen it as proof of some grand plan for them all. Nate simply thought he'd managed to stumble forward this time instead of backward.

So, the hard-nosed spinster turned businesswoman, Zelda Smith, was the notorious Lady Silver. He had never met her without her veil on, but he'd heard plenty about her from her patrons throughout the *ton*.

It made a sort of sense, he thought. Such an enterprise would surely not operate under the sole purview of a married lady, and the very business of scandal and gossip was necessary to inspire the prints sold from her shop and the others like it.

He himself had been featured in one of her satirical cartoons, some years ago. He never had the pleasure of seeing the piece, but he was told it was an amusing rendering of his work browbeating several Jamaican plantation owners into paying their taxes as agreed to the Crown. All in all, such things could actually benefit one's reputation in the long run, and so he hadn't minded in the least.

It was also an excellent way to leverage the type of blackmail that he'd found in those letters to Lady Hansen. Now the question arose of just how this society came to be in the first place and who, if anyone, they answered to in the government. There was no obvious connection, as he had expected there would be, in identifying Lady Silver herself.

When they stopped again for late-afternoon repast, he saw to the refreshing of the horses while also securing a second driver. This way, they could continue to travel through the night with no necessity arising for another awkward evening in a shared inn bed. He imagined they might both sleep better on opposing sides of the carriage anyway.

He rather imagined his little wife breathed a sigh of relief alongside him. She had buried herself into a book following the explosive revelations of their earlier conversation and had barely come up for air since. She'd even taken it with her into way stations to read while she ate. In fact, he was reasonably certain she had finished the damned thing and started it over again just in an effort to avoid conversation.

She had peeped up at him over the fraying cover of the book a few times, her eyes magnified by those round spectacles, and each time, he'd met her eye with a smile. He knew it was a little unkind, but it was only that she was so very amusing when flustered. He had never met a woman of breeding before who was so expressive with every little thing she felt.

Her lips would purse at things she found objectionable and her eyes would narrow if she was feeling suspicious of his sincerity. Sitting across from her during conversation was quite the visual entertainment. Still, teasing people was not an activity he much bothered with, unless one could classify his manipulations during negotiations as teasing, and he did not.

He would have to engage her in a gambling game of some sort, just to observe all of her peculiar little tells. How such a woman managed to conduct espionage was beyond him.

She seemed to wait for him to doze off before arranging herself on her side of the carriage under one of the blankets. He never got to witness her ritual of settling into sleep, and instead always seemed to find her rapidly changed from a state of complete awareness to her almost childlike pose with her hands folded under her cheek, spectacles hidden away somewhere, her breathing even and lost in the oblivion of sleep.

Of course, it would usually be too dark to study her any further shortly thereafter, as the carriage rumbled along through cobbles and dirt and the occasional paving that hadn't been retouched since Ancient Rome. It was not the most restful sleep of his life, but it was still an improvement on those days prior to the wedding.

He couldn't wait to be back in London and to fall asleep in his own, fine bed. The thought that he would not be alone in that bed any longer was not one he allowed to pester him. It was a problem for tomorrow.

Fog hung thick over London upon their arrival, a heavy veil of icy air that shimmered with the looming promise of snow.

Far from the bustling streets and fashionable squares of the Season, the city in deep autumn was a place for the workmen and the poor, bundled up in their patched coats and scarves and gloves. It was bleak and misty and far too forbidding and quiet to interest those who enjoyed the trappings of wealth and warm hearths in sprawling country estates.

Nathaniel watched his wife as she gazed, wide-eyed, out of their carriage window at the much-changed city. The scene was enhanced by the ominous glow of the sunset, which thickened the crowds on the streets with an eagerness to return to their homes before dark. The book she'd been immersed in was in her lap, with one of her slender fingers holding the place where she'd last read, but it seemed much forgotten for the first time in days.

She had leaned so close to the window that her little, upturned nose was almost flush against the glass, her lips parted in surprise as her breath created a small cloud of fog to appear and vanish with every breath she took. As ever, it was a pleasing sort of entertainment to observe her, unkempt hair and all.

She had done her best to maintain the coiled bun at the back of her head, but her hair had become more unruly by the day, refusing to stay in place and dropping tendrils down that she had taken to just shoving behind her ears. He imagined he hadn't fared much better, in truth, and both of them were looking forward to baths and rest.

He would have a guest room made ready for her. Yes, that would be best. They could both recover from their journey without being concerned with waking or otherwise disturbing the other. His staff knew well enough to keep their silence, and they would be much better off with a night of proper sleep behind them than they would be going directly to Bond Street to present their failure to Lady Silver ... or, should he think of her now as Aunt Zelda?

He shook his head, repressing the urge to sigh at the strangeness of it all. Once they were in the city, every street seemed to take as long as a full day on the road in the country, as though block by block they began their journey anew. When he was little, he used to bounce his legs or fidget with his hands when he felt this way, as though time were moving as slowly as it deliberately could, just to torment him. He'd gotten enough raps across the knuckles for it that the habit was fully quashed in adulthood, but damned if he didn't sometimes wish he could indulge in a bit of childish restlessness.

His townhome was modest by his own design, chosen for its unique location, which happened to be both convenient to the requirements of the Season and secluded enough that he rarely dealt with unexpected visitors. Even the gravel of the drive seemed muted under the wheels of the carriage as they pulled into place, yet of course, somehow his staff was at the ready to assist them with disembarking and finding their way inside.

"The lady will require a bath and a bed," he said to the butler, tossing a glance over his shoulder at Nell. "I would like the same, please. Dinner should be served quickly rather than opulently, if you catch my meaning, and both of us should be roused early in the morning. If you can find a lady's maid on such short notice to attend our guest, it would be most appreciated."

He didn't stop to get a nod of assent, trusting instead that his instructions were taken with the same level of professional reverence to which he was accustomed. He saw himself up the stairs and into the bedchamber, stripping himself of his cravat and jacket along the way. Just a few moments of rest in his own bed was all he needed, then he could rise, wash, and eat something as he planned for tomorrow.

A claw-foot tub and soaps from his preferred apothecary would make a world of difference. A belly full of something other than the wayfarer's rations they'd eaten along the way would fortify him. He'd sleep well and awake refreshed and attack the challenges of the day as precisely as he always did.

Yes, just a little bit of rest first, he thought as he climbed into his imported sheets and sank his cheek into eiderdown pillows. Just a bit of stillness first, he promised himself, and closed his eyes against the sounds of his household being roused back to life.

CHAPTER 5

*I*t was the first time in over a week that Nell felt truly warm, all the way down to her bones.

She had been ushered into an armchair at the back wall of a large bedroom, where a fire was promptly coaxed into a roaring largesse. The servants milled around her, bringing in a porcelain tub that looked like it could hold three of her, and transporting both her suitcase and the stolen one into the room.

"When will my husband be joining me?" Nell asked, eyeing the steam rising from the tub. She wanted to languish in that water, but the idea of Atlas walking in and seeing her nude was not one she was quite ready to entertain. At least, not yet.

"Your husband, ma'am?" a maid asked with a frown. "The master said it was only you staying for the evening. Should we be expecting another guest?"

Nell opened her mouth to respond and then closed it again,

color rising in her cheeks. "No," she said thinly. "I am just very tired. I got confused for a moment."

The maid tilted her head with a little smile, her wide blue eyes apparently suspecting nothing of the scandalous truth. She looked a little older than Nell herself, full figured and curly haired, with wisps of honey blonde escaping from her cap around her ears. She turned and bustled over to the luggage to begin the process of unpacking. "Travel addles my brains too," she said cheerily. "But why leave London at all, when everything you need is right here? Well, aside from your husband, I suppose!"

"Leave the brown one be," Nell said quickly, gripping the arm of the chair as she watched the maid hesitate over the two valises. "The blue one is mine, though there isn't much inside. Two dresses that should be laundered, plus the one I'm wearing now. If you wouldn't mind just laying out a shift for me to sleep in and pressing the last clean gown for use tomorrow, that would be perfect."

"Right, I can do that, ma'am, no problem," she said, swiping up the blue bag and carrying it to the cushioned bench at the foot of the bed. "My name is Sarah, if you're wondering. I've been with Mr. Atlas for some years now, but you're the first guest we've ever entertained in my time here. Might I ask your name, ma'am, just as to know what to call you?"

"Eleanor," she replied. "Or Nell, if you prefer."

Sarah bit her lip, a dimple appearing in her left cheek. "I could hardly call you by your Christian name, ma'am! The master would have my head!"

Nell hesitated, uncertain if her husband had deliberately concealed their marriage from his staff or if this was a simple oversight. Perhaps he remembered her concern over the gossip reaching her family before they did, and was acting in her personal interest. Yes, that must be it.

"You may call me Mrs. Applegate, if you like," she decided, erring on the side of caution.

"And are you to be with us long, Mrs. Applegate?" she asked politely. "I will be better able to accommodate your comfort if I have ample time to prepare."

"I can barely keep track of my home from one day to the next, Sarah," Nell said with what she hoped was a friendly quirk of her lips. "A woman's position is ever changing."

"Truer words," Sarah agreed with a little chuckle.

Another duo of servants with steaming water came in and dumped their bounty into the tub. They paused this time and gave Nell a little bow each, as though to silently indicate that this was the last of the water for her bath.

Sarah looked up at them with her brow furrowed, impatience on her face. "The lady will be needing towels and soaps, of course," she said. "And a new sponge."

The two men exchanged a glance between them, but did not argue, turning on their heels to see to this additional task. All the while, Sarah shook her head, muttering about the uselessness of men.

She had the dirty dresses bundled up under her arm and Nell's last clean shift spread on the bed, ready to be donned en route to blissful slumber in an actual bed.

"We have food coming up shortly," Sarah told her. "I will

bring it in personally. Do you require a privacy screen for your bathing? Any particular toiletries?"

"No, thank you, Sarah," Nell answered, blinking at the luxury being put on offer to her. "What's here is more than enough. I am going to wash my hair tonight, however, and I do not trust myself to stay awake until it is fully dry. Might you aid me in braids or rag curls before I sleep?"

Sarah nodded, her pink cheeks flushing with pleasure. "I would love to, Ms. Applegate. Let me get these dresses to laundry and bring your food up. Feel free to hop into the tub as soon as the gents bring your soaps and towels. No one else will be walking in to surprise you."

Nell nodded, her legs aching as she pushed to her feet. How on earth did one end up just as sore from a lack of movement as from heavy exercise? She hadn't felt this stiff since a very long uphill climb during a visit to Edinburgh some years ago. Hopefully a nice, hot soak would be just as tonic now as it was then.

The two male servants returned with a selection of oils and soaps for her to choose from, a handsome yellow sponge that must have been imported from the Mediterranean, a pot of some sort of moisturizing cream, and two fluffy white towels to wrap herself in when she finished her bath.

Later, it would seem to Nell that as soon as the door closed behind those two servants, that she vanished from her position by the fire and appeared, somehow immediately stripped of her clothing, in the searing embrace of the bathtub.

Of course, evidence that she had crossed this distance by human means was evident, both from her footprints on the carpet and her clothing strewn on the floor, but as she sank down fully into the bath, embraced by the floating dots of rose oil that gave it a lovely scent, she couldn't be bothered to conjure up any memory but the present, submerged like a sea nymph in a blissful cocoon of perfect warmth.

MORNING ARRIVED FAR TOO QUICKLY.

Nell would have loved to stay in this absurdly large, wonderfully lush bed for days, until she felt strictly human again. But alas, she was the one who requested to become involved in her aunt's affairs, and so now she must face that duty head-on.

She had sat by the fire after her bath, her eyelids drooping as Sarah eased a wide-toothed comb through her hair. It was no surprise that it was full of snarls and knots, after the way she'd mistreated it on the road, but Sarah's gentle fingers and cheery rambling about topics Nell could barely focus upon was soothing enough that she didn't mind the process of having them worked out.

Once her hair had been returned to a presentable, combed state, the drying effect of the fire had already done much of its work.

"What a lovely color," Sarah cooed as she began to wind Nell's tresses into a braid. "I wish mine was so straight and fine."

Nell had scoffed at that, but thanked her for the compliment as she nibbled on the food that had been brought up. By the time she finally crawled into that luxurious bed, she barely had time to pull the coverlet over her body before she had found herself rendered entirely unconscious.

That is until morning made its unwelcome appearance, as it always does. She was roused by Sarah, who had returned to assist her with her hair and clothing, beaming ear to ear, as though the rising of the sun was just the most thrilling thing ever to have happened.

"I would stay in that bed for the next week if I could," Nell had confessed, dragging herself back into the chair where her hair had been braided the night before. "I've never had the pleasure of one quite so luxurious."

"Oh yes, the bedding abovestairs cost so much, it'd make your eyes water," Sarah whispered conspiratorially. "So it's a waste, isn't it, that we rarely entertain guests, and never overnight?"

Nell did not respond, though it was more uncomfortable concealing the truth of her name and status in the light of day. Surely Nathaniel himself would clear up her identity in short order, and she could apologize for the deception to Sarah immediately thereafter.

"There, now, that's a lovely curl," Sarah said approvingly as she shook the braid from Nell's hair, leaving it in a shiny curtain of golden brown that fell nearly to Nell's elbows. "Shall we leave a bit down around the face and in the back? I think the shape of the curl would make a fetching look."

"Oh, if you like," Nell said, glancing back at her. "I usually just wind it into a tight bun."

"Oh, that's a shame," the maid replied with a click of her

tongue. "If my hair were so biddable, I'd style it in all manner of ways."

And so, with the primping and pampering of Sarah's attentions, Nell found herself laced into her last clean gown, a thick weave of light blue, and her hair arranged to sit high on her head save for a spill of curls over her shoulder. She didn't mind the effect at all, even if it had taken an unseemly amount of time to arrange such a fashion.

She was led to the dining room and informed that the master would join her momentarily. She sat, upright and nervous, resisting the urge to crane her neck around every few seconds to check for her husband. She had left her spectacles and her book in the bedchambers, else she might have resorted yet again to the company of a thinly written sleuth and his daring deeds.

When he finally arrived, she nearly jumped out of her skin from the start it gave her, being that she had stared straight ahead in silence for what felt like an eon.

"Good morning," Nathaniel said airily, stepping over to the head of the table and seating himself. He blinked at her, the shadow of a little smile turning up the corners of his mouth as he took in her hair. "Did you sleep well?"

"Oh yes," she said quickly, still frozen in place. "Very well. I cannot tell if your bedding is particularly luxurious or if it was simply quite the contrast from the carriage bench and horse blankets."

"Perhaps a bit of both, hm?" he chuckled, motioning for a footman to bring them hot tea and frothy milk. "I thought perhaps we might discuss our plan of action before heading to Bond Street to see your aunt? I want to make sure we have an approach that works in tandem rather than accidentally stepping all over one another when we attempt to explain our conundrum."

"I rather thought we'd just toss the suitcase at her and flee before any repercussions could occur," Nell replied, lifting the tea to her lips.

Atlas stared for a moment, then finally shook his head and leaned back in his chair with an incredulous look on his face. "You really are full of surprises, Miss Applegate."

"Nell," she corrected, setting her teacup down and reaching for her cutlery. This breakfast looked like ambrosia compared to all of the tavern meals they'd eaten on the road, and she fully intended to enjoy every bite of it.

"Nell," he agreed, toying with his own fork while still considering her. "You think she will be angry, then?"

Nell gave a light shrug, finishing the bite she had just taken and dabbing at her lips before answering. "Anger isn't really what I'd call it. Aunt Zelda is a calculating woman, and I'm certain that whatever penance we must do for mucking up such a simple assignment will have all sorts of hidden pitfalls folded into it. We must simply stay on our toes and prepare for the unexpected."

"How does one prepare for the unexpected, pray tell?" he asked with some amusement. "Isn't that rather contradictory?"

"You are a politician, Nathaniel," she replied evenly. "You know what I mean, even if you might phrase it differently. After all, you must be prepared to speak when the opportunity to hold the floor arises, without knowing ahead of time what was said before or what will come after."

"Granted."

It was unsettling the way he watched her. He had done it the whole time they'd been in the carriage, like she was some book to be studied and memorized or a puzzle that could be unlocked. He seemed to have very little interest in his food, only picking at a piece here and there, all while wearing that expression of contemplation and observing her quite a bit more keenly than she was prepared to tolerate while doing something so undignified as eating.

"Thank you for seeing to everything last night," she said, hoping to snap him out of his reverie. "A hot bath was just what I needed."

"Mm, did they manage to find you a lady's maid? I don't keep one on staff here for obvious reasons, unfortunately."

"They did. Sarah," Nell replied politely. "Though she said she had worked for you for some years. Perhaps she had a skill set you simply weren't taking advantage of?"

"Perhaps so."

He seemed unconcerned with such coincidences and banal matters, which of course was only another opportunity to have him falling back into his unsettling observation of her.

"She did not know that I am your wife," Nell said, softly enough that the footmen standing at the doorway to the dining room could not overhear. "I hardly knew how to introduce myself."

"Ah." His cheeks pinkened a little and he cleared his throat.

"My apologies for that. I thought it best we recover fully before deciding together how to forge ahead. I hope you have not taken offense. I was admittedly a little too focused on my own recovery to think the situation through."

"Only a little offense," she told him, raising her eyebrows. "I suppose you are right, though. We should plan how we are to handle our situation before we set out for Bond Street. Shall we discuss such matters here, or somewhere more private?"

Nathaniel's eyes glittered, like polished amber flecked with gold. Without taking them off her, he dismissed the two servants and asked them to shut the doors behind them.

She held her breath, her heart speeding most unexpectedly at this development. When he leaned forward, she thought she might be faint.

"Yes," he said softly. "Let us speak plainly, wife."

CHAPTER 6

athaniel had spent a great deal of time that morning debating upon how to dress for this appearance with Lady Silver. Often, before undertaking a delicate negotiation or a new acquaintance, he would have time to gather gossip about the target or otherwise observe them from a distance before such a time as he made himself known.

That was not an option with Zelda Smith. He knew her name, of course, as any member of Society ought to, but he had never patronized her shop, nor made an introduction. He might have seen this woman a number of times without her veil and not realized it. From the beginning, he'd had no idea what to expect, and after a bit of conversation with her niece, he was even less sure of himself.

"She's not a bad sort," Nell had assured him, those big gray eyes of hers blinking at him with guileless sincerity across the breakfast table. "It's just difficult to tell sometimes whether or not she is angry."

"I can't imagine what that's like," he'd replied somberly, hoping it would make her laugh.

Instead she tilted her head at him, resting her chin upon her hand, her plate of fruit and toast forgotten, and said, "Perhaps you will be able to read her better than I. After all, you are also a bit of an enigma."

"Only because the truth is so very boring," he'd replied with a wink, though his joviality sounded much more at ease than he felt. That joke did not make her laugh either. Why did he care so much whether or not the strange little duckling laughed, anyhow?

She did look much improved without those spectacles perched on her nose and her hair slicked back in a severe little knot. Her dress was still less than fashionable, but it was at least clean, and the pale blue color did suit her, bringing out the stormy color of her eyes. Perhaps he could fashion her into something presentable, should he need a wife on his arm for any future dealings. She certainly had the constitution for it, if not the presentation.

He shifted uncomfortably in the seat of the carriage, stealing another look at her across from him. She was still fascinated with the view from the windows, watching London come alive without the gentry present to interfere. She had wrapped herself in a woolen pelisse in a faded olive color that had the appearance of something well-loved and often worn, which was to say, a little worse for the wear. He frowned, taking in the simple weave of her knitted gloves and the scuffs on her boots.

She had said her parents were not wealthy, but her aunt certainly was. Surely hosting one's niece for her education and financing a London debut at the cost of turning a child into an agent of deceit should merit a few trips to a respected seamstress. It was too late in the year for the shops he would have chosen in the Season, but surely he could find someone in the city to outfit his wife in a way that befitted her.

He had a sneaking suspicion that she would never have complained, or even noticed at all that the quality of her clothing was so inferior to his own. The fact that he took affront to this realization, rather than relief, was a bit discomfiting. She would learn to value herself on par with the more privileged of the *ton*, he thought. Just as he had, against the odds.

Yes, a clothier would be his first priority, once this business with the Silver Leaf was sorted.

"Is it always so gray here?" she mused, glancing over her shoulder at him. "I wonder if I simply do not notice when it is warm outside with so much distraction about."

"I don't mind it," he replied with a shrug. "It makes a fire inside all the more luxurious when it's wretched without, after all, and the sunny days all the more treasured."

She smiled at that, seemingly genuinely charmed by this bit of cynicism in a way that his jests had not accomplished.

"You are exactly right," she agreed, clasping her hands together. "There is a kind of beauty in every setting. What a timely reminder, Mr. Atlas."

"Nathaniel," he corrected with a quirk of his lips, pleased at the way she blushed and bit her lip. "Or Nate, if you like."

"Nate," she said, testing the sound on her tongue. "That is a nice nickname. I shall venture to remember to use it."

"You must," he said seriously, "else our matching first initials will go unnoticed by passersby."

She finally giggled, raising her fingers to her lips and shaking her head. She turned back to the window, releasing another little titter, to resume her observation of the passing scenery.

Nate was so pleased that he'd finally gotten a laugh out of her that he was damn near giddy. He checked himself, a bit puzzled by his elation over such a simple, meaningless exchange. Perhaps the girl's oddness simply made her a more enjoyable opponent in games of social chess. Yes, that was likely it, combined with the fact that he'd had no company other than hers for well over a week.

They arrived at Bond Street to an almost eerie quiet, with most of the shops and boutiques lining the area already shuttered for the winter. Mrs. Smith's Fine Prints, however, was still open for business, its beveled windows glistening with early-morning frost. The signage swinging over the door appeared to have a fresh coat of red paint declaring itself to the world.

His little wife gave a shiver that he suspected had little to do with the chill in the air. She gave a meaningful little glance to him over her shoulder, her mouth drawn into a flat line of acceptance, just as the door was pulled open by their driver, allowing the pale morning light to flood in.

They were greeted at the door by a slender woman of middling age, with a friendly round face and a mop of brassy hair. He braced himself for the recognition in her face when she saw him, but she only spared him a glance while embracing Nell. From the doorway he could make out a great selection of satirical cartoons, stationery booklets, pamphlets, and more organized throughout the modest little space.

"Oh, little Eleanor, you must be frozen to the bone!" the woman tutted, ushering them inside and knocking the door shut with her hip. "The frost is unseemly early this year. Is the gentleman with you?"

"Yes," Nell said softly, looking from the woman over to Nathaniel. "Mr. Atlas, this is Harriet Goode. She helps run the shop with my aunt."

"Pleasure to meet you," Mrs. Goode said with a wide, earnest smile, striding forward to shake his hand. "I'm sure you'll be wanting Zelda. Why don't you come upstairs and I'll get you some tea while we wait for her to return. She popped out for pastries with your brother."

Nell froze, seeking out his eye from over Mrs. Goode's shoulder. "Peter is here?" she asked in an airy voice that did not at all match the expression on her face.

"Mm, he came in the night before last and said to expect you soon after. Come along!" She crossed the floor and opened a door that led to a staircase, allowing them to scale it ahead of her.

Abovestairs was a handsomely outfitted flat, a fair amount more opulent than the shop underneath. They were, as promised, placed in front of a fire with two scalding hot cups of tea, while Mrs. Goode fussed over their lack of biscuits until the chime of the downstairs bell forced her to return to her duties.

"It's a good thing, isn't it?" Nate asked, dropping a cube of sugar into his cup and giving it a gentle stir. "Perhaps Peter has already taken the initiative to explain the bulk of our misadventure, and all we have left to do is await our sentence."

"Peter has a tendency to dramatize things," Nell said with a grimace. "He might have spun a tale far more dramatic than the true series of events. Once he has done that, it is often difficult for me to set anyone's understanding of a story back to rights."

"Fanciful, is he?" Nate responded with a chuckle. "I genuinely would not have guessed it of him. He barely spoke in the month we spent at Somerton, to me or anyone else within my hearing."

"Yes, well," Nell said with a sigh, "once he builds up the courage to speak to you, he might never stop again."

"Fascinating," he murmured, sipping at his tea.

The sound of the bell ringing again downstairs was followed by a swell of voices, then heavy footsteps on the staircase. Nell straightened, gripping her teacup with a white-knuckled propriety that made Nathaniel feel a bit of her nervousness himself. He had not yet decided what to expect here.

The door seemed to be blown open by the pure force of the woman who burst through it. She was wearing a close-fitting, well-made gown of deep purple, and her stark white hair had been fashioned into a curling coif at the back of her head. She was chattering away to a harried and overburdened Peter Applegate as he scrambled in behind her, his spectacles slipping down the length of his nose as he struggled to balance several boxes of fresh baked goods in his arms.

"Oh, Peter," Nell tsked, rising to her feet and shoving her teacup onto the table in front of her in one smooth motion. She scooped several of the paper boxes away from him, allowing him to regain his balance and his dignity, all to the complete obliviousness of their aunt, who had simply continued to walk in and was pulling off her gloves next to a hallway mirror, still chattering away in one long, unbroken stream of gossip.

"And I said to the man, slander is what you're doing right now to my place of business, for I can prove the veracity of my claims and the ineptitude of yours. I swear to you, I thought he might weep, but at least it shut him up for a few moments so I could make my escape." She stopped for breath, frowning and turning over her shoulder. "I say, are you even listening to me? Oh, hullo, Eleanor."

"Good morning, Aunt Zelda," Eleanor replied in a tone that spoke to her weary familiarity with such antics. "Where shall we put the pastries?"

"Oh, should've left them downstairs. Now someone will have to take them back again. Just there on the coffee table for now, if you please." She turned from her spot, her gloves held tightly in her hand, and gave Nathaniel the iciest smile he'd ever seen in his life. "This must be your husband."

"Madam," he said, rising and giving a stiff bow. "It is an honor to meet you."

"Oh, stop it, both of you," Nell huffed, breezing past her astonished brother to drop the boxes onto the coffee table and flip open the lid of the one at the top of the stack. "He already knows who you are and you know who he is. Oh, you got *pain au chocolat*! You must have been expecting me."

"I'm always expecting you, dear," Zelda Smith said, her smile warming considerably as she turned her eyes toward her niece. "That way, I can never be wrong."

"Perish the thought," Peter Applegate muttered under his breath.

If she had heard the comment, Mrs. Smith gave no indication. She gave Nell a quick embrace, but pulled back quickly, patting at her carefully coiffed, stark-white hair and glancing in the mirror that hung next to the doorway.

"Would you like a pastry, Nathaniel?" Nell asked, turning to look at him with those big, guileless eyes. "They aren't as pretty as you might expect, but the taste is divine."

"No, thank you, my dear," he replied with what he hoped was an affectionate smile. "Perhaps I'll have more of an appetite once our business with your aunt is concluded. After all, I believe we have a great deal to discuss."

"Not so much as you might think," Peter replied, though he was looking at his sister rather than Nate.

"It was a clever gambit. I'll give you that," Mrs. Smith said, plucking an apple tart from the paper box and arranging herself on the chair across from Nate. "Splitting your efforts doubled the chances for success, and only at the cost of your liberty, my dear niece."

"I found the documents," Peter told her, the words falling quickly from his mouth. "It is all rather a stupid story, but

Alex did indeed take them from the Corden home by accident. They were recovered fully, alongside the coin."

"I see," Nell said with a little frown, her enthusiasm for her pastry dropping significantly. "And Alex himself?"

"Perfectly well," Mrs. Smith said with a haughty sniff. "Though that fiancée of his demands a series of rather lofty introductions come spring on his behalf."

"Fiancée," Nell echoed. "Do you mean Miss Blakely?"

"Oh, whomever," Mrs. Smith clipped with a shrug of her shoulders. "Lady Somers soon enough, I suppose."

Nate kept his expression neutral, but did meet his wife's eye as she turned toward him, her brow furrowed in concern. He did not know what reaction she expected, but the absence of one entirely seemed to ease some of the stiffness from her little shoulders, at the very least.

She presented such a tragic figure, standing there with her eyes wide, absently picking at the flakes of pastry crust gripped in her hands as she anticipated some display of jealous outrage. He had the strangest urge to immediately rise to his feet, wrap her in his jacket, and lead her back outside into the safety of their carriage.

Of course, that was absurd. If anyone needed protecting here, it was Nate himself. He was the only one who wasn't neck deep in this family's mysterious doings, after all, and he'd gone and married into it thinking to give himself an advantage to his own ends.

He sighed, glancing up at the slim and unimposing figure of his wife's twin brother. Peter was significantly taller than Nell, but just as slender of build. His hair was the same dark brown as hers, ruffled from the wind and what was likely an utter lack of concern for his appearance.

Between this man and Mrs. Smith, a woman whose formidability was somewhat softened by her age, he thought he and little Eleanor stood quite a good united front, should the necessity arise to stand against them. After all, Nell was an Atlas now. That was how marriage worked. She was his now, not theirs.

When he turned back to Mrs. Smith, he saw her peering at him with her eyes narrowed, as though she could hear every insulting thought that had just spun through his head.

"Nellie, Peter," she said, "would you two be dears and bring the other box of pastries down to Harriet? I would like a moment to get to know my new nephew."

"Oh, but ..." Nell began, her voice thin and nervous.

"Come on," her brother cut in, placing a hand on her shoulder. "It will give us a moment to talk too."

She looked over at Nate again, as though hoping for his input. He gave her a little nod, which she returned, turning on her heel and stepping back out onto the stairwell ahead of her brother, who soon followed, leaving him alone in the silent loft across from an unveiled Lady Silver.

CHAPTER 7

*N*ell had never felt quite so harried in her life.

She took the stairs two at a time, bursting out into the shop well ahead of her brother, and walked immediately forward to brace herself against the counter. She drew in deep breaths, telling herself that all was well, all was as it should be. In fact, it was better than they had anticipated! So, what in the world was the matter with her?

Peter had recovered the documents somehow, hadn't he? Yes, she had run off and eloped for what amounted to no good reason at all, but what did that matter opposite a successful mission? Oh, God, what must Nathaniel be thinking of her right now? He must at least suspect that she had known all along that Peter had the documents, and that she was nothing more than a scheming, aging debutante who'd seen the opportunity to snag a husband and taken it by any means necessary?

Didn't you? a voice in her head whispered.

"Nell!" Peter hissed, appearing at her elbow and sliding the box of pastries carelessly down the counter. "I have been beside myself with worry! I've been waiting here for three days, just sick with not knowing what had happened and how that rogue reacted when you failed to retrieve the documents. How could you do something so dangerous? How could you?!"

She could feel him seething next to her and knew his eyes were boring down on her, waiting for her to turn so that he might properly stare his fury into her face. It was a very good reason to remain as she was, looking at nothing more than the bit of marble countertop between her hands.

Harriet was in the opposite corner of the shop, assisting a patron in choosing from the new prints. All of them were engrossed in their conversation and blissfully unaware of the sharp whispering between two young people at the rear of the room.

"Eloping is hardly the most daring thing I've done, Brother," she said as evenly as she could. "I daresay it was sensible, as far as Society will be concerned."

"Well, yes," Peter replied, exasperation making his voice crack. "They weren't in the room all those times that the bloke casually suggested murder as a solution to a variety of problems. At best, he's simply depraved, but he could very well have a long history of butchering people who've gotten in his way, and now you are bound to him. Forever!"

"Yes," she agreed. "I am married to a wealthy, influential man who will give me a comfortable, respectable life. I am no longer the inevitable spinster daughter, dangling like a yoke around our parents' necks. I am not the tragic wallflower with a line of prettier sisters stifled in my shadow, awaiting a proposal that shall never come. I will not apologize for my decision!"

Peter was silent for so long that she gave up on her determination to avoid his eye. She eased her grip on the counter and turned to face him with a little sigh of defeat.

He looked as though she'd just dropped a bushel of rocks on his head, his face blank and stricken, arms hanging limply at his sides. He was staring at her, evidently gobsmacked by her words, though surely the facts of her situation had not come as any sort of surprise to him.

"None of us consider you a burden," he finally stammered, lifting his hands slightly, as though he were offering his words on an invisible platter. "We never would."

"It does not matter if you have these thoughts or not," she said, reaching out to grip one of his outstretched hands. "Reality is hardly shaped by the graciousness of a patient family. You cannot deny that I had no prospects, nor can you believe that our sisters would have had the opportunity to seek Aunt Zelda's patronage if I had remained her loyal spinster protege. She was determined to shape me into her image, Peter. I only want my own image, whatever it may be in the end."

"What about him?" Peter asked, rather than argue with the things she said. "How will you stay safe, alone with Atlas? What if he becomes angry someday and puts his hands on you?" He hesitated, a look of horrified realization passing over his face. "Or has he already?"

She snorted, shaking her head to stave off the desire to laugh at the question. "He hasn't touched me at all, in fact," she said with a little shrug and a baleful smile. "Not even a kiss after our wedding vows. I do not think you have anything to be concerned about, on that front. I rather think he plans to tuck me away somewhere and continue on with his life as it ever has been, which will leave me free to create a future all my own. It will be an amenable outcome for us both."

"Hm," Peter grumbled, his face a mask of doubt. "We shall see. I suppose we ought to go up and interrupt them now, in any event, before they start plotting things without us."

She inhaled deeply and nodded, giving her brother's hand one final squeeze. "Yes," she said. "Now, despite your private concerns with my choices, I must ask for your sympathy. Will you stand by me whilst Aunt Zelda's disappointment is presented, likely at length and with great fervor?"

"Of course I will," he said with a little sigh. "We can disappoint her together."

NATE WATCHED his wife scurry away with a kind of helpless paralysis, seeing no obvious route of escape as Lady Silver turned her shrewd, gleaming eyes toward him.

Nell had those eyes, he realized, though while hers reminded him of storm clouds over the sea, her aunt's were pure, polished steel. Or perhaps silver was the more appropriate comparison, he thought with a glimmer of amusement.

She took her time pouring herself a cup of tea, dropping a single cube of sugar into it with a resounding *plop*, all the while watching to see what he might do or say. It was a common technique in negotiations, he knew. Silence often prompted much more fascinating insights spilling from the lips of the person opposite you than any question or query might do.

Luckily, he was well practiced in the art of remaining silent, and simply settled back into his chair, lacing his fingers together, and gave her a placid smile as she began her ritual of stirring the sugar and milk into her perfectly curated cup of tea.

She seemed to find his reaction amusing, or at least he thought that's what the glint in her eye conveyed. She took a delicate little sip of the tea, so little that he couldn't be entirely sure she'd actually consumed any of it, and made a long ritual of setting the cup back in its saucer and adjusting it to her aesthetic satisfaction.

"It was an unexpected move, on your part," she commented lightly, glancing up at him as though she'd just remembered he was there. "What could a girl like Eleanor have tempted you with, especially opposite that glittering diamond of a socialite you were courting? It is hardly a wonder that I am suspicious."

"Suspicious of what?" he queried, his posture still languid but fixed. "In order to pursue the thief, it became necessary to compromise your niece. I did what any decent man might do."

"A decent man might have pursued the thief with Peter rather than Nell," she replied.

"Your nephew was not roused by the commotion, and there was precious little time to take action. All the same, I find it surprising that you, who seem to dote on the girl so much, think so very little of her appeal as a woman."

She gave the faintest snort, leaning forward to snatch her teacup back up. Evidently he had won the first round of will against her. "Overtaken by lust, were you?" she snapped. "Mr. Atlas, I love my niece, but let us not pretend she is a skilled seductress or otherwise some tempting English rose, just begging to be plucked."

"She has other qualities," he said, careful not to allow a sharp edge into his words. "I have come to believe we will be rather well matched as husband and wife."

She grinned at him, her teeth flashing like a cat's just before it pounces. "Have you, now? Oh, I'm certain you've got the next several years planned out already."

"I have an inkling," he said with a shrug. "One must not barrel through life completely unprepared."

"Indeed not." She took another sip of her tea, considering him. "As it happens, I have a task for the two of you that is immediately benefited by these hasty nuptials. I expect you to accept it and graciously, for you have robbed Eleanor of a prosperous future."

"What future is that? I am hardly destitute."

"No, but your money is yours, not hers. A spinster has far more freedom and fun than a wife does, as far as I'm concerned. It was my hope to shape her into my successor and leave her this shop. I still might."

"The shop?" he repeated with a raise of his eyebrows. "Not the Silver Leaf?"

"They are one and the same. Do not be insolent with me, young man." She tutted, setting down her teacup without the faintest concern for how pleasingly it landed this time. "It is too late to grouse over it now. What's done is done, and I expect such brashness to benefit all of us in the end."

"I'm listening," Nate said, giving a respectful tilt of his head. He did not want to push this woman to antagonism, no matter how tempting the verbal jousting was. "How may we serve?"

"Good of you to ask. You will take your new wife home, first and foremost, and send out proud announcements of your wedded status."

"I have already brought her home," he said. "I can send out notices today. Eleanor led me to believe you would wish to have the information first."

"She is correct," Mrs. Smith said, without elaboration. "However, you have not yet brought her home. Your townhouse in London is little more than a pied-a-terre for your constant political ventures. It is not where you install a wife. You must take her to your ancestral home, in Kent."

"Kent?" he repeated, momentarily dumbfounded. He blinked, forcing himself back into his bearings despite the queasy swell that rose in his stomach. "No one has lived at Meridian in decades. It is likely little more than a ruin now."

"You'll find that isn't the case," she replied with a smirk. "I'm sure you already know that I was a great intimate of your parents, Nathaniel. Did you think I'd let you leave their home behind to crumble into the dirt? No. No, my boy, no. I made a promise to your parents and I have kept it. You will need to provide dressing and a staff, but Meridian's shell has been well kept these last years. I will fetch you the keys. Your aunt keeps the other set, since that nasty business with your uncle. Shame about that, honestly. Just a moment."

"My parents," he echoed hollowly.

It was too late. She had risen and floated off to some unknown destination in the rear of the flat, just as Nell and her brother reappeared from the top of the staircase.

She looked around with her brow furrowed and turned to meet Nate's eye with far more concern than he thought the situation merited, even considering all the context.

"Ah, good," Zelda sang, clipping back into the room with a set of brass keys on a large ring. "I shan't have to repeat myself now. Eleanor, you are to make to Kent with your husband here and take up your rightful place at his ancestral estate."

"Kent?" Nell said, her eyes wide and darting from aunt to husband. "You are from Kent?"

Her brother stood next to her with a scowl on his face, his arms crossed over his chest.

"Mm, near Dover," Zelda confirmed on Nate's behalf, her arm jutting out to proffer the keys at Nell directly rather than offering them to Nathaniel. "You are to make yourself visible and amicable to all the people worth knowing in the area, but there is a particular family you will wish to lavish extra attention upon. It is imperative that you get an invitation to the winter masquerade at an estate called La Falaise. It is a very exclusive affair."

"Is it?" Nate asked, his voice a little louder than strictly necessary. "I've never heard of La Falisse nor a fashionable winter masquerade in Kent."

"And for good reason," Zelda said with her back still to him. "Now, let us all sit down, have a nice cup of tea, and I will give you your assignment. Isn't that lovely? No need to trudge to Seven Dials or put on a silly costume. Do sit down with your husband, Eleanor, your tea has gone cold."

Nell gave a little sigh, squeezing her eyes shut for the briefest moment, then marching forward to obey her aunt's commands. When she settled down next to him, he reacted in instinct and reached for her hand.

If she was surprised, she did not show it. She kept her eyes forward, but gave his fingers a little squeeze. The gesture might have been gratitude or perhaps reassurance, but was regardless a comfort in this confusing whirlwind.

She did not comment upon her aunt and brother ogling their clasped hands as though it were something crude and unfathomably shocking. She stayed calm and cool, and did just as he had done some moments before. She allowed the silence to settle over them, which would force Lady Silver to speak first.

It was a mercy that his wife knew how to navigate this encounter, for Nate did not trust himself to speak any longer.

CHAPTER 8

"They are people, Nathaniel, not furniture! You can't simply parcel the lot up and ship them to the coast!" Nell cried in exasperation, following her husband around the foot of his bed while he tossed items into his valise. "We can hire new staff in Kent."

"I don't see what difference it makes," he huffed, sidestepping her approach with the elegance of a man who had avoided a great many unpleasant things in his life. "This is a house. Meridian is a house. They live in the house where they work. Why should they mind which house it is?"

She crossed her arms over her chest, her face screwing up in irritation. "Will you stop and listen to me for a moment? These people live in London! They likely have lives here, maybe even families. You cannot uproot an entire household and ship it east like a trunk of belongings. You will have to consult each and every one of them and take only the ones willing to make this change, which might be far more permanent than some winter ball we must attend."

"Fine," he said, snapping the lid on his valise shut and securing it. "Shall I poll them? Or would you prefer to?"

"They still don't even know who I am," she shot back. "They're likely all scandalized that I'm in your bedchamber right now, even without all the noise you're making throwing things about."

He hesitated, his hand going slack on the handle of the valise before he could toss it into the pile of luggage he'd been amassing. He turned to look at her, standing there with her back up and her chest puffed out like a prim little pugilist just before a match. It made him sigh, allowing a tendril of guilt to slip through the cracks of his outrage.

She had chattered at him all the way back from Bond Street and he hadn't really heard a word of it. His head was still spinning from the sheer gall of that woman, Lady Silver or Mrs. Smith or whoever she was, and her handing the keys to Meridian over like she had any right to the place! It was amazing to him that he'd remained seated when she mentioned his parents, rather than vaulting across the room and locking his hands around her throat.

Still, none of that was Miss Applegate's fault, was it? She had sat there next to him, holding his hand like he was a frightened schoolboy, and had looked to him first before answering any of her aunt's demands. In fact, he was increasingly suspicious that the girl didn't really know the nature of her family's work, even if she was neck-deep in it.

"I am sorry," he said finally, turning and collapsing to sit on the edge of his bed. He motioned for her to join him, amused despite himself at the sudden panic that sparkled in her face. "Come now, I won't do anything untoward."

"I know that," she said quickly, dropping her crossed arms and pacing over to the bed. She perched herself on the corner farthest from him, ankles linked and hands folded in her lap. She stared at him with those wide, gray eyes like he might pounce upon her at any moment.

He did his level best to control the twitching smile that threatened to escape onto his face, and instead put on his best expression of penance. "Eleanor," he began. "Nell. I apologize for my behavior. You recall in the carriage when I told you that I am without origin?"

She nodded, rapt with attention, but did not make a sound.

"Perhaps you believe this to be untrue now that you know I was born in Kent and lived for a time in an old house that belonged to several generations before me. You must understand that what I told you is what I believe. I have no feelings for that place nor that house that are not mired in something deeply unpleasant. I wish to God we were being sent anywhere but there. I do not intend to keep a permanent staff on once our task is completed, and as such I feel it is most pragmatic to simply move my current, trusted staff for this temporary interlude."

She bit down on her lip, likely stifling the urge to ask for details of these unpleasant memories he referenced, and cast her eyes to the side, avoiding his own gaze.

He watched her, still plagued with the feeling he had misused her somehow. "I will make an announcement to the staff forthwith," he told her gently. "I shall explain that we only wished to tell your family in person before making our union public. It is the truth, isn't it?"

"It is," she agreed, her voice soft and distant.

Silence hung between them, punctuated only by the whistling of the wind outside.

"I am sorry, Nathaniel," she added, suddenly raising her chin to meet his eye. "I feel I have dragged you into misery, and I do not know how to fix it."

He was stunned, scrambling for a moment to find the words to reply to her. *She* was sorry? Good God, how was this woman involved with anything that happened in the shadows? She was innocent as a lamb.

"You have nothing to apologize for," he told her. "This has been a bizarre and unprecedented time for both of us, I'm sure."

"We don't have to go," she said, blinking up at him with those big, trusting eyes. "We can simply decide not to be part of the Silver Leaf anymore, if we wish. I do not think Aunt Zelda would retaliate, though she would doubtless be displeased."

He sighed. This was probably the intelligent solution to their plight. He could not explain to her why it was impossible, why he had spent over a decade seeking out answers that he would never find if they did the sensible, safe thing and chose to withdraw. "I'm afraid I'm a man of my word," he said. "We will go to Meridian and see this mission through, and then we will decide if we wish to continue on with your aunt's machinations."

She nodded, sucking in a great breath of air as though to fortify herself. "Why did she have the keys to your family's house?" she asked in a tone that did not expect an answer. "What did she mean by what she said to Peter? I feel more lost now than I did this morning!"

"As do I," he replied grimly. "In regards to her holding the keys to my family's estate, I am just as baffled as you are. She didn't seem even remotely concerned that I'd draw up charges against her for meddling in my property. She knows I cannot without raising a great deal of questions that have no convenient answers."

She gave a little grimace, shaking her head at what must have been a lifetime of her aunt's antics. "She has known of you for far longer than you've known of her."

"So it seems," he replied evenly. The sentiment was not wholly correct, but it did unsettle him that Lady Silver had apparently seen him coming years and years away. It had not been expected, especially knowing what he knew of her.

"So, it's Kent then?" she asked, tilting her head. "And an announcement of our union?"

"So it seems," he agreed, pushing himself back to his feet. He offered her his hand and assisted her to standing as well, looking down into her eyes. "Shall we introduce you to your staff, then, Mrs. Atlas?"

She gave a shy smile, biting down on her bottom lip. Despite the annoyances swarming around them, it gave him a little thrill to see her so bashful at his behest.

"Nathaniel," she said softly, taking a step forward, closing the space between them, leaving her hand in his. "I know you did not marry me for the reasons most men might run off with a girl. I would still like to make an effort to be happy in our union, to be the wife you might have wanted, if things had gone more predictably."

He could feel the way she held the breath in her lungs, her

dark lashes flickering as she blinked away the embarrassment of her words. His first instinct was to play the romantic hero. He was good at it, well versed in sweet words and doting mannerisms that sent debutantes into a pliable muddle of infatuation. It would placate her, he knew, perhaps even thrill her, but he found himself hesitating from the artifice.

She was never going to be the bride he had envisioned for himself, slippery and cool and nurturing ambitions that spanned Society from end to end. To tell her otherwise would be lying, and he rather thought that she'd spent her life around quite enough dishonesty.

"If you do not wish to share a bed with me, I understand," she added, lifting her chin against the blossom of heat that spread over her cheeks. "I should never insist upon such a thing when it is not wanted."

He blinked at her, tempted yet again to laugh at such an absurd statement. He didn't. He knew well enough how that would seem to her, in such a moment of vulnerability.

"I think that it is a worthwhile endeavor," he told her, lifting her hand to his lips for a gentle kiss. "I should like very much to attempt happiness as man and wife, even if it is not what either of us might have imagined. It is all strange and new to me as well."

She gave a tenuous little smile, the color remaining high in her cheeks from the brush of his lips. "Shall we speak to the staff together, then?"

"Yes," he agreed, tucking that little hand into the crook of his arm and motioning toward the door. "That is a splendid idea."

CHAPTER 9

$\mathcal{I}$n light of everything that had happened, Nell found that she couldn't begrudge her new husband the necessity of immediately packing up their things and venturing out onto the road again. After all, autumn was quickly falling away to winter, and it would be best to avoid first snow if they could, especially since they did not yet know what awaited them in Kent.

"Something you said earlier made me realize that we can simply parcel up and ship over some of the more pressing necessities, my dear," Nathaniel had told her over an early supper. "I do not trust that much remains at Meridian that we will wish to use for any length of time, so at the very least a bed and some basic washing items should be sent ahead of us."

"I gave you that idea?" she had marveled, recalling no such suggestion.

"Quite. You said we can't simply ship the staff over like so much furniture, which made me realize that we *can* ship over the actual furniture. You are a clever one, you know."

"Oh." She had blushed, turning her attention onto her food in an effort to hide the flush of pleasure that had risen in her cheeks. Her head would be spinning for hours, she knew, from the events of the first half of their day.

"We will send some things tonight, I think, and set out at first light tomorrow," Nathaniel continued, oblivious. "I don't relish sleeping in that carriage again."

Of course, she wished more than anything to suggest they do nothing of the sort. Stopping along the way at coaching inns would be far more comfortable for them both and would give them the opportunity to share a room and a bit of privacy on this next trek. Now that she'd reclaimed her things from her aunt, she had proper sleeping attire and a few dresses that might serve to flatter her meager charms more effectively than what she'd worn thus far as a married woman.

Still, she couldn't bring herself to mention sharing a bed again just yet. He hadn't been unkind or rejected her outright earlier, but he hadn't exactly expressed a passionate intention to make good on their spousal duties either. For the first time in her life, she dearly wished she'd spent more time gossiping with the girls she'd known at school. Perhaps a few of them might have given her some guidance in the business of seducing one's husband.

Her own mother had never offered much in the way of guidance on such matters, for she was spoiled by a long and loving marriage with a man who doted upon her every word. Perhaps she might write and ask anyhow, she thought, no matter how embarrassing such a thing might be. After all, her parents had sired many children and were still very affectionate with one another, despite a lack of wealth or luxury.

She wondered with a smirk what Aunt Zelda might suggest on the matter. She surely had knowledge of such things, no matter how distasteful she found them. Nell had seen some truly shocking prints drawn up of various affairs between the rich and influential over the years, though she'd always quickly looked away rather than studying them for a glimmer of useful information.

Ah, perhaps it was hopeless. She should be floating on clouds of euphoria at having been presented to the household staff as Mrs. Nathaniel Atlas, not dwelling on her own superficial grievances. It was common enough anyway, for a woman to have her own bedroom in her husband's house. In fact, Mrs. Arlington had told her pupils more than once that this very thing was the key to matrimonial harmony. There was no shame in it.

He had presented her as though she were a precious treasure he had unearthed by nothing less than divine will, and while the staff was ogling her with bald curiosity, he had presented them with the mysterious offer to join him in Kent for the next several months, leaving the final decisions in the hands of his butler and whisking her off to the dining room before she could so much as breathe.

He was truly magnificent. She had never seen anyone hold their own with such casual disinterest against her aunt. Nathaniel had sat next to her, holding her hand in what must have been a true and devoted gesture of sympathy, while they were barraged with cryptic instructions that would throw their lives into further tumult. He had borne it all with a polite non-nonchalance, and when she had finished, he simply agreed to her terms, as though it were no bother whatsoever.

Peter had offered to accompany them, his brow still furrowed in senseless worry over Nell's safety with her new husband. Zelda had responded in no uncertain terms that she had her own plans for Peter and "his sword arm," whatever that meant. He had appeared just as baffled as she was, but they could draw no further details from their aunt at that time.

"We have two tasks to attend to tonight before we depart London in the morn," he said, startling her out of her reverie.

She blinked back to the present, realizing she'd been gripping her fork so tight that it had put angry, red rivets in the flesh of her hand. She dropped the offending item immediately, and quickly lifted her head to meet her husband's eye.

"One of us must write the marriage announcement for the *Evening Standard,* and a generic one for some of the smaller circulations. The other will need to take up the task of compiling a list of purchases to be made ahead of our arrival in Kent. We will send a rider out tonight ahead of the furniture transport. Do you have a preference in the matter?"

"I am capable of either," she replied honestly. If nothing else, Nell knew she was useful.

"Then if you don't mind, I much prefer the frivolous matter

of penning an advantageous set of announcements," he said with a little quirk of his finely sculpted lips. "I hope you do not think me vapid."

"Never," she assured him, perhaps a little more reverent in her tone than she had intended.

That was how she had come to find herself next to Sarah, the maid who had assisted her the night before, with a stiff bit of parchment balanced on a book in her lap.

"Pardon my saying so, ma'am, but I truly think we are all going to arrive in Kent and realize we've forgotten a great many important things."

"Oh, doubtless so." Nell sighed. "That is always the way with any travel, isn't it?"

"Oh, I wouldn't know, would I?" Sarah said with a grin. "I've never left London."

"Never?" Nell said, aghast. It wasn't that she herself was terribly well traveled, but to never leave the confines of London seemed impossible. It was a place the whole of Society could only tolerate for half the year, while they all spent the other half recovering from the endless bustle in various country hideaways. "Do you mean to join us in Kent, then? It is, of course, your choice."

"Oh, yes, I might as well." Sarah shrugged, her good nature seemingly extending to uncharted adventure. Her blue eyes sparkled, dimples deep in her cheeks as she spoke. "I'd like to see the ocean, after all. And I hear the countryside is full of strapping men in need of a good wife. Maybe I'll find one out there, hm? Anything's possible."

"Certainly possible," Nell agreed. "I found a husband, after all."

"And how," Sarah agreed with a little giggle. "The master is quite the catch."

Nell tilted her head, considering the other girl. She was unmarried for certain, but perhaps she might offer something in the way of feminine guidance, along the lines that she had been contemplating earlier. She couldn't ask right now, of course. There was no telling how much of a gossip the girl might be or where her loyalties might truly lie, but maybe, if they continued to get on so well ...

It was worth considering, anyhow.

"Plates and cutlery will be necessary, though I rather think purchasing them in Kent is more sensible than transporting a large amount of fragile china, don't you agree?" Nell said absently, scratching at the list she was building. "What about books? Is Mr. Atlas a great reader?"

"There's a small library here," Sarah replied. "He most often prefers his study, though."

"Well, at the very least I will want something to read along the way," Nell said. "I suppose stocking a library in Kent is not a major priority, as much as it pains me. Someone ought to employ a stable hand and general tack and supplies to receive us. I do not know what state the stables at Meridian will be in, but it will benefit us more to repair them than to pay to have the mounts lodged elsewhere. Do you know how much of the staff intends to join us on this caper, by any chance?"

"I haven't heard of anyone who doesn't wish to go," Sarah

said earnestly. "It's a strange and exciting prospect for the likes of us. I doubt many will pass up the opportunity."

"Well, at least there's that." Nell sighed. "Transport for so many is going to be a bit of a pain to arrange, but at least we know the quality of each worker from the outset. I think this is as thorough as the list is going to get, Sarah. If you can't think of anything else, you might as well deliver it to Mr. Humphrey now."

"Yes, ma'am," Sarah said, coming quickly to her feet to bob a curtsey. "Will you want another bath tonight? Will you and the master be heading out into the city? I can return to help you dress if so."

"No, no," Nell said, shaking her head. "We must rise very early to begin our journey. I will likely retire soon. If you could just show me to the library you mentioned, I will choose some books for my journey."

"Of course, ma'am," Sarah said brightly, motioning in the direction they were headed. "It's just across from the master's bedchambers. It's a big house, but you get used to it."

It was a big house. Not quite so big as the country estate where she'd passed the majority of the autumn, to be certain, for it was still wedged into a row of London, where space was scarce. Still, it was much larger than the home she'd been raised in as a child and of course much larger than her aunt's outfitted flat above the print shop.

She felt a pang of regret that she must leave so soon, before having a chance to properly explore the place. Though, of course, they would be back in the spring when Parliament resumed ... or, Nathaniel would be anyway. He might not wish to bring his wife along for the Season. Many men did not.

She frowned, waving off the maid and stepping into the library, a tidy room made up of four shelves, two matching chairs, and a fireplace. Nell had always thought that reading spaces were messy by nature, a place where thoughts and belongings were toppled and built upon and rearranged too often to keep any sort of order. Evidently, her new husband did not subscribe to that line of thinking.

There was very little fiction to speak of on the shelves she was tall enough to reach. Only mythologies and a few classic novels were present, perhaps as a matter of academic necessity rather than a joy in the embrace of fantasy.

She brushed her fingers over the carefully alphabetized volumes of reference and research. Machiavelli gave way to Milton who led to More. None of these books were strangers to her, but none were beloved friends either. She settled on a collection of poems by Alexander Pope, which certainly would have never been available to her at Mrs. Arlington's, and a brief history of Kent, which she did not know much about at all. After a moment of deliberation, she also grabbed a volume of translations titled *Tales from the East*, which sounded intriguing, if nothing else.

When she stepped out of the library, intending to make her way back to her chambers, she found herself rooted in place, staring at the closed door of Nathaniel's bedchambers with a sudden flash of inspiration. She knew nothing of seduction, admittedly, but she did know quite a lot about rationalizing her desires until other people saw the sense in them.

She bit her lip, her mind racing with different ways she

might execute her idea. She squeezed the books to her side, nervous energy making its way up from the soles of her feet to the speed of her heart, and decided that she must take advantage of her status as Mrs. Atlas while she could, lest she be left behind and never have another chance to do so.

Nate was soaked to the bone, clenching his jaw tightly to prevent his teeth clattering together. Why he'd taken it upon himself to hand deliver the blasted wedding announcements to his chosen publications was currently beyond him, though surely he'd had a valid reason at the time of setting off.

He rode up to his townhouse on a very agitated horse, his breath condensing into great clouds of fog that he left in his wake. The rain was not falling hard anymore, but even the thin sheets of it that slapped down from above were like a gifting of chill, delivered directly to the flesh.

He had attempted to wait it out, stopping at an empty pub near the offices of the *Evening Standard* and nursing a glass of whiskey for the better part of an hour. If he could have, he'd have taken a carriage home and sent someone to retrieve his mount, but with the household scrambling for an early departure, he simply couldn't afford to create more work for any of them, nor could he dawdle about in a pub for the entirety of the evening.

It was already dark so early in the day by this time of year, and he'd lost his race home to the rapidly dimming light of dusk.

He stepped around several men hauling a hardwood bed

frame onto a carriage, scrambling to keep the pieces shielded under a waxed tarp. He hoped to God the mattress didn't get ruined in this weather before it could reach Kent, lest he and his new bride have to make do with blankets on a bare, likely very dirty floor.

He stepped into the house, shaking himself free of one layer of raindrops as he doffed his hat and coat, handing them off to a waiting footman.

"Do you need a bath, sir?" the lad asked him, taking in his bedraggled appearance.

"No, just a towel or two and my pyjamas should suit me," Nate answered. "And perhaps a stint standing a little too close to the fireplace."

"At least your bed is already warm," the young man said with a little blush. "Mrs. Atlas retired some time ago."

"Did she, now?" he replied, curiosity besetting him. "Let us hope I do not wake her with my chill, then. See that these clothes are dry before they are packed up for shipment, and I will take a spot of hot water, after all. Just a basin for a quick toilette, if you please."

"Sir," the footman said, already turning to scramble off after his task.

Nate resisted the urge to quiz the footman further and instead made haste toward his bedchamber, deeply curious as to what he might find inside. She had said not more than a few hours ago that she would not force herself into his bed if he did not want her there, and yet apparently she had done just that.

He sighed to himself, relieved that the clinging fabric of his clothing was so cold as to combat any dangerous thoughts the premise might otherwise inspire. The girl was no scheming seductress, not by half, and he had no desire to damage her delicate frame or her burgeoning trust in him as a husband by losing himself to brutish, animalistic drive in the bedchamber.

He must tread carefully. He would eventually bed her, yes, and perhaps even beget an heir, but it must be at a time when he had greater control over himself. His life had seen more tumult in the last two weeks than it had since he was a lad of ten, and as tempting as it was to lose himself in pleasure with his sweet little wife, he must take care with the process of seduction, he must be measured and tactful.

After all, if their first encounter was frightening or painful for her, she might not be willing to repeat it. He rather suspected that in ignoring his baser urges for so long, indulging them once would ignite an overwhelming appetite.

How did one bed a virgin, anyhow? He frowned, hesitating just outside of his bedroom door. He hadn't felt this unprepared in many years. It was a silly thing, but he had a sudden impulse to study as though he were walking into an exam or a particularly delicate negotiation.

What sort of man balks at a willing girl in his bed? his mind taunted. *Which of you is the virgin, after all?*

He took a bracing breath and turned the doorknob in his hand, refusing to be hobbled by the prospect of something that promised to be pleasant, even if it had sent his heart thudding with anxious doubt. He didn't know what he expected to find within, but reality was a far cry from a demanding wife, demanding carnal attention.

Nell was indeed in his bed. She was asleep, seemingly not by her own design, propped up on pillows with a book splayed open on her chest. Her spectacles had emerged from her luggage and were currently balanced precariously on the upturned tip of her nose, threatening to leap to their doom at any moment.

He released a gust of air, suddenly feeling quite absurd. Not wishing to have her disturbed, he left the door cracked slightly ajar, so that the washbasin could be brought in as quietly as possible.

He made his way to the bed, noting that she had chosen the left side as her own, and carefully lifted the spectacles from her face, careful not to touch her lest she wake. Unable to resist the curiosity, he held them up to his own eyes, peering through the rounded glass at the world as she must see it without them.

It wasn't terrible, he decided. He could make out everything in the room, but if he were asked to read from the book she held, he wouldn't have been able to. An average debutante would have worn them as seldom as possible, but today was the first time he'd seen her without them for hours on end. There was a mild temptation to wander toward the mirror and see how he looked in them, but he thought it best if he didn't indulge in silliness.

Instead, he folded them up and set them gently on the table next to her, considering how he might lift the book away next without disturbing her sleep.

The door creaked, giving him a start. A maid nodded

respectfully to him, quickly depositing a steaming bowl of water in a wire basin frame and scurrying back out, drawing the door silently closed behind her.

He decided to leave the book in place for the time being, so that he might wash and warm himself to a presentable state before risking waking her. He stripped his wet clothes off and draped each piece on the chairs before the fire, shivering as his clammy skin was exposed to the air.

A cloth dipped into the hot water did wonders to ease the chill away, though he did rather wish he had a bath to soak in now that he'd had a taste of heat. He stepped into dry, woolen pyjamas that had absorbed some of the warmth from the fireplace, and pushed his damp hair back from his face.

One never appreciated how wonderful being dry and warm was without a harsh reminder of the alternative.

"Nathaniel?" Nell murmured in a groggy voice from the bed.

He turned to find her, still clutching the book to her chest, staring at him across the room. "I didn't mean to wake you," he said softly. "My apologies."

She shook her head, rubbing at the sleep in her eyes and pushing herself up to sitting. The book fell away from her night-rail, revealing a tantalizing amount of bare flesh along her shoulders and decolletage. It was not the delicately inviting negligee one might see on a new bride, but rather a serviceable and well-loved item that belonged to a maiden. Why was that somehow even more provocative?

Her dark hair was braided down her back, a few wayward

curls escaping around her face, and the modest swell of cleavage hinted at a bosom more ample than he had anticipated on such a petite frame. Looking at her like this made him wish he had invested more time in learning how to be a rake.

"They took my bed," she said, stifling a yawn behind her hand, "to Kent."

"Ah. Yes, I saw them loading it up for transport," Nathaniel answered thinly. "Do you need anything? I was just about to turn in myself. We have an early morning ahead of us."

"Mm, no," she said, eyelids already drooping again. "Just come to bed. Please."

Those words somehow made him wish to do anything other than sleep. However, fleeing into the house proper in his bare feet and pyjamas, on the run from a wife who likely weighed less than some of the books she read, was such an absurd proposition that he forced himself forward, putting to use his years of experience at donning a calm facade.

She had turned to her side, adjusting her pillows to a reasonable height. When he pulled back the blanket to climb in next to her, he was gifted a view of her slender, pale legs peeking out from the rumpled hem of her night-rail, which had ridden up past her knees.

He swallowed, deciding that turning away from her was indeed the safest way to sleep, and did his best to ignore the scent of lavender and mint that drifted up from the sheets as he settled into place.

The lanterns were already extinguished, the only light in the room coming from the fireplace. It was plenty enough light to expose him as the lecher he was if he happened to roll onto his back. He gritted his teeth, attempting to summon calming thoughts as she settled in behind him.

"Good night, Nathaniel," she whispered, her hand briefly touching his back.

"Good night, Eleanor," he replied, knowing he wouldn't sleep at all.

ight I give you a kiss goodnight?

The question played itself over and over in Nell's mind, pushing itself forward onto her tongue, curling into almost-words, her heart beating hard, urging her to just say it. She lay there, frozen in place, her mind screaming at her to be brave. It should not have been soothing, and yet somehow she was asleep before she could even get out a single syllable, her tongue left in knots throughout the night.

When she awoke, Nathaniel was gone. The spot where his body had been in what seemed like just moments ago was empty and cold, and it was too late to say anything at all. She had gone to all the trouble of cooking up a plan, of having her bed dismantled and taken away, only to fall asleep before executing it. *Twice!*

Oh, she could just scream.

Nell wasn't accustomed to failure. Getting good marks, seeing ideas through to fruition, that was who she was! This was no different than a subject at school, was it? It was a challenge, a task, and she had faltered at the finish line.

Up until now, she had never set a goal for herself that she was not certain was in her reach.

"Good morning, ma'am," Sarah said brightly from the windows, oblivious to her mistress's clamoring internal crisis.

It was the light she was letting in that had pulled Nell from her tormented slumber. Glancing up at it now made her blink rapidly, a thousand pink orbs exploding in front of her. It was a bright morning.

"The rain has cleared right up, so the roads should be good once we're out of London," Sarah commented, smiling out at the fine weather as though she'd summoned it herself and was pleased with her work.

"Where is Nathaniel?" Nell asked, her voice croaky and dry as she fumbled out of her blankets, into the land of the living. "Where is my husband?"

"Oh, he took off before daybreak," Sarah answered, turning on her heel to bustle over and retrieve a tray of breakfast food for Nell. "He said he wanted to ride ahead to Kent and make sure the basic necessities were sorted before his bride arrived. Very thoughtful of him, to be honest. Lots of the girls belowstairs have been swooning over such a gesture. You are a lucky woman, if I may say so, ma'am."

"Of course, thank you," Nell replied, for lack of anything else to say. She allowed the maid to put the tray in her lap and without much considering the offerings, chose and bit down on a plank of dry toast. She forced herself to chew, grateful that the task would prevent her the freedom to make any facial expressions, lest she give away her discontent with his sudden departure.

He had run away from her! She should be horrified and embarrassed, but instead, just now, she rather wanted to strangle him. Or perhaps she wanted to strangle herself. It was hard to know how she felt anymore.

"I can ride with you in the coach if you like, ma'am," Sarah continued, already at work setting out a dress for the day. "But if you're not wishing for any company, I will make myself scarce. There are plenty of places to sit within the carriage train. Some of us are staying behind for the next days to continue packing up and closing the house, but I feel it best I be on hand for you as we go."

Nell paused, reaching for a glass of water to wash down the harsh remains of the bread, which were sitting heavily in her slender throat. Once she could speak again, she turned toward Sarah with what she hoped was a confident visage. "Surely you don't mean to pack up *all* of the furniture to send to Kent? It would be quite the expense of both time and resources to pack up the entirety of the house. We only agreed to basics, didn't we?"

"Well, yes, ma'am, of course, but basics add up to quite a lot of items, and some heavy lots besides."

"Nathaniel wishes for the master bed to be left here," she said suddenly, the coolness of her tone giving the command a weight of authority. "It is heavy and made of precious materials that could easily be damaged en route. We will have no need of guest quarters for only a few short months, after all, and can make do with the furniture from the room I took the first night. Leave this one as it is."

"Oh," Sarah said, her bright blue eyes wide and alert. "Yes, of course. I will tell the men. We shan't be packing up anything cumbersome beyond what went last night. No rugs or tables or anything of that sort."

"Good," Nell replied. This time, she lifted a piece of toast and took her time coating it with a soft layer of butter and a dollop of marmalade. This petty act of defiance had somehow soothed her soul. "Only one wardrobe for us as well. It should be sufficient. Tell me, how many days is the journey, by your reckoning?"

"Well, I wouldn't rightly know, ma'am, but some of the more worldly staff have made estimations. They say that by horse, the way the master went, it is likely less than two days through. For us, in the coach, mayhap three, but that is all dependent on the roads and the weather."

"I see." Nell desperately wished to heave a great sigh, for the only thing that made the prospect of another long leg in a rumbling carriage less appealing than it already seemed was the absence of her new husband as a diversion. "I should like if you rode with me, Sarah," she decided, pleased with the way the girl's face lit up. "I do spend quite a lot of time reading during these trips, if you don't mind stints of silence."

"Oh, not at all," Sarah said breathlessly, clasping her hands in front of her in barely contained excitement. "I have some knitting to attend to and perhaps I will snag a book from the collection myself! I never make the time for such pleasures."

"Then it is settled," Nell said with a tilt of her head. "Let us make for Kent and Meridian House."

"Yes, ma'am," Sarah replied gleefully.

NELL FOUND that she was rather adept at being the mistress of a domain. Never before in her life had she been the one to issue orders to others. Never before in her life had she lived anywhere but under another mistress's roof, be it her mother's, her aunt's, Mrs. Arlington's, or most recently the Viscountess Somers.

Without any practice whatsoever, she was able to speak with enough authority to be obeyed, and as such, her coach set off first, with two drivers and Sarah in tow. She explained to them the method Nathaniel had used to hasten the arrival time from Scotland to London, with refreshed horses at coaching inns and shifts between the two men up top. It was not an instruction that was received happily, but it was received, and that was all that really mattered in the end, wasn't it?

She wore her blue dress again, but reverted back to her sensible bun, her dark curls coiled and pinned into submission. She tucked herself into the corner of the carriage that she had become accustomed to and attempted to begin the journey by delving into the work of Alexander Pope, a man whose work was deemed inappropriate for the library at her finishing school.

Sarah sat opposite her, happily clacking her knitting needles together as lengths of woven textile emerged from the other end. After about an hour, Nell found the knitting process rather more fascinating than Mr. Pope's cynical views on life itself and the unavoidable futility of it all.

Perhaps it hit too close to home just now.

When they made their first stop, Nell was able to negotiate a refreshment period for their party, with a hot meal and a portion of time in one of the coaching inn boarding rooms, a dormitory of cots near the barn, where the gentlemen were able to nap if they so wished before setting out again. Nell herself felt too restless to sleep, and Sarah appeared happy to tuck herself near the fire at the inn and pelt the other travelers with curious questions.

They were no more than a day from London, but to the wide-eyed maid, they might as well have crossed the ocean and arrived on unknown shores.

Once back in the carriage, Sarah chattered wistfully about the things she'd been told of the town of Canterbury, and what it might be like to visit. "People take religious pilgrimages there," she said breathlessly. "It's quite famous!"

"It is," Nell had agreed with amusement. "I have not been either. It is likely in the history of Kent I took from the library in London, though. If you've a curiosity about the place, do have a look inside."

"Oh, yes, ma'am, that sounds splendid." Sarah sighed, standing immediately and bracing her hand against the top of the carriage so that she might dig through the bag with the books in them. "Do you want this other one, then? You don't seem to like the one you've got."

"Yes, might as well," Nell said with a sigh, holding out Mr. Pope's anthology in exchange for the impulsively borrowed

Tales from the East. "Perhaps this one will be a little more optimistic about the state of the world, hm?"

"Well, we are headed southeast, ma'am," Sarah said earnestly. "It seems appropriate."

Nell had chuckled to herself, settling back against the carriage window with her feet propped on the other side, and opened the cover of the book.

Tales from the East, it said. *A collection of magic and myth from afar.*

She didn't recognize the name of the translator, but did note that the book had been published by Oxford University. She wondered idly if her brother might know the man who'd done the translations. Perhaps the world was smaller than any of them realized.

It was a strange thought to have ahead of being catapulted into a world of fantasy quite alien to Nell. Here there were no knights in shining steel, nor lords and ladies at the forefront of all. Instead of English gardens and meandering dales, there was golden sand and tropical trees, filled with birdsong and the chatter of monkeys. Heroes were not the rich and powerful, but rather a fishmonger's wife who takes wishes from a magical catch, a concubine eager to run away with her lover, or a band of thieves after a treasure that certainly did not belong to them.

Each story was a little longer than the one that came before it, each trace of magic a little bolder and more fantastical. Nell thought that the man who'd translated this work had done a capital job of building one's immersion into the strange and foreign.

When she stumbled onto a story called *Ali with the Large Member*, she realized that this book too was likely not intended for young women. It was a strange story about the male anatomy and how those who possess a particular organ are prone to become obsessed with every aspect of it. Having only seen nude men in tasteful sculpture, Nell thought that the degree of concern over such a thing was well and truly overblown, even if the story itself had brought blood rushing into her cheeks.

The book was long and so dense that Nell often finished a story only to read it again twice over, simply to absorb everything woven inside. More than once she found herself reaching for a lantern so that she might continue to read through the dark hours of their journey.

She found herself at sea with djinn and mermaids, at a royal court studded with rubies as a sultan demanded the culprit of a murder in just three days from a man who would pay with his own life if he failed. She gave herself chills reading of a haunted mansion, full of trickster spirits, eager to sap the life from humans in exchange for pleasant dreams.

On the second day, as they stopped for luncheon and rest, Nell took the liberty of ordering baths for all four of them, so that they might feel a little more human for the final leg of their trip. She encouraged everyone to take their time and feel restored, as she did not fancy the prospect of arriving on Nathaniel's doorstep as bedraggled and unkempt as she'd been at the end of their last journey.

Despite the urge to fall back into her book, Nell committed to a nap after her bath, leaving her long mane of hair over the end of the cot, so that it might dry while she slept.

By the time she woke, it was already dark, and she reasoned that they might as well spend the night. The drivers in particular expressed great gratitude at this idea, and Nell took Sarah abovestairs to share one of the nicer rooms with a larger bed for the evening, rather than continuing to board in mixed company after dark.

"You seem to like your book as much as I like mine, ma'am," Sarah said happily as she combed through the tangle of Nell's curls before bed. "Might we trade once we've both finished? I've never had such time to read about England before, and I find it is giving me great pleasure."

"Does it?" Nell asked, pleased. "What have you learned?"

"Oh, a great many things, ma'am. Did you know that England used to be Italian?"

"Italian?" Nell asked, turning her head for a moment.

"Yes, ma'am. Kent in particular was part of Rome all through the old times. Even the great King Alfred, who I take was quite the effective bloke, couldn't take Kent for the Saxons. The book says the Roman influence is alive and well today. I wonder if they're all dark and Italian-looking there!"

"I doubt it," Nell said with a laugh. "Rome was basically the whole of Europe back then. They're likely just as English as you and me. You know, I am from Winchester, west of London. There, we are Saxon down to our bones. King Alfred is buried just a short walk from my parents' home."

"Perhaps you're finally taking Kent for the Saxons then, ma'am," Sarah giggled. "Else you're joining the enemy."

"I suppose we shall see," Nell replied with a little smile. "God willing, I'll do my forebears proud."

"Oh, I'm sure you will," Sarah said, wrapping off the end of Nell's braid. "So long as we don't turn into heathens by Christmas, I figure we've held strong."

"Ha," Nell said, climbing into the bed and snuggling down into the covers. "By the time you finish *my* book, you'll wish you were a heathen all along."

"Splendid." Sarah yawned. "I'd make a right pretty heathen, ma'am. I look well in furs."

Nell fell asleep smiling, her mind spinning with a strange tapestry of thoughts that resulted in spectacular—if incoherent—dreams.

CHAPTER 11

*N*athaniel was not a coward.

He didn't think he was a coward, anyhow. He hadn't run from anything since he was eleven years old, hiding in the stables to avoid his uncle's strap. Yet here he was, halfway across the nation, because a sweet little woman wanted to share his bed.

It was absurd. He was being absurd.

He had faced down far more harrowing confrontations than bedding a willing wife, and one who was more appealing by the day besides.

He couldn't rationalize what it was about her that was suddenly so vexing. Perhaps it was just the way between men and women, that if they spent enough time together, certain urges would emerge. That must be it. He had never had trouble resisting temptation before, when he'd been the one and only king of his private life.

It was her constant presence that was muddying his mind. It could happen to any man. Hell, it likely did happen to a great majority of them. Nate should be congratulating himself on how rare an occurrence this was rather than lashing himself over his weaknesses.

She was a woman and he was a man. This was just the nature of things. Framing her as some particular breed of female allure was just his primal impulses urging him to action.

Still, every time he thought about this particular marital duty, his lifelong survival tactics for maintaining a cool head seemed to fail. His general strategy of finding some sensible means to dismiss both his urges and his panic as irrational nonsense was just as useless as his attempts to occupy his mind with important business he must still attend to.

It seemed like every time he had a moment of quiet in which to formulate coherent thoughts, he found himself pulled into various fantasies about what she might look like under all of those boxy, unfashionable clothes. Once he got himself into that particular state of fervor, there was no careful calculation to be had, no calm execution of a plan that would ensure an optimal outcome.

He might have cried if he were prone to such things. As it were, he was not, and instead settled for riding horseback, hell for leather, in cold, misty weather en route to Kent. Why send a missive when one could simply arrive on his estranged family's doorstep, after all?

Why indeed? He was not above sleeping in a stable or two to hasten his arrival. Patience had never been his strongest virtue anyway. It was hard to dwell on such silly problems when your body ached and your skin had gone numb from the unflinching onslaught of cold. And one never much dreamed during sleep borne of such deep exhaustion.

Once he had passed through the county border, past the wooden sign that proudly declared *Invicta* between a crude painting of two white stallions, the memories of this place began to replace his disjointed thoughts concerning Eleanor.

His cousin, Kit, still lived in his childhood home, a homestead surrounded by fruit orchards that stood close enough to Meridian to reach by horse in under an hour. As children, Kit and Nate had often visited every afternoon in the summer, in one home or the other.

Navigating to the Cooper home was second nature to Nate, even after all these years. Some things were permanently etched into the memory, no matter how far afield destiny might take a man.

He had seen Kit in London this past Season, recently returned from war and decorated. He had been as he always was, bright-eyed and eager to explore what the future might hold. Optimistic and hungry for life, now that he could settle his family's debts, free of his wastrel of a father.

They had spent a few nights together, sipping port at White's, but both had been so occupied with their own business that it seemed they hadn't seen each other at all, in the end. Nate had rather brusquely declined an invitation to visit Kit in the autumn, which was less than ideal as a backdrop for showing up at his doorstep out of the blue, much less as harried and unkempt as he likely appeared.

Still, he did not hesitate nor consider finding lodging elsewhere. Despite it all, he knew he would be welcome, and when Kit answered his knock at the door, he didn't speak a word of complaint. He didn't speak any words at all. He simply offered a welcoming embrace, given freely with no expectation of answers as payment.

It wasn't until the next morning that Nate felt truly human again. His clothes were a bit worse for the wear, having been hard-worn through his journey, but a shave and a bath and a spot of breakfast in a comfortable chair were enough to calm some of the feral panic he'd been indulging for the last several days.

Upon arrival, his cousin had led him inside and immediately seen to his comfort and repast, insisting that explanations could wait until the morrow. It had been a relief, for another hour or two on that damned horse and Nate was certain he would have keeled out of his saddle and spent the night in the grass.

Kit was gone in the morning, attending to some business in the fruit orchards he'd recently purchased back into his family's name, and so Nate dined alongside his aunt Susan, who patted him on the hand by way of greeting, and was perfectly happy to sit in comfortable silence until he deigned to speak.

Silence had been a means to survival when Uncle Archie was still around, his temper always teetering right on the edge of explosion, and even with him rotting away in some debtor's prison on the other side of the world, the habit still loomed heavily over them.

She looked much the same as she had the last time Nate had seen her, slender, but strong, with a posture that would not be humbled by any misfortune life threw at her. She had a few new lines around her sweet blue eyes and some of the sheen in her light hair had given way to silver. Her smile was still warm, her eyes crinkling with pleasure at having found him seated at the table, and her hands still bearing the telltale calluses of a woman who spent entirely too much time at a loom.

"I have married," he said to her, to break the silence.

It was perhaps too abrupt an announcement, said in too loud a voice, for her head snapped up in surprise, making him wince.

"Have you?" she said softly, reaching forward again to touch his hand. "When?"

"Within the last month," he replied vaguely. "It was an elopement, which is why I did not reach out to the two of you to attend. There was no formal wedding."

"Oh," she replied, considering him. "I would never have thought an elopement to be something within your purview, Nathaniel. She must be quite the woman."

"Her name is Eleanor," he said, "she will be joining me in a few days' time. We were hoping to spend the remainder of the holiday season at Meridian."

At that, her eyes widened considerably, her hand tensing on top of his own. "Nathaniel! I do not even know if Meridian is safe to live within anymore," she whispered, as though the house might overhear. "It has been unattended for a very, very long time. Why not simply stay here, with us? You are most welcome."

"I cannot. It must be Meridian," he replied with a weak smile. "It has evidently been cared for enough to still be habitable. A friend of my parents' has been seeing to the general upkeep of the estate, though it has remained unoccupied throughout my absence. We are hopeful that we can make a home of it again."

She appeared too stunned to formulate a reply, blinking at him in astonishment.

"I shall tell Kit when he returns," Nate said, patting the hand she had frozen atop his. "Hopefully he will be willing to assist me in some of the restoration."

"But what of your wife?" Susan asked, clearly a little scandalized. "Where is she?"

"She will be joining me in a few days' time with some of our furniture from London and a small staff to assist us with restoring Meridian to its former glory. She is looking forward to connecting with some old friends here. You might be familiar with the Dempierre family?"

"Me?" Susan said with a little laugh. "I think you well know I don't walk in such circles, Nathaniel. I know *of* the Dempierres, but I certainly have never spoken to any of them. I couldn't afford the privilege!"

"Wealthy, are they?" he replied, as though the information were of no great import to him. "It is strange that I don't know of them, then. I don't recall any Dempierres amongst the *ton* during any Season in recent memory, and yet my wife insists that they have quite the social clout."

"Well, they are French, aren't they? They keep to their own. Bit sore about the plight of exile, I imagine. They live in a little castle on the cliffs and host survivor's balls and all manner of other foreign pageantry." She hesitated, a scandalous thought causing her eyes to widen. "Nathaniel, Is this bride of yours from France?"

"She is from Winchester, my dear woman, fear not," Nathaniel replied, unable to stop a chuckle from bubbling over. "I shouldn't do something so shocking without at least sending warning first."

"I daresay you would," she admonished, not unkindly. "You've marched down your own path since you were old enough to crawl, haven't you?"

He gave an apologetic shrug, still smiling. "I suppose I do have a tendency to plot independently for my future. It may become more difficult now that I have a wife."

"I certainly hope so," she answered, dabbing at her lips with a napkin. "Well, if you're determined to live at Meridian, we might as well go see how the place stands, don't you think? Kit won't be back until after luncheon, and it's a short ride from here. Do you have the keys?"

"I do," Nate said, raising his eyebrows in surprise. "I will fetch them. I suppose there's no time like the present, and I admit I'm curious as to how the old place is faring these days myself."

"I'll get my shawl, then," she said, pushing back her chair. "There's no telling what we'll find. God help us."

Nate watched her go, popping a final morsel of his breakfast into his mouth. He wasn't sure what memories were about to be stirred from deep slumber within him, and perhaps it would have been better to risk the unknown alone.

All the same, it was a comfort to see his aunt again. Perhaps he wasn't without origin, after all.

CHAPTER 12

By the time the sun had started to set, Nate and his aunt had realized just how enmeshed they'd gotten in exploring the rooms of Meridian.

As though by magic, the first carriage bearing a haul of items from his London townhouse had arrived, with items that could feasibly make up a bedroom, only an hour or so after Nate and Susan had begun their task. It was good fortune, for they were able to single out a room to sweep and dust to a satisfactory state so that things might begin to come together that very day.

There was still quite a lot of furniture in the old place, most of it shrouded in large swathes of white fabric, haloed with dust. He and his aunt had inspected a few things, a piano in the parlor, the dining table and chairs, and even the crib in the old nursery seemed to be salvageable, while other things, like the twenty-year-old mattresses left to decay in their frames, would have to be disposed of.

"Kit will be wondering where on earth we've gotten to,"

Susan said, peering out at the dull glow of the setting sun. "There's no dinner on, either. I suppose we might go retrieve him and take our supper at the public house?"

"I'd like that," Nate agreed. "You've done quite enough labor for the day."

They returned to the Cooper house, a bit dustier than Nate would have preferred, and gathered his cousin to set out for a ready-made dinner at the cozy little pub that had sat on the corner since the Tudors had reigned.

"I'm amazed that it's held up so well," Susan told them, settling on a hearty shepherd's pie and a glass of ale. "Whoever your mysterious caretaker was for all this time, he did a wonderful job beating back the consequences of time."

"I can't believe you intend to live there," Kit said, his eyes narrowed over his own glass of wine as he studied his cousin. "You seemed very much decided on never wanting to set foot in that house again."

"Well, time changes a man," Nate replied with a shrug, hoping that a meaningful glance in Kit's direction would silence any further questioning along these lines. "And so does marriage. It wouldn't do to put my new bride up in London all year 'round, would it? We will make new memories to overshadow the old ones."

"Yes," Kit agreed, his eyes still narrowed with suspicion. "I have no doubt on that accord."

"Tell us all about her, Nathaniel," Susan said, reaching over to clasp his hand across the table. "If my own son won't marry, I'll have to take my joy in your own union. What might we expect of your Eleanor?"

What might they expect? Nathaniel hadn't the faintest idea, but he gave his practiced politician's smile, and sang her praises as though there was no doubt at all in his mind, all the while ignoring the keen way his cousin watched him with an uncomfortable intensity, likely seeing right through every layer of artifice, no matter how carefully constructed.

IT WASN'T until Susan Cooper had retired for the evening that Kit spoke freely.

"I want to see it," was the first thing he said.

"You want to see what?" Nate had asked, already fantasizing about plodding back upstairs and kicking his boots off.

"Meridian. Let's ride out now. It is still early, and there will be plenty of time to return if you wish it. If you don't, I understand you now have a bedchamber prepared for you, oh lord and master."

Nathaniel sighed, running a hand through his hair and looking away from his cousin.

Growing up, people had often thought them brothers. Kit was just two years younger than Nate, and the resemblance was often described as uncanny. Kit was fairer, with golden blond hair and his mother's soft blue eyes, and a fair bit more muscled, due to his penchant for taking the hard way 'round in life. He wore his hair longer and his clothes plainer and his emotions more honestly.

Tonight, with Kit towering over him, arms crossed over his chest and a frown cut deep into his face, Nate rather thought his cousin was the manifestation of his own conscience. Kit was a reflection of himself without the shadows and the artifice, and he was the only person in the world who wouldn't happily swallow his sugared half-truths and be grateful for the pleasure.

It was a damned nuisance.

"I'll saddle the horses," Kit said, as though the matter was settled. "Grab some lanterns and oil. I'll meet you outside in a few minutes."

There was no point in sighing again, but Nate did it anyway. When he stepped outside, Kit tossed him a set of reins and wordlessly mounted his own horse, ready to set out. They rode in silence, which was just as well, for Nate was not prepared for the lump of dread that rose up in his throat at the sight of Meridian cresting the horizon, lit only by moonlight.

It had not seemed half so ominous by the light of day, not half so full of pain and secrets. There was no turning back, however, and if he was determined to follow through with the task set to him by Lady Silver, he must set his jaw and brave it out, like any other man would.

Kit's face was dour as they arrived, each movement he made somehow heavier in the wake of all the history that hung around this place. It was a rare thing to see Kit without a smile on his face, truth be told, which only added weight to the dread Nate was nursing.

He drew the ring of keys from his coat and strode forward, determined not to let this play out any longer than it needed to. His staff were sleeping at a local inn tonight, so the house would be empty for likely the next day or more, while things were set to rights inside. The hinges on the door did not squeak or protest, instead swinging open at the merest suggestion, as though it were well accustomed to inviting visitors inside.

Kit sucked in his breath, stepping over the threshold and into the gallery with his lantern held high in front of him. The candlelight cast a faint glow throughout the large, empty room, its chill magnified by the Italian marble in the floors and the cold, tarnished brass on the fittings. It might as well be a ruin or a cave in some unknown corner of the world for all the resemblance it bore to what it once had been.

"We've only just started our work," Nathaniel said dryly, stepping around his cousin and motioning to the left-hand staircase. "You'll have to forgive our lack of progress. Come, I will show you the bedroom we're currently outfitting if you like."

Kit nodded, his eyes wide, taking in the surroundings as he followed, each footstep echoing throughout the cavernous insides of the unfed beast that was this house.

They passed the nursery, the door hanging open on hinges that would need replacing, and the cradle inside haloed in eerie moonlight on a threadbare rug. Kit seemed to shiver, huddling into his coat a little more after that.

When they reached the bedroom, Nate was pleased to see the bed had been fully assembled, complete with linens, and the floors swept and tidied. There was even fresh wood in the fireplace. He could easily pass the evening here if he so chose.

"I'll light a fire," he said, walking past his stunned cousin to go about the business of bringing some warmth into this place. It gave him an excuse to keep his back turned, to occupy his hands and mind while Kit came to whatever conclusions he was going to come to.

He discarded his gloves and knelt at the hearth, gathering the tinderbox and a bit of kindling to go about his work. He couldn't remember the last time he'd had to light his own fire. Something about seeing the sparks jump to life and mature into mighty flames was deeply satisfying.

By the time he stood, the fire was building nicely, and the warmth was most welcome.

The light that flooded the room seemed to highlight the bare walls and naked floors. The room had been stripped clean, without even curtains to darken the world without. He tried to remember if there had been decor of any sort in here this morning. There had been a rug, he knew, when he'd walked through with his aunt, but he couldn't form a clear memory of the walls.

This had been his parents' room.

Kit set down his lantern and crossed the room, taking a seat on the edge of the bed with his elbows balanced on his knees. He shook his head, staring into the fire rather than looking directly at Nate. When he spoke, his voice had lost its sharp edge, blunted by the shock of coming back here again.

"Who is she, Nathaniel?" he asked. "What are you really doing here?"

Nate didn't answer immediately, leaning back against the mantle of the fireplace and attempting to organize his thoughts in a way that would be the most palatable.

"Do not lie to me again." Kit sighed, running a hand over his face, rubbing at his eyes. "I always know when you're lying."

"You do," Nate replied evenly. "You are the only one."

"Not your wife?"

"Least of all my wife." Nate shook his head, glancing out the naked windows to the sloping hills below the house, a blur of blackened grass and skeletal trees in the darkness. "I think you know that I would not have come back here of my own accord. It is an unpleasant necessity for the good of everything, and I would simply like to make it as tolerable as I can. You oughtn't harry your mother with more worries, least of all on account of me."

"I will worry about my mother, Nate." He was frowning again, such a stern judge of all things right or wrong. "Who is this girl you married? What are you involved in? Just have out with it now and spare us both the boredom of a long game of block and parry."

Nate drew a bracing breath, deciding there was indeed no point in a long game of subterfuge, at least where Kit was involved. He crossed his arms over his chest, leveling his cousin with his best serious stare. "My sister would have been twenty, this past spring. Did you know that?"

Kit flinched, clearly surprised by the direction this had taken. "Yes, of course I did. It was a tragic thing that happened to them, Nate. It was cruel and unfair."

"It wasn't an accident," Nate replied. "You remember your father's rantings about my parents being caught up in shady dealings? Of being executed as traitors with a baby in tow as collateral damage?"

Kit squinted at him, confusion evident on his face. "My father is a delusional madman. He sees plotting and conspiracy everywhere. He once accused us of feeding information to the vicar, remember? He chased us around the lawn with a polo stick. His insistence that your parents were in bed with silver spies was just more lunatic ranting."

"You're not entirely wrong," Nate said smoothly, resisting the urge to admit he was, in fact, passing information to the vicar during the incident in question. "Archibald Cooper was a paranoid, unsteady, untrustworthy fool. However, in this particular matter, his grandiose beliefs happen to have been correct. My parents were indeed involved with a contingent of spies. They are called the Silver Leaf Society, and I have spent years seeking out answers as to who they are and what agenda they serve."

Kit did not immediately respond, his mouth opening and then snapping back shut as his hand came back up over his eyes. He groaned, likely regretting his demand for the truth.

"My parents worked for the Silver Leaf Society. It has been confirmed beyond any doubt, but beyond that, the details remain a mystery."

"What details?" Kit asked, as though he did not truly want the answer.

Nate frowned. "You know very well. They departed Dover, sea-bound for Calais with my baby sister in tow, and none of them ever returned. Your father said they were disposed of for treason by agents of the Crown. It's an unpleasant reality, but I am inclined to believe him until I see proof otherwise."

"You can't seriously believe that! You must realize how unhinged it sounds!"

Nate held up a hand, continuing to speak, with no sympathy stirring in his chest for the shock he was dropping on his cousin. "After a great deal of time and effort, I have finally made my way into the ranks of this secret society. *That* is why I am here. I must play the part of a loyal lackey until I have uncovered the whole of the truth. After that, I intend to expose and destroy all remnants of their murderous ranks, and I've made great progress in doing so."

"And the girl?" Kit asked, his voice thick with exasperation. "Your wife?"

Nate hesitated, no simple answer rising to his thoughts. Eleanor was not only a member of the society he intended to upend, she was the heiress apparent to take over the whole operation. Her expressive little face floated up in his memory, so void of evil or malice, and he found he couldn't quite categorize what part she played in all of this anymore.

"Nate!" Kit snapped, glaring at him.

"I am protecting her from them," Nathaniel decided, feeling the truth of it down to his bones, "lest her innocent heart sends her headlong into unsalvageable danger." *Or unfathomable corruption.*

"Ah, yes," Kit said, sarcasm dripping from his words. "Nathaniel William Atlas, defender of fair maidens. What on earth has gotten into you? This is madness! You have a good life in London. A promising future! The past is well behind us by now. What could have possibly possessed you to go digging into things that could get you hurt, much less some innocent girl standing obliviously in the crosshairs?"

"She was standing there before I found her, Kit." Nathaniel pushed himself off the wall and paced the length of the floor, nervous energy rattling him too deeply to remain still. "I need to see her safely attended to, provided for once I've shone a light on the dark dealings within which she has found herself entangled. You must not say any of this to her, however. We are here on a simple mission for the Silver Leaf, and we will execute it faithfully, as we must."

Kit waited for Nathaniel to turn back and face him, his lips pressed tight together in disapproval. "What mission is this?"

"We must be invited to a winter masquerade ball put on by a family called the Dempierres. From what your mother told me, they sound difficult to simply encounter in social circles of the area, so I must needs research them and plan for our course of action."

"What are you going to do to them?" Kit pressed. "At this masquerade ball?"

"Nothing," Nate replied with a shrug. "We are simply to attend and observe, at least so far as we know now. I would not play at mischief that could get anyone hurt."

"No?"

"No," Nate snapped. "Knowing how the Silver Leaf dealt with defectors some twenty years ago, I found myself testing the waters in my first mission, to determine if they were still willing to use lethal means to punish those who might turn their backs on the Crown."

"And?"

"If they are, only the woman who runs things knows of it. All of the agents I have worked with reacted with bald-faced horror at the very concept of violent retribution, even under significant pressure. Which is just as well, for I might have had to risk losing my progress to warn some poor idiot who was in their way, had they been amenable to lethal solutions."

Kit just blinked at him, his face slack with disbelief. It was, Nate supposed, quite a lot to throw at a person all at once, but Kit and his damned persistence had brought it upon himself.

"Nate," Kit muttered, flopping back onto the mattress to stare at the ceiling. "You are a bloody fool."

Nate looked at him a moment and then gave a begrudging nod. "Yes," he agreed, "I suppose I am."

CHAPTER 13

*S*hambling through the roads into Kent County was almost surreal. This trip had been days shorter than the one she'd taken south with Nathaniel not a week past, and yet, somehow, throughout this one, she'd almost come to believe she would never arrive at her destination.

There was no mistaking it. Signposts began to display familiar city names, many of which sent Sarah into a flurry of trivia recently learned from the history book she'd borrowed.

They stopped for a late breakfast at a way station in a thicket of rapidly balding trees, where the ground was a patchwork of gold and rust from the blanket of leaves. Nell had a cozy mug of steaming hot chocolate with a modest breakfast of porridge and honey, and watched from the window as more leaves floated down to carpet the earth on every gust of wind.

When the driver asked for directions to Meridian House, the reaction was as though he'd asked for the location of the underworld. It took some coaxing and convincing before the locals would proffer directions, and even then they warned that no one had lived in that house for nearly twenty years, and their trip was in vain.

Nell asked Sarah to arrange her hair again in the carriage, her pulse coming quicker at the realization that she would be with Nathaniel again very soon. She wished she could step from the carriage in stunning silk skirts and the sway of a woman who knows how to enchant a man, like the courtesans in *Tales from the East*. What she wouldn't give for that kind of prowess.

As it stood, she simply hoped she was presentable enough, for today felt like the first day she would truly live as a woman grown and wed, arriving at her homestead for the long winter. Whether she was feeling anticipation or fear seemed irrelevant, for the quickened breathing and racing heart were the same either way.

"You must be missing Mr. Atlas something fierce," Sarah said with a knowing smile as she twisted and pinned Nell's wayward curls into order. "If I had a husband like that, I'd be desperate to get back to him too."

Nell bit her lip, her cheeks warming at the thought of it. "Sarah, have you a beau back in London? Or perhaps elsewhere?"

"Me? No, not anymore," Sarah said cheerily. "I was wooed for a bit by a baker's boy, but it wasn't meant to be. My mother scolded me red for cutting him loose. Said I was spoiled for choice and would regret it, but I don't."

"You didn't love him?" Nell asked, curious.

"Not the way a wife loves a husband, no." Sarah sighed, securing another pin and picking up a new coil of hair. "My mum always scolded me for liking the beautiful ones. 'Don't pine for the pretty ones, Sarah. You can't trust pretty men,' she always said, but I'd like to learn that lesson on my own, given the opportunity, thank you very much. Besides, plenty of ugly blokes are untrustworthy too, aren't they?"

"I suppose that's true," Nell agreed, frowning. "Would you say Nathaniel is a pretty man?"

"Oh, by God, would I," Sarah snorted, raising a hand to stifle the unladylike sound. "Apologies, ma'am. I forget myself."

Nell turned to look at her maid, whose cheeks were still pink with amusement, her hand covering the smile on her lips. "You may always speak freely with me, Sarah," she assured her with a conspiratorial smile. "And rest easy, if you'd answered any other way, I'd know you surely for a liar."

The two of them had giggled over the moment, falling back into comfortable silence as the carriage ambled its way over the final stretch of road to their destination.

Meridian House was built into a sloping rock face, with a tumble of flat, green land sprawled out around it, dotted with fruit trees. It was nowhere near as grand as a country manor like Somerton, where she and Nathaniel had passed the prior month, but rather stately in its practicality. Timeless. It was an heirloom estate, grand enough to have a name, but modest enough to allow for neighbors.

They were not the first carriage to arrive in the drive that day, judging from the unloading in process as they approached the drive.

A man she almost mistook for Nathaniel was shouting orders at workers while they heaved some particularly heavy piece of covered furniture free from its secured place on the transport wagon. He must have been a relative, she realized, for even from a distance she could see the likeness in the two men. This one was not as richly colored, nor as sleek, and he did not possess the elegance of motion that her own husband did, but they were undoubtedly kin.

He waved in their carriage with a smiling enthusiasm Nathaniel never would have displayed so openly and approached himself to open the door for them, extending a hand to assist Nell out into the bright afternoon sun.

She took care stepping out onto the uneven cobble, which was much in need of mending and overgrown between the pebbles. While she found her balance, the man was occupied assisting Sarah out next, then speaking to the driver with instructions for stabling the horses and taking some rest inside the house.

"Nell!" called a voice from the house, sending her spinning in its direction with her heart directly in her throat.

Nathaniel strode across the lawn with an expression on his handsome face that at least seemed pleased with her arrival. He was sharply dressed, his boots glinting in the sunlight as he approached her, holding out his hands for hers in welcome.

She did not rightly know what gesture was appropriate, and so gave a tenuous smile back and reached her own fingers out, allowing them to be wrapped in the warmth and strength of his large, strong hands. She did not trust herself to do much more. When he leaned forward and pressed a soft kiss into the swell of her cheek, she thought very well that she should be hailed a heroine for not slumping to the ground in a dead faint.

"You've made excellent time," he was saying brightly. "I did not estimate your arrival for another night or two at least. You must forgive the state of the house, but you know as well as any that it is a work in progress. Allow me to introduce my cousin, Christopher Cooper. He is assisting us with putting the house back in order."

The other man appeared again, giving a little bow in greeting. "No one calls me Christopher," he told her. "You must call me Kit, as everyone else does."

"Well, then you must call me Nell," she said with a smile and the shadow of a curtsy. "How wonderful to meet you, Kit. I was not expecting family to herald our arrival."

"Oh, your husband has seen to a great many things in anticipation of your arrival," Kit told her, a distinct note of playful ribbing in his sparkling blue eyes. "I've never seen him quite so determined."

"I find that hard to believe," Nell demurred, pleased despite her awareness that this must be little more than routine flattery.

"I have taken a few liberties," Nate confirmed in a low voice, drawing her attention back to him, only to immediately be snared in the hypnotic pull of those chameleon's eyes, as dazzling as the autumn foliage around them. "I imagine you'd like to rest before I bombard you with all the particulars, however. It has been a long journey."

"It has," she agreed, breathless.

That knowing little smile curled at the corners of his mouth. He gestured toward the doors to Meridian, tucking her hand into his elbow with that same, practiced motion he'd used back in London. "I will show you to the bedroom," he said. "You've earned a spot of relaxation."

She allowed him to lead her away, catching only the barest flicker of bafflement in the face of his cousin as they passed into the house, sheltered from the bright illumination of the afternoon sun.

Bedroom, he'd said, as though there were only one so far. If she'd been alone in the stairwell, she might have given a little jump of victory at the outcome of her little ruse, regardless of its failure back in London.

"I have been making inquiries," Nathaniel said low and deep, in a whisper meant for only her ear.

She knew it wasn't intended to be seductive, nor even particularly intimate, for it was simply Silver Leaf business. All the same, she couldn't stop the gooseflesh from rising on her arms. No one could rationalize that tone of voice with her silly physical reactions, now could they?

"The Dempierre family rarely mingles in local company. However, they are fond of a particular clothier in Dover proper, a Frenchwoman whose designs apparently were so luxurious that they put her life at risk during the initial uprising. I have already visited the shop and commissioned several things for you. It is my hope that you can gather information while you are being fitted."

"I likely can," Nell said cautiously. "It depends on the

temperament of the seamstress, or, I suppose, those in her employ."

Nathaniel gave her a little smile, as though he were genuinely pleased with her response. "I never doubted it," he assured her, leading them to a halt to open the door to the master bedchamber.

The trappings were very simple. There was a bed with lots of lovely, soft pillows and warm blankets, though, and that was all she really cared about. Furniture would simply be ornamental in the wake of Nathaniel's absurdly luxurious bedding.

She walked forward, taking in the scope of the room. Temporary curtains had been hung, just plain bolts of black fabric, blocking the light from the room. She gripped one and flung it back and was momentarily struck dumb by the view.

From here, high on the vantage point from the hilly terrain, one could see for miles out. A sloping terrain gave way to a sheer drop, and beyond that was nothing but shimmering blue water, stretching endlessly into the horizon.

Nathaniel approached from behind, stopping short of touching her, with his hands folded behind his back. "Do you approve of the view, my dear?" he asked, as though he knew that she did.

"Oh, Nathaniel," she said, turning over her shoulder to gaze up into his face. "Do you know I have never seen the sea before? And there it is, right outside my window!"

The teasing amusement slid from his expression, seemingly

driven away by the surprise of her words. "Never? How can that be?"

She laughed, turning the full way around to face him, and leaning back against the window sill. "Winchester to London to Bath, and even up to Yorkshire are the extent of my life's travels. None of those places have a coast."

He gave an incredulous little breath of laughter, shaking his head. "I cannot imagine it. I will have to bring you closer soon, and perhaps when it is warm again, you might swim in it."

"Oh, I cannot swim," she said hurriedly. "I would sink to the bottom like a stone anchor and you'd have to find a new wife."

He did not respond immediately, his eyes scanning hers with an unreadable look on his face. "Well," he said softly. "We can't have that, now can we?"

She blushed, realizing the silliness of what she'd just said. She opened her mouth, intending to diffuse the awkwardness of the comment, but found herself suddenly pulled close to her husband, engulfed in his delicious scent.

His lips descended onto hers in a quick and decisive motion, though they landed with unspeakable softness and warmth. He held her with one arm around her waist and his other hand cupped against her cheek, and he kissed her as though he truly wanted to.

Nell had never been kissed before, of course, but she thought that one could very likely tell the difference between a reluctant kiss and a sincere one. In her estimation, this was a sweet sort of kiss, not the demanding, passionate sort in books and giggling gossip, but perhaps one born more of affection than urgent need.

Perhaps he had come to *like* her. Surely that was better than simply desiring her, wasn't it? She couldn't work out just now why that might be, but she knew that for the moment, it was all perfectly thrilling, regardless.

She allowed herself to release the startled tension in her limbs, to lean forward and soften her lips against his in what she hoped was a show of acceptance and pleasure at the gesture. She let her thoughts scatter into ambiguous sensation, reveling in the way this felt.

He pulled back before she could properly lose herself in the swirling of strange and alarming sensations that had begun to stir within her. He was still wearing that bemused expression, though he did not look displeased.

They stared at one another for a long beat of silence, Nell wide-eyed and Nathaniel contemplative.

"I shall leave you to your rest, Mrs. Atlas," he said finally, with a little bow of formality.

"Oh," was all she managed, and no other words even came to mind until he had already shut the door behind him.

SHE HAD BEEN SO COMPLETELY certain that she would get no rest at all after that kiss. It was no wonder she felt so disoriented when she woke, over an hour later, still sprawled on her back in the luxurious feather bed. She had been contemplating the patterns of plaster on the ceiling, her body still warm and tingling from her first kiss. She did not even remember closing her eyes.

When she flung back the makeshift curtain for a second time, the sun had progressed well past its apex, and while still bright and whole, had sunk to somewhere behind the house. From the bedroom at this hour, nothing was visible of direct sun, save for the glints of golden refraction in the expanse of the ocean in the distance. She closed her eyes, imagining that she could smell the salt in the air from where she stood, and imagining further that her husband had returned to claim yet another kiss from her by this window.

Even though neither thing became a reality, she was still smiling when she opened her eyes again.

The room was just as sparse as it had been before she'd dozed off, though someone had come in to light the fire while she'd slept. She eyed the bell pull next to the bed and wondered if it was functional still, and even so, if it would ring rooms that servants had already settled into.

She felt more refreshed than she would have expected, and found that there was a spring in her footsteps as she made her way from the room and down the stairs to the foyer. Workmen were resting on the lawn, some of them napping in the tall grass and others having a spot of food. The door stood open, allowing in a stream of crisp autumn air, which wove its way through the ground floor as though it were perfectly at home.

She did not see Nathaniel among the workers without, nor did there seem to be anyone milling about within the house. She turned on the spot, craning her neck down the twin hallways that diverged from the center of the room, each weaving its way beneath a different staircase. It was anyone's guess which way the kitchens were, which she imagined were the access point to the servants' quarters.

"Ah, you're awake!" called a cheerful male voice from behind her. "I trust you had a pleasant rest?"

Nell turned back with what she hoped was a smile that appeared gracious rather than relieved at the sight of Kit Cooper approaching the front doors. "I am fully restored," she said. "This house is wonderful, but I am terrified to go exploring lest I get permanently lost!"

"It is a beautiful home," Kit replied with a shrug, "or at least it has the potential to be. I imagine you are looking for Nate."

"I was, yes. He mentioned that it was only a short ride into the city center, and I thought I might pick up a few things from Dover and familiarize myself with the setting. If I knew where my maid had gotten off to, I'd likely take her along as well."

"Well, Nate took the carriage into town to pick up some lumber and mortar for our repairs, but if you don't mind riding horseback, I would be happy to accompany you into the city."

"Horseback would be preferred, after the last few weeks," she said with genuine relief. "I would be most grateful for the company. Are you certain you aren't needed here?"

"Oh, I'm certain I am." Kit laughed. "That's why I'd love to have an excuse not to be. Besides, it will give me a chance to get to know my new cousin. I'll get us saddled up and we'll be off."

"Splendid," Nell replied with a clap of her hands. "I shan't be a minute."

She had never been much inclined to dramatics or hyperbole, but she thought that perhaps this day had been the best she'd ever had. The thought gave her a lightness that sped her way to collect her coat and hurry off onto the next adventure.

CHAPTER 14

The city of Dover was not as grand as London nor as elegant as Bath, but Nell thought that it was quite possibly just as historically rich as her home city of Winchester.

As they slowed to a canter to approach the city stables, Kit pointed to a large, medieval structure that sat several leagues off from the city itself, and explained that it had been some kind of castle or fort or lighthouse since the first men had come to Britain.

"How fascinating," Nell had breathed, craning her neck over her shoulder for as long as she could until they had ridden too far to continue looking. "I don't suppose it is open to the public? I visited a very old Roman fort in York just some months past, but it was nothing near as grand as that."

Kit chuckled, shaking his head. "Sadly, not until the war and all its subsequent skirmishes are over. The castle has seen an unbelievable amount of renovation and improvement since France started smoldering, and now is a garrison and armory. If you ride out to the cliffs beyond the castle on a clear day, you can see the French shores. Some say it is our most crucial stronghold, conflict or no."

He dismounted and held his hands up to assist her down from her mount, a sweet-tempered if somewhat elderly mare that he'd introduced back at Meridian as Apple. "Her full name is Apple Tart," he'd explained with a little frown, "but I always got the impression she didn't appreciate being called a tart, and so I shorten it now, in her dotage."

He escorted her onto the high street and toward the clothier Nate had chosen, keeping a leisurely pace and pointing out landmarks along the way.

"I confess I do not know how long such endeavors take for ladies," Kit told her, nodding toward the glossy wooden sign above the clothier. "Shall I return in an hour? Two?"

"One hour should be sufficient," she assured him. "I will not be undertaking too much today, but would very much like to see the progress being made. Once both Meridian House and myself are up to standard, I very much wish to have you and your family for dinner."

"You are too sweet for the likes of Nathaniel," he assured her, waving her off as she rang the bell to the shop.

She realized she had not asked Kit if he had a wife or children. He simply seemed the sort to have a cozy homestead with many little ones pattering about. He was a softer version of Nathaniel, she thought, unburdened by the concerns of ambition. He likely had a vocation all his own and reveled in working with his own two hands. The thought made her smile, wondering how he must have clashed with her husband when they were boys, at odds over what games to play.

The first thing that struck her as she pushed the door open was the smell of dried flowers. It wasn't overpowering enough to be unpleasant, but it was surprisingly strong, perhaps heightened by the warmth coming off the central fire. Rather than a little bell over the door like her aunt kept at the print shop in London, this place had opted for three chimes, which grazed one another with delicate notes that floated out over a luxuriously appointed room, decorated in cream and pink.

"We are in the back!" called a woman in lightly accented English. "Come along, if you please."

Nell clutched her reticule to her middle, stepping around the cluster of cushioned chaises that were grouped around the sales desk. She had not removed her coat, nor her scarf and gloves, for she did not know where to put items in a place that already appeared to be so very, very full.

She felt a rather drab contrast to the surroundings, in her clothes of muted gray, black, and blue, with her old coat and scuffed shoes to match. She would have reached up to smooth her hair, but she told herself she was more sensible than that.

Her footsteps were muted by the plush carpeting, which also seemed to soak up the sound of voices that were coming from behind the dressing screen in the rear part of the shop. "Hello?" Nell said, stopping just short of peering around the screen and perhaps catching someone in their particulars. "I am here to speak to Madame Bisset. My husband placed an order for me."

"Oh! Mrs. Atlas, you come at last," cried the same voice, evidently delighted by this surprise. "You may come around. We are simply sharing a glass of wine. Would you like one?"

"Oh, I ... yes, why not," Nell replied uncertainly, toeing up to the edge of the screen and peeping around, as though she still wasn't certain she had permission to do so.

A young woman was reclining in a pink chaise longue, over-stuffed and lined with brocade like the ones in the front room. She had honey blonde hair piled up on her head and was sipping from a glass of white wine in nothing but her shift and bare feet. She tilted her moss-green eyes up to meet Nell's and gave nothing but a little giggle by way of introduction.

"*Sois sage!*" tsked a second woman, who stepped over the first. This one was significantly older and fully dressed. Her hair was a startling shade of artificial red, bound up in a spray of ringlets and silk flowers that Nell found somehow flattering, despite their suitability for a woman in her latter years.

This older woman turned her attention to Nell, holding out a glass of wine and offering a wide smile. "Please join us, Mrs. Atlas. I am so pleased to finally meet you in person! Your husband is *most* generous, and so I must congratulate you on your match. I am Silvie Bisset, and I welcome you!"

"Oh, thank you!" Nell said, extending her hand. "It is lovely to meet you. As you know already, I am Eleanor Atlas."

"This poorly mannered layabout is Giselle Dempierre," Madame Bisset said with an affectionate roll of her eyes. "We call her Gigi."

"They call me a great many things," the blonde woman said, dimpling at Eleanor. She had no accent to speak of, but spoke each word with a certain leisurely disregard that outed her as foreign. "But you may use Gigi if you please. I was just coveting some of the pieces your husband purchased for you. Madame Bisset was being a horrible witch and refusing to sell me some of your things without your knowledge."

"I am too old for such silliness," Madame Bisset sniffed. "Besides, look at poor Mrs. Atlas, forced to wear such ill-fitting garb until I may remedy it. It is unconscionable! I must fetch my tape and pins. Please, just a moment. Pardon me, Mrs. Atlas."

Nell watched the clothier scurry off, her bright red ringlets bouncing with her haste, and felt profoundly unsure what to do with herself. She was holding the glass of wine in one gloved hand, reticule in the other, and was still standing ramrod straight in the middle of the strangest room she'd ever set foot in. It would have been overwhelming on its own, but she had also apparently encountered directly a member of the family she had only been hoping to discreetly observe.

Giselle Dempierre giggled again, seemingly very enter-tained by the dowdy Britishness that Nell radiated. She made a show of leaning forward and setting her glass down on a glass table, then stretching her arms over her head, arching her back like a cat's to display her elegant figure. "You may as well undress," she said sweetly, curling back into the chaise like that self-same cat. "Dear Silvie can't very well measure you in all of ..." she hesitated, her eyes scraping over Nell's modest ensemble as though it were a morbid display. "Well, all of *that*."

Nell gave a nervous nod, looking about for other surfaces before realizing she'd have to set her own glass of wine next to Gigi's.

She turned her back to the other woman, hoping the rising blush in her cheeks was not visible, and peeled off her outerwear carefully. She folded each piece and stacked them into a small pile next to the privacy screen. It occurred to her as she sat to remove her boots, seemingly to the great amusement of the other woman, that while she had not exposed herself to the target in the spycraft sense of the term, she certainly was putting herself into a vulnerable place far sooner than she had intended.

I am literally exposed, she thought, giving rise to a flutter of anxiety in her chest. Worse, she had no idea what to say to the other woman.

Once she was down to her shift, she reached for the glass of wine and tipped it into her mouth, grateful for the soothing warmth that spread into her limbs. She knew she ought not ask for another glass so soon, but she rather thought she was going to need a few bottles to soothe her startled nerves.

Madam Bisset returned, piles of lace and satin and velvet and fur in her arms, topped with a precariously balanced pincushion. She nodded in approval that Nell had already removed her apparently ill-fitting vestments.

"Your husband estimated your frame very well!" she said with a suggestive smirk, taking in Nell's figure as it appeared in her sensible, well-worn shift. "I shall be able to send you home with a few items tonight, if you like."

"Well," Gigi observed, making no move to reclothe herself or leave Nell to her privacy. "Who wouldn't like that?"

NATE WASN'T sure if he was indignant or embarrassed.

The last time he'd seen his little wife, he'd kissed her. He hadn't planned to kiss her. Eventually, yes, but not the instant she arrived and so suddenly. Then he'd realized that if he kissed her for any longer, he wouldn't be able to stop and beat a hasty exit. Now, she was missing!

Well, not missing entirely. She had gone into Dover with Kit, from what he'd pieced together, but she hadn't so much as left a note behind letting him know where she'd gotten off to.

The last glimmer of twilight was hanging in the sky. He'd stopped himself from pacing around the foyer like a worried governess and instead had taken to the dining room to write some much-delayed correspondence to his various contacts through Parliament. Trouble was he couldn't keep his focus on the dry, boilerplate sentences for long enough to get them adequately onto paper.

He hadn't been able to stop thinking about that kiss. He had kissed Miss Blakely once, at a ball in London, toward the end of last Season, when it became apparent that they were both amicable to the idea of matrimony. It had been a fine kiss, if not somewhat methodical, and he'd had no problem breaking away after it and sending her on her way. He certainly hadn't had to force himself to step backward before the desire to taste her deeper had overtaken him.

He shook his head, heaving a short sigh. He had thought himself a master of his own baser desires if the likes of Gloriana Blakely hadn't tempted him to dangerous thoughts. She was, after all, considered one of the most beautiful debutantes London had ever seen. Yet, here he was, married to a woman he had initially found mousy and forgettable and somehow she had driven him to the type of distraction he hadn't dealt with since his youth.

Her maid had unpacked her modest assortment of things, hanging up no more than half a dozen dresses in the wardrobe and depositing a book and Nell's spectacles lovingly on the nightstand, where his wife would surely wish them to be. Was she content with so little? It certainly seemed that way, though Nate could make no sense of it.

He'd spent his entire life hungry for the next step, the next achievement, the next victory. He should have been burning bright, eager and anticipating that his largest endeavor, his most carefully kept goal, was finally so near completion. Instead, he kept forgetting the Silver Leaf entirely while considering upholstery and carpeting and a trousseau fitting a beloved bride. He had lost himself in exploring this old tomb and in anticipating his wife's arrival.

Now that she was here, he could only hope that the monotony of the days going by would temper his ardor and allow the space for his old spark to reignite. Such breathless nonsense wasn't sustainable. Everyone knew that.

The sound of voices and the door opening in the foyer brought him immediately to his feet, his eye going immediately to the mirrored panels on the far wall so that he might smooth his hair back into order. The unmistakable sound of his wife's voice layered over Kit's booming laughter sent a spike of alertness into his chest, spurring him in the direction of the commotion.

Nell was pink-faced and grinning, bundled up under so many layers that she might have been a woolen doll. She was carrying two paper boxes, both long rectangles, and Kit seemed to have four more of the same size.

"Oh, Nathaniel!" she cried upon seeing him, her face lighting up as though she were delighted. She carefully deposited the boxes she was holding on the floor and rushed to him, flinging her arms around his middle as though he were a dear old friend. "Oh, thank you so much! I have never had so many fine things! I had such a wonderful day!"

He did not wish to become amorous in front of his cousin, and so he dropped a tight-lipped kiss onto the top of her head and muttered some platitude about it being no trouble at all.

Kit watched them with his eyes narrowed, the same way he'd stared at Nate that night in the pub.

"I'm afraid I've had some wine," Nell whispered, releasing him and stepping back. She tilted her head up to meet his eye, her gray eyes sparkling like moonstones. "Quite a lot of wine," she amended, pressing her lips together as though this were a jest between the two of them.

"I'll simply have to drink some and catch up with you," Nate replied, using the voice he had perfected for charming dinner conversation. It made Eleanor beam up at him, but only narrowed the curious stare from Kit. Nate simply lifted his chin, issuing a silent dare to his cousin. "Come, we can have a bite to eat and you can tell me all about it. Kit, will you stay for dinner?"

"I wish I could," Kit replied, handing the boxes he was carrying to a servant who had come to collect them. "I've business to discuss with my mother. You two will have to come to dinner at mine very soon, especially now that your wife has some proper dinner attire."

"Oh, that sounds lovely," Nell said. "Doesn't it sound lovely, Nathaniel?"

Kit gave an infuriating wide grin, loving that their audience was oblivious to his antagonism.

"It sounds worth considering," Nate replied evenly. "Let's get you out of your coat and get you fed, hm? Kit, shall I see you outside?"

"If you like," Kit replied with a shrug. "I do know my way back."

"I'm not convinced you know as much as you believe you do," Nate said cheerfully, patting Nell on the shoulder as he strode across the room to hasten his cousin through the door. "Go on then, out with you."

Kit chuckled silently, though Nate could see the way his shoulders shook anyhow. His horse was still saddled and waiting for him in the drive.

"She did have quite a lot of wine," Kit told him, approaching the horse and patting its nose. "I think it was that seamstress plying her with an elixir for impulsive shopping. However, you'll be pleased to know she patently refused to add anything to the already exorbitant purchase you have set into motion."

"I wouldn't mind if she had," Nate replied. "Is that what is in those boxes? Clothes?"

"Yes, but not nearly the whole lot. I think it's mostly under-things and a new coat, though of course I didn't inquire. We didn't have time to stop by the cobbler, so you'll have to make another trip for that."

"Not a bother. I suppose I should thank you for seeing to her needs, but you might have scrawled a quick note so that I didn't have to interrogate half the staff to find out where you'd gone."

Kit's widening smile only deepened Nate's frown. "My apologies," he said, as though he wasn't sorry at all. "Don't let me keep you any longer. You clearly are eager to spend time with your beloved."

"You sound surprised," Nate said coolly.

"I am surprised!" Kit replied. "Unlike you, I enjoy a good surprise. Now, go back inside. I'll return in the morning and we can open up some of the rooms on the ground floor, hm? Maybe I'll finally find those dice I lost when we were small."

Nate scoffed but gave a begrudging half smile. "Perhaps. Stranger things have happened."

Kit did not reply to that, but Nathaniel felt his sentiment all the same in the way he smirked. He gave a curt wave and turned on his heel and returned to the house in search of his bride.

CHAPTER 15

*N*ate had the strangest urge to knock before entering his own bedroom, even though he knew he was expected. Upon returning to the dining room, he had been informed that the lady of the house had wished to dine in the bedchamber, and that unless he was opposed, they would be serving him up there too.

He wasn't sure how they were going to manage that with nothing but a bed and a wardrobe in that room, but he was certainly willing to try.

He steeled himself and pushed the door open, revealing the glow of candlelight and a small, makeshift arrangement of a coffee table that had once been in the drawing room and two cushions from the parlor couch serving as chairs. An old privacy screen had been set up beside the fireplace, and from where he stood, he could see shadows moving about behind it.

There were servants in the room, which made his trepidation about entering even more ridiculous. One was arranging the food and wine onto the low table, another unpacking the paper boxes from Dover, while one set lanterns around the perimeter of the room for want of a functioning lighting fixture in the dark.

"Sarah, might you hand me one of those lanterns or just a candle if you have it?" Nell called from behind the screen. "I cannot see a thing back here."

"Yes, ma'am, of course," said the curly-haired maid who had arrived in the carriage with Nell this morning. She handed the box she was unpacking to the other maid and swept up a lantern to attend her mistress, stepping around Nathaniel as though he were just another piece of furniture.

"Would you like anything else, sir?" a footman asked quietly, gesturing to the strange dinner arrangement on the floor. There was a bowl of cherries in the center of the table, two empty glasses, a bottle of wine, and two plates heaped with meat and potatoes.

Nathaniel thought his wife might benefit from a glass of water rather than more spirits, but when he turned to address her through the screen, all coherent thought died in his throat. The illumination of the lantern made the silhouettes of the two women behind it crystal clear, down to the individual strings in the stays that the maidservant was currently loosening around Nell's torso. The light traced the curvature of her legs, even with the ghost of her shift flowing over it through the barrier.

He realized in one horrifying flash that if the footman turned around, he would also be treated to this marvelous view.

"Nothing," he said, perhaps a little more curtly than he'd

intended. "You are all dismissed. I will ring if we require anything further."

"Sir," the footman replied stiffly, beating a hasty exit rather than linger with an agitated master. Mercifully, this meant he did not turn back around.

"Sarah, you may go," Nell's soft voice murmured from behind the screen. "If you could just pass me the new dressing gown first, I will braid my own hair for bed."

"Yes, ma'am," the maid replied. She stepped out from behind the screen, forcing Nathaniel to feign deep interest in the state of his cuticles until she had passed the dressing gown over and said goodnight to her mistress. She did, however, get a clear look at how poorly the privacy screen was performing insofar as protecting Nell's modesty.

Nate did not look at her face as she passed by him on the way out, but he could swear he felt the knowing smirk that was likely on her face as she breezed past. Once the door was closed again, he was free to ogle the display, which he managed not to do for all of four seconds as he made his way to the foot of their bed to remove his boots.

It was only that the eye couldn't help but be drawn to the moving shadows behind that screen. She moved so elegantly, with a slow deliberation that was likely because she was a touch intoxicated. Though, he would wager that she had always taken great care with what little she owned, which meant she did not undress or discard garments with haste, even with the clearest mind.

He dropped the boots onto the floor and gave up on attempting to convince himself he was interested in anything other than this unintentional seduction.

She pulled the pins out of her hair and shook it free, long, wayward curls falling down to her elbows. He realized he had never seen her with her hair down. He had not imagined it so long and wild. How had she fit such a luxurious mane into those prim little buns that were always just a little lopsided?

She drew her shift up over her body and tossed it over the top of the screen, bending forward to retrieve one of her new garments from its box. From where he stood, his breath static in his lungs, he could see the detailed shape of her breasts and the tantalizing way they shifted their weight as she tipped herself forward. Her bottom rounded pleasantly and gave a delightful little bounce when she shook out the garment she held. She pulled it over her head with care, shimmying it down to its proper place rather than tugging at it.

She extended an arm and retrieved the dark blue dressing gown he had commissioned for her from where it hung on the corner of the screen. He had chosen the fabric with her coloring in mind and had detailed the shape he thought most flattering to Mme. Bisset: cinched at the waist and generous flow at the bottom, so that even her feet would be insulated by the warm and intricate fabric. She sighed happily as she put her arms through it, hugging it to her for a moment of girlish indulgence before tying it into its proper place and smoothing it down her legs.

She stepped out, the robe swaying gracefully at her hips, her hair a glorious tangle over her shoulders, and gave a little start to find him sitting there, eyes locked on her.

"Oh! Nathaniel!" she squeaked, touching the sash at her waist as though she had just realized she wasn't fully dressed. "I hope you do not mind my impromptu dinner arrangement, but I was dreadfully uncomfortable and desperate to change into the lovely things you bought me."

"I do not mind in the least," he assured her hoarsely, followed by a hasty clearing of his throat.

She hesitated, bashful and oblivious to the vision she presented. All that dark hair tumbling down on either side of her pale face, those big gray eyes set off like diamonds by the deep royal blue of her collar. How had he ever thought her mousy or plain?

"Won't you come sit?" she finally said with a little smile, kneeling down onto the pillow closest to the screen. Her robe and nightgown spilled out around her legs in shades of ink and turquoise. She reached for the wine and poured a modest amount in both cups, her hand steady despite her previous indulgence.

"I know it looks silly, but I have been reading so many tales of the Orient where they described eating this way, and I desperately wanted to try. I wouldn't have been able to justify it once we were properly sorted with furniture here."

Nate took a bracing breath, unsure about the wisdom of standing in his current condition, but he quickly moved to kneel opposite her while she was distracted with the beverages. He cleared his throat, chiding himself to get his impulses under control, and gave her what he hoped was an assuring smile. "It is charming, Nell. I am so pleased that you approve of the items I chose," he said softly. "If I may say so, this particular ensemble suits you very well."

She blushed, lifting her wine to her lips to cover a smile. "Thank you," she said after a moment. "It was a very productive outing. In addition to collecting some of my new clothes, I have made the acquaintance of one of the Dempierres."

"Have you?" he marveled, this bit of information at least pulling his mind in a safer direction. "How did you manage that?"

"It was pure happenstance," she told him. "She was in Madame Bisset's shop when I arrived and she ... she stayed throughout my fitting. I believe she found me amusing."

"You are amusing," he assured her, carving a bite of his steak.

"Not amusing in the way of someone who tells jests," she said slowly, tilting her head in thought. "More like one is amused by an uncoordinated puppy or a man who slips and falls on the street. I was a curiosity, I believe."

Nathaniel frowned. He knew exactly what she meant. He had often found her amusing in much the same way, though he saw his own amusement as affectionate and this stranger's as hostile. He felt suddenly stifled and pushed himself to his feet, making to remove his jacket.

She watched him, her expression more curious than anything else, and nibbled at her dinner as he shook off his cuffs, cravat, and waistcoat, drawing a deep and satisfying breath of air, unrestricted. "I've a mind to change into my pyjamas as well," he said to her, giving her a smile that he had been told was friendly. "You look so very comfortable there in your own."

"I am, yes," she said brightly. "I have never owned anything half so fine. I could live in this one ensemble forever and never want again, and yet, I've brought home several more!

It will make me presentable for dinner with your family or to send my card along to the Dempierre household."

"Is that what you plan to do?" he asked, returning to his cushion with significantly more freedom of movement. "Send a card?"

"Well, Gigi—that is, the Dempierre girl—she scheduled another fitting with Madame Bisset in a week's time. I thought perhaps I would happen into the shop on that same day and hope for another chance encounter. If that fails, then yes, I think sending a card is our best option, now that I am known to one of them."

He nodded, considering it. "I think it's simple and straight-forward," he said. "If she finds you amusing, as you say, she may be eager to interact with you further."

"Once the house is ready, we should host a gathering here and invite them all," Nell continued, popping a small piece of potato into her mouth. As she reached for her wine glass to take another sip, Nathaniel was treated to a tantalizing glance of cleavage. "Something intimate that will garner conversation. Depending on when this masquerade is held, we may have precious little time to ingratiate ourselves with this family."

"Hm? Oh, yes, naturally," he said, perhaps taking a bit too deep a drink of his own wine and forcing himself to focus on his plate.

She went quiet for a moment, perhaps simply out of enjoyment of the dinner. He did not know, for he was trying his damndest to keep his head down. The crackle of the fire and the scraping of their forks on the plates were the only sound for a stretch of time, then the clatter of cherry pits into a dish as Nell sampled the fruit from the bowl.

"Why did you kiss me?" she asked suddenly, her voice piercing the silence like birdsong.

"What a question!" he replied immediately, unable to hide the curl of his lips. "Must a man have a reason to kiss his own wife?"

She leaned back on her hands, studying him, illuminated by the glow of the lanterns that lined the perimeter of the room. "You hadn't done it before."

"No," he allowed. "But I should have."

She pursed her lips, considering this, but could not make sense of it based on the way she shook her head. "But what made you kiss me then, in that particular moment?"

"I couldn't say for sure," he confessed, allowing his eyes to roam over her form. Did she know what she was doing? Did she know how she looked, reclining like that? "It seemed like the natural thing to do and I desired it. Do you wish for me to refrain from doing so in the future?"

"What!" she exclaimed, pushing herself up to a rigid posture with her eyes wide. "Of course not! I simply haven't the faintest idea which behavior to replicate if I'm to inspire you to do it again!"

This admission hung heavy in the air for a beat, with Nathaniel uncertain he had heard her correctly.

"Oh," she groaned, burying her face in her hands. "I'm sorry. The wine loosened my tongue, and I did not think before speaking."

"Perhaps we should both think a little less and speak our minds more freely," he suggested, reaching across the table to pull one of her hands from her face and into his own. "Do you want me to kiss you again?"

She peeked up at him through her one revealed eye and gave an almost imperceptible nod.

"Good," he whispered. "Come here."

She swallowed, blinking a few times as though she had to assure herself she had heard correctly. Perhaps without her spectacles, she had come to be distrusting of all of her senses.

She did not stand, for he was still seated and holding her hand. Instead, she pulled herself in a little crawl around the table and came to kneel next to him with her knees brushing his own. She was trembling slightly, her cheeks pink with anticipation.

He couldn't help the smile that tugged at the corners of his lips, and rather than her mistake him for laughing at her, he leaned forward and put those lips to better use, slanting over hers as gently and carefully as he could manage.

She gave the loveliest little sound of pleasure and placed her hands tentatively on his shoulders, attempting to return the kiss by mirroring the ways he used his lips.

He chuckled, helplessly charmed by her innocent enthusiasm, and darted his tongue out to taste the sweet curve of her bottom lip. He cupped her cheek and dragged his thumb down the line of her jaw, urging her to open that willing little mouth a bit so that he might taste her tongue as well.

She seemed to enjoy this, her hands slipping forward, tracing the back of his neck. She again mimicked his own motions, curious to meet his tongue with her own. She was obviously a devoted student with a gift for quick learning.

She shifted forward, just one tug away from being in his lap, her fingers exploring the muscles of his neck and shoulders as she tested different angles for kissing and finding a new delight in each one.

He groaned, unsure how much more of this he could take, and pulled slightly back, dropping a kiss on her chin and meeting her eyes with his own.

"Nell," he said, stroking the side of her face and allowing his fingers to twine into her loose hair. "What do you know of the wedding bed?"

"I understand the mechanics, in theory," she said in a breathy voice. "And am becoming more versed on its appeal by the moment."

"I wish to bed you," he told her, aware that his voice had dropped deeper, more urgent. "Would you like that?"

She bit down on her bottom lip, the way he was finding she was wont to do when excited, and gave a quick, jerky nod. It was enough.

He pushed himself to standing and offered her his hand to draw her up as well. It was no great challenge to sweep her petite little frame from the floor, and unfathomably satisfying to hear the way she squeaked in surprise.

He knew he was going to have to keep his head. Unchecked, he imagined that he would brutalize the poor girl for a minute or less and then collapse into a relieved heap of unconsciousness for the next several days. That could not happen. She deserved so much more.

Besides, he reasoned that she would be more likely to allow him to repeat the activity if he took pains to make it bearable.

He set her gently onto the bed and trailed his fingers down the column of her throat, between her breasts, and down to the knot she had tied at her waist with the dressing gown's sash. He watched her face as he tugged the knot free, holding her eyes until he could peel the robe open, exposing her delicious little body in the fine weave of muslin and lace that he'd chosen for her.

He leaned forward to press his lips into the curve of her throat, tasting the pale flesh there while his hands explored the texture of the nightgown, dipping into the curve of her waist, enjoying the swell of her thighs and the softness of her middle. He was slow and gradual to cup her breast, wanting to draw out the anticipation, to feel he had earned its softness and weight in his hand.

She gave little gasps, some of pleasure, others of surprise. When he leaned back and peeled his shirt off over his head, she had a moment to catch her breath and perhaps to enjoy some of the anticipation he himself was feeling.

She pushed herself up to sitting, pulling her arms out of the dressing gown and tossing it onto the bedpost, her eyes wide and bright, framed by such a lovely dark fringe of lashes. She stared unabashedly at his exposed chest, at the spray of curling hair over his heart and the plane of hard muscle that led to the line of his trousers.

She extended a hand tentatively, pressing the pads of her

fingers into the warm flesh beneath his collarbone, tracing her nails lightly over it, seemingly fascinated with the sensation. "I have never touched a man before," she whispered, seemingly to herself. "I have often wondered if your skin would feel like mine: soft and warm and smooth."

"And?" he asked, allowing her to explore as he stroked the strands of her hair that fell over her shoulders.

"It is lovely, but different." She spread both hands over his chest, stretching her fingers apart, tracing them back over his shoulders and down again over his ribs.

He twitched, reaching down instinctively to grasp her wrist before it could trail any farther, but not quick enough to stop his involuntary recoil.

She raised her eyes to look disbelieving into his eyes. "You are ticklish," she realized, a grin spreading over her face. "Mr. Atlas is ticklish."

"Nonsense," he whispered, unable to suppress a little smile. "I simply want your hands elsewhere."

"Oh?" she whispered, her eyes dropping to where he was leading her touch and widening as she realized his intention. "Oh!"

He released a hiss of breath, his vision seeming to darken as she allowed her sweet little hand to be pressed into his arousal. She did not flinch nor shy away, instead inching herself forward on her knees and taking it upon herself to stroke his length through the soft leather of his trousers, seemingly fascinated by this part of him.

He wrapped her hair around his hand and dragged her lips back to his, kissing her hard this time, demanding entry to her mouth rather than requesting it. With his other hand he returned to her breasts, shaping them into his palm and dragging his thumb over the tightening peaks of her nipples, delighted with the way she fed him little moans between her kisses.

He pushed the straps of her nightgown off her shoulders, tasting his way down the column of her throat and into the recess between her breasts, nudging down the sagging fabric until her pert, rosy nipples sprang free, tightening into erect points as gooseflesh spread over the milky expanse of her chest.

She followed his example, yet again. If he could remove her clothing, then why not the other way around? Her fingers were nimble and efficient, jerking free the ties at his waist and pushing the unbound leather down around his hips so that she could draw him fully out into the firelight.

The sensation of her hands on his bare cock was the thing that pushed him fully into primal need. There was no waiting anymore, not until he was sated. He flicked his tongue over one of her nipples and stepped backward off the bed just long enough to peel off the last of his clothing, all the while watching her kneeling in the middle of his bed with her chest exposed, her breath coming heavy and exiting through her swollen lips.

She looked like a sacrificial virgin, delivered into his bed and exposed for his pleasure in a ring of flickering flames, willing to be taken, anxious to hand her innocence over to his own depraved desires.

She did not shy away from his nudity, nor did she seem alarmed by the sight of his rigid erection. She moistened her lips and pushed her nightgown down over her waist and hips, leaving it in a pool around her knees so that he might see her exposed as well, and gaze upon her body uninhibited.

There were many things he intended to do with that body, many things he intended to indulge in once his animalistic frustration had been sated. He crawled back onto the bed, scooping her up with an arm behind her waist and lying her flat on her back.

"Oh! Careful!" she gasped when he pulled the nightgown along her shins and free of her feet. "It is delicate."

He nodded, too muddled to assure her that he could buy her two hundred identical nightgowns and still be willing to rip them to shreds in return for being allowed to remove them from her. It was not the time, and he did not trust he had the vocabulary. He laid it carefully over the dressing gown she'd looped over the bedpost and turned back to her, reclining back on his silk pillows.

She was the delicate thing here, the treasure he did not wish to damage. He pressed her knees gently apart and touched her, feather-light, at the core of her pleasure. She gasped, but did not seem to find it objectionable. Rather she spread her knees farther apart, leaning her head back onto the pillows and closing her eyes, as though she trusted him completely to do with her as he willed.

Be careful, her voice said again in his head. *I am delicate.*

He tested her entrance with his fingers, pleased to find her slick with her own desire. He would go as slow as he could stand. There would be time for abandon later, in the long lives they would spend together sharing this bed. The thought sent a bolt of heat through him as he climbed over her and positioned himself at her entrance.

"Stop me if I hurt you," he whispered, his voice strained with the last remnants of his self-control.

She nodded, seemingly eager, and shifted her hips forward, drawing the tip of him into the warm well of her body.

His eyes flickered shut, his head spinning as he began to ease himself into her, little by little, building a gentle rhythm as her wetness accommodated them both. She gasped sharply some seconds in, at the point where he assumed he had pierced her maidenhead, but she did not stop him, nor did she cry out in pain.

He pressed his forehead into hers as her arms wrapped around him, the softness of her thighs resting against his hips. He knew he would explode quickly, that this was a poor showing for her first encounter, but he could not stop himself anymore than he could prevent the sun rising. Not this time.

Once he had managed to sink himself into her enough for a steady rhythm, his body took over his senses. He did not lose his gentleness, but the sounds of her little gasps and the feel of her gripping at his shoulders and raking her fingers through his hair were somehow louder than any thought he'd ever had.

How he had managed to go so many years without indulging in this want, this *need,* was incomprehensible. He could not imagine this degree of pleasure from another woman, nor did he wish to.

He felt her soft, sweet little body welcoming him, and it was enough to push him over the ledge, as though a thousand years of restraint had finally breached a crack in the dam. He pumped his seed deep into her, groaning softly as he dropped his face into her hair and gradually slowed his thrusting to rocking to stillness.

She gave a shuddering breath, and cradled his head against her shoulder. She stroked his hair and let him lie there atop her until his breathing slowed.

When he looked up at her, wondering what apology he could possibly proffer for such a short and likely unsatisfying performance, she kissed him before he could speak.

"Will you hold me, at least until I'm asleep?" she whispered against his lips, and he felt the curve of her smile there when he said he would.

In the end, however, it was he who fell asleep first, wrapped in a comforting embrace.

CHAPTER 16

*N*ell did not sleep for a long time. It was well that Nathaniel had found his own rest so quickly, for she certainly would have insisted on being held for quite some time as she waited for oblivion to find her. She stroked his hair, resting her cheek on the soft crown of his head, and inhaled his scent as the minutes ticked past.

He had been so rigidly still when they had slept side-by-side in the coaching inns and in London. He had breathed so silently that she had at times thought perhaps he wasn't breathing at all. Tonight, he seemed for the first time like a warm, flesh-and-blood man, one who stirs in his sleep and breathes with enough force to be heard. It was as though he'd gone from marble to flesh all at once.

When he rolled away from her, curling onto his side against a pillow, she smiled. It wasn't because he had released her, for she knew that was not done deliberately and held no deeper meaning, but rather because some part of himself that he kept so firmly under lock and key seemed to have escaped in the act of their intimacy.

She slipped quietly from the bed and tiptoed to the end to gather her shift to her and tug it back over her head. She held it up above her waist and made her way to the wash-basin to quickly rinse the maiden's blood from her thighs, exceedingly mindful not to stain her new things.

The fire was burning low, but she looked into it for a while, marveling at the way her skin felt so aware of every brush of the fabric that covered it. It was as though her sense of touch had been kindled past its previous limits and for the first time, she was truly within her own body.

She was tired, yes, and she knew she should sleep, but at the same time, she felt that she could run the length of the grounds and dive into the ocean and swim all the way to France without a moment's regret or doubt. It felt as though she were right on the cusp of something, which was ridicu-lous, because she had already discovered so much in the last hours.

She covered their discarded food with the cloth napkins that had fallen to the floor, and paced the perimeter of the room, extinguishing each lantern with a quick gust of breath, until only the glowing embers in the fireplace were left to give shape to the surroundings.

When she was finished and ready to climb back into the bed, she indulged in one final moment of whimsy, spinning in a circle to send her nervous energy out into the universe on the bell of her skirt. It was something she might have done as a child, and even one spin left her stifling her giggles, a bit lightheaded and dizzy. Perhaps girlish spinning and several glasses of wine did not mix well.

It was the closest she got to really considering what had

passed here tonight, and what it might mean for the future. These were thoughts for tomorrow, when her head was clear and the sun shone bright. Tonight, she was simply a creature of sensation, driven from one impulse to the next.

She climbed into the bed, drawing the coverlet up over both of them, and curled her body around Nathaniel's back, burrowing her cheek into the warmth between his shoulders. She thought that if she must lie here awake for hours more, she would at least do so happily in this position.

It's funny how quickly one can fall asleep once she abandons all hope of doing so.

IT WAS the clanking of dishes that woke her.

Nell had slept so deeply that it seemed only a moment ago that she'd crawled into bed, and yet it had clearly been many hours. The sun was bright in the window, the black makeshift curtains flung back for the day, and servants were clearing away the remains of their little dinner from the floor.

She spared a moment for quiet relief that she had put her nightgown back on, for she threw off the coverlet from her body before remembering what had passed here the night before.

"Good morning," said Nathaniel from the wardrobe, where he was rolling up his shirtsleeves opposite a thin, propped-up mirror. He smiled at her in reflection, sending her heart directly into her throat. "I hope I didn't wake you."

"You didn't," she assured him, rubbing the sleep from her

eyes and stifling an early-morning yawn. "I usually rise before the sun. It was an unusually deep sleep."

"Was it?" he asked, turning to face her, obviously pleased with the idea. "I also slept better than I have in ages. It is a relief to be done with the traveling for a spell."

She blushed, reaching for her sumptuous new dressing gown as she slipped from the bed. Somehow in the light of day, she felt less certain about her body in such thin material. Perhaps it was a silly thing to be bashful now, but here she was, all the same.

"I am going to open some of the rooms on the first floor this morning, after breakfast," he continued, oblivious to her sudden reticence. "There's no telling what we'll find. I also have a carpenter coming today to install proper lighting in this room and the dining area. You are not required to assist in the labor, of course, I simply think it is prudent that I inspect each room before the staff flocks in, so that I will know if aught goes missing. My aunt would be delighted to show you around the grounds today instead, if you prefer it."

"I would love to see the grounds, but I would much rather become acquainted with the house first, if I am to be its mistress. Besides, I must confess I'm dreadfully curious about what's in some of these old rooms," she said, passing him to draw some items from the wardrobe. "I shall wear one of my old frocks so that the dust won't be an issue. I don't mind a bit of muck, but I would hate to stain one of the new ones."

"It isn't just dust. There might be rodents or other nasties in the unattended areas," he warned her. "We found an unseemly big spider in the kitchen on the first day."

She chuckled, shaking out her patched travel dress and tossing it on the bed. "I grew up alongside a twin brother, sir. I assure you I have met my fair share of nasties. So long as they aren't the venomous sort, I will stand brave against them."

"As you say," he demurred with a little smile. "I confess I'm not fond of insects myself, so perhaps your bravery will embolden me as well. Pray, do not tell your brother of this weakness. I shouldn't be able to regain my sense of dignity."

Nell shooed him from the room, giggling to herself, and rang for Sarah. It was a simple thing to get buttoned into one of her serviceable old dresses in comparison to the layers and endless buttons and bows she'd had to navigate at the clothier's yesterday.

She pinned her hair into its customary bun, and after a moment of deliberation, decided on wearing her spectacles downstairs today. After all, it was going to be dark and dusty in those old rooms, so she would surely be aided by improved vision, wouldn't she?

Hopefully Nathaniel did not mind them nearly as much as her friends from school did. Surely he saw the practicality of optimized eyesight at necessary junctures? He seemed a practical man in some ways, though she knew he had a penchant for beautiful things.

She averted her eyes from her reflection as she passed by their little mirror, reminding herself that she had never cared for such vain concerns and it would be a waste of her finer qualities to begin obsessing over them now.

She considered her husband over breakfast, which they passed with sparse conversation as they cracked their eggs and nibbled at their toast. He made no comment on her spectacles, if indeed he noticed them at all. It was as though nothing at all had changed since yesterday, when in truth her entire life had been redefined.

She noted a light soreness of her person, though it was not wholly unpleasant to be reminded that Nathaniel had desired her. It was difficult to know how well the encounter had gone for certain, though she hoped that the way he had slept afterward meant that he had somehow become more at ease with her. Surely he had, after all of that?

It was no wonder girls got themselves into trouble so often in Society. She had never understood before why it was so difficult for some girls to simply behave and be where they were supposed to be, but if someone like Nathaniel had attempted to coax her into dark corners prior to their marriage, she knew without a doubt she would have followed. Even if she had much to learn about pleasing her husband in the bedchamber, this first experience had been scintillating, and she hoped to repeat it soon.

"Will Kit be joining us today?" she asked as the plates were cleared away.

"Not until after luncheon," Nathaniel had responded with a wave of his hand. "He is negotiating with the orchard foremen today so that he might retain a trusted staff come spring. The land changing hands so many times in the past years has created an unstable network of workers, which of course means a substandard harvest. It will likely take several more years to return everything to its former standard."

"Orchards," Nell had pondered as they walked to the first of the unopened rooms. "What do you grow here? Apples?"

Nate nodded, his hand drifting thoughtlessly to the small of her back as he guided her through the labyrinth of hallways, unaware of the thrill it sent through her. "And pears and the cherries we had last night. My aunt has a talent for potting and preserving. We also had rotating fields for barley, rye, and radishes once."

"How did they come to disrepair?" Nell asked curiously. "Kit seems an earthy and responsible sort."

"He is. The problem originated before Kit was old enough and educated enough to manage the fields. My uncle, that is, Kit's father, was not a responsible land owner and had an unfortunate habit of getting involved with dodgy investment schemes and using our land as collateral. So, Kit has spent the better part of his life attempting to reclaim what once belonged to our families and see the fields back to fruition."

Nell took this in, biting her tongue on the questions that rose immediately to mind regarding this uncle and Nate's personal history with him.

She tucked away her curiosity for a more opportune time as they arrived at their destination, and stepped back as her husband used his body weight to push open the first in a set of double doors which required a coat or three of fresh paint. When it gave way with a thin crack of splintering wood, a cloud of dust did indeed emerge from within, sending both of them recoiling down the hallway until it settled.

It was immediately clear that this had once been a ballroom.

Some of the wall hangings were covered with sheets, which gave Nell some hope that they might have weathered the years without much damage. Sunlight slanted in through the smudges and streaks of the long-neglected windows, highlighting their footprints on the deep, burgundy wood that made up the floor. Couches lined the walls, all of them covered in carefully tucked layers of fabric. In the corner was a small, raised platform with a set of instruments which had *not* been covered and had accrued a thick layer of dust in the years of misuse.

She went to the instruments first, her eye immediately drawn to the elegant shape of a pedal harp, carved in exquisite relief. She could no more resist the allure of such a thing than she could forego her love of stories or her taste for summer melon. She stepped around the piano as though it were of no consequence, drawn like a maiden to an enchantment in a fairy story.

The harp was taller than she was, but most harps were. It was much finer than the instrument she had played at Mrs. Arlington's under the steely-eyed tutelage of a Welsh master, a man who had considered Nell his personal prodigy. Up close, she could see the workings in the wood, animals in the style of a Renaissance painting frolicking over the curves and dips, chasing one another up the central core of solid spruce.

She reached out to touch it, knowing that the strings were old and out of tune, and knowing full well that the entire instrument was covered in dust. Still, a quick *glissando* under her fingers drew out a bright ring of off-key music.

"Do you play?" Nathaniel asked, startling her as though she'd been caught in something untoward.

She whipped around with an apologetic smile, her hand going flat against the strings to silence their thrum as the dust clouded out from the disturbance. "I do," she said once the tone had been silenced. "I used to be quite adept, but I am over a year out of practice."

"We will have it restored," he said with a firm decisiveness. "I wish to hear you play."

"Oh!" she said, her cheeks warming under his attentions. "That would be lovely, Nathaniel. Truly. It is a beautiful instrument. It has exceptional carving along the wood. It is a shame it has been left unplayed for so very long."

"Yes," he agreed softly. "Beautiful instruments are meant to be warm and oft visited. With enough affection, I'm certain you can make up for its neglect."

She gave a nervous laugh, stepping off the platform with her hands twisting together and avoiding his gaze. Something about what he had said had sent jitters clattering through her in the most nonsensical way. She glanced up at the walls, looking for anything that might be more worth studying than her gorgeous husband.

He had seen her naked last night. He must be thinking about it every time he looked at her. He must be remembering the things she'd let him do to her. Why was everything so much more embarrassing in the light of day?!

"I am fond of the baroque pieces," she blurted out in a high, nervous voice. "I once spent two months memorizing the whole of *Passacaglia* for no reason other than knowing I couldn't take the sheet music with me when I left Bath! It is my favorite piece, though it is quite long."

"You are full of surprises, Miss Applegate," he replied.

"Nell," she corrected automatically, only to realize as she spoke that he had said the name in a tone that implied the error was deliberate. She turned, her brows furrowed, and found him leaning against the wall with his arms crossed over his chest, watching her with a wry smile. "Ah. You are teasing me."

"I am," he confessed, spreading his hands open in a gesture of apology. "I can't seem to help myself. I swear it is not mean-spirited, Eleanor. I find your reactions when you are flustered very endearing."

"You do?" she asked, genuinely surprised. "I cannot imagine why."

"You can't?" he repeated, raising his eyebrows.

Nell attempted to sputter out her befuddlement, but when the words would not come, simply reverted to a sigh of exasperation. "It would certainly explain things, if my distress was amusing to others. Glory used to prod me so, and when I was worked up into a proper steam, she'd suddenly embrace me, laughing as though I'd told the finest jest she'd ever heard! It drove me absolutely barmy."

He chuckled, which only made her sigh again, her arms flopping down to her sides.

"Nell," he said sweetly, pushing himself off the wall and walking toward her. Slats of light danced over him as he went, changing the glimmer in his eyes from gold to green to gold again. "Have you ever met a person who is oblivious to their own charm? Someone who you find yourself growing fond of almost by accident, as though it were sprung upon you when you were looking the other way?"

"I don't think so," she replied, drawing her eyebrows together as she considered the question against those in her acquaintance. After a moment, she shrugged and said, "I tend to know right away whether I like someone or not."

He reached her, gathering her hands into his and looking down at her with an expression of clear skepticism. "Is that so? Is your opinion of me the same today as it was that night when you handed me the letter at Almack's? Is it the same as it was even a few weeks ago, when we departed Somerton together?"

She frowned, averting her eyes as she considered this question. "I have always ..." she hesitated, not wishing to humiliate herself. "I have always found you appealing, though I suppose as one gets to know another person, more concrete features of the other begin to take shape."

He lifted her hands to his lips, lingering over her fingers with a soft kiss. His eyes sparkled with amusement at her obvious discomfort, as though to demonstrate the strange line of reasoning he'd just described. "So it is different, now that we are married?"

"It is different now that we have spent a great deal of time together," she huffed, doing her level best not to chew on her lip. "And of course, after ... erm ..."

"After last night?" he prompted, tugging her closer to him, so that she had little choice but to meet his gaze or to stare directly into his shirt. "There is nothing to be embarrassed about, Nell. We are married. It is a thing married people share."

"I know that!" she breathed, certain now that her entire face was as bright as the bowl of cherries from the night before. "That is not what I meant, anyway. I meant that before, you were this enigmatic figure, this question I could not answer, and while you are still a man of many puzzles, I feel those questions pressing less on me when we interact."

"I will answer any questions you have," Nathaniel said to her. "What would you like to know?"

Have you ever killed a man?

She shook her head, dispelling the thought. It would not suit the tone of this moment, nor the fledgeling intimacy that they had begun to build.

What is your interest in the Silver Leaf Society?

Who are you really?

Why would you agree to marry me?

He sighed, using his finger under her chin to tip her head up, where he dropped a soft kiss on her forehead. "You are right that I have been less than forthcoming about the details of my past," he said, completely misunderstanding her silence. "Perhaps tonight, I can tell you the whole sad story and give you some context as to why I'm such a chilly prig more oft than not."

"I would never call you that," she protested, though to be frank, his nearness was making her head swim. All sorts of memories that a lady ought never harbor were sparking to life amidst her confusion and his nearness.

The ache between her legs was a reminder of what had occurred, and while not exactly pleasant, it was somehow delicious in its own way, a secret reminder of how she had changed. She licked her lips and took a bracing breath. "I am not embarrassed," she assured him, this time managing to keep his eye without losing her nerve. "Not in the least."

He grinned, sliding his fingers along the length of her arms and drawing her against him. "I am, to be truthful. It was not my finest performance."

"What do you mean?" she asked, her voice gone breathy and soft. She found herself leaning onto her toes, wishing to be close enough to kiss him again, the way she had last night.

"I will show you," he assured her, "soon. Perhaps even tonight."

Nell could feel her heart thudding insistently against her ribs, as though demanding she react in a more demonstrative way than she was. She looked at his face, his lovely face and perfect, sculpted lips and wondered what it might feel like to be the sort of woman who kissed a man of her own volition, with pure confidence that it would be well received.

A sharp rap on the wood of the open door cracked the surface of her trance, drawing her quickly and harshly back to earth. Behind Nathaniel, one of the footmen was hovering next to the door, looking supremely uncomfortable.

"What is it?" Nathaniel sighed, releasing Nell and turning to face the poor lad, who looked as though he wished to be anywhere else on the whole of the planet.

"Visitors, sir. Here to see Mrs. Atlas."

"Me?" Nell said, sharing a look of surprise with her

husband. "Who is it?"

"It is a Lady Dempierre and her daughter, sir," the lad answered quickly. "They've come down from Dover. The younger lady says she is recently friends with Mrs. Atlas."

This time the look shared between Nell and Nathaniel carried a sight more weight.

"We are hardly dressed to receive company, Stuart," Nate said. "Do we even have a room available in which to make conversation?"

"The drawing room has been cleaned out, sir, and has plenty of natural light. That is where we've put the two ladies, though we will move them if you so wish."

"No. It will do," Nathaniel said, running an agitated hand through his hair. "It's too late to make any other impression, after all," he added, for Nell's benefit.

"It appears that sometimes, the mountain does indeed come to Muhammad," Nell muttered, looking down at the dusty fingerprints on her skirt. "I suppose we must make the most of it."

Nathaniel was looking at her sidelong, as though something she'd said had caught him off guard. He blinked, shaking the confusion away, and held his arm out to her. "They intended to surprise us," he said. "So let's surprise them in turn and appear from the trenches of our own labor. The unexpected often gives one opponent the upper hand, after all."

Nell was grateful to have her husband's lead to follow, for she had no idea if that was true or not, nor did she have the first notion of where the drawing room might be.

CHAPTER 17

*N*athaniel could have strangled that footman for interrupting them. He'd like to do it twice over for the news he brought, which had thoroughly shattered the moment for the foreseeable future. Of course he knew it was not poor Stuart's fault that the Dempierres were apparently ahead of the game, nor that Nathaniel would rather have hosted them in a barren orchard rather than let anyone see the house in its current state.

Meridian might not be his most beloved possession, but he did not care to see it exposed so when he was fully aware of its potential grandeur. Further, he did not like that his little wife was fussing at the dust on her skirts with her brows drawn together in dismay. It must have been a deliberate thing, to take them so unawares. It made him uneasy.

She pressed her spectacles up from where they were teetering on the tip of her nose and glanced at him with a sudden thought. "Ought I remove them?" she whispered as they walked from the ballroom. "I know they are not fashionable."

"Absolutely not," Nate replied firmly. "This is your home and your time being requested in a manner quite brash. If you see more comfortably with your spectacles on, then I should hope you never take them off again."

"Except to sleep," she said with a little smile. "I've broken more than one pair that way, much to my father's dismay."

He patted her hand, nodding to Stuart to lead them into the drawing room and greet their guests.

Both ladies were standing near the fire, speaking in low voices to one another, and dressed artfully enough to attend any ball in London at a moment's notice. They looked quite a bit alike, with dark blonde hair coiffed up into a spray of silk flowers and cheekbones sharp enough to be cast into relief, even in the middle of the day. They turned in unison, both of them immediately putting on gracious little smiles at their arrival.

"Oh, it is you!" the elder Dempierre woman exclaimed, leaving her daughter's side to rush toward Nate. She reached up and cupped his face in her hands as though they had known one another their whole lives, her mossy green eyes sparkling with unshed tears. "Oh, Nathaniel, you are a man grown!"

"*Maman!*" the younger Dempierre hissed, gathering up her ruffled skirts and marching over and tossing a conspiratorial smirk at Nell. "You mustn't rush at strange men like that!"

"Oh, be quiet, Gigi," she crooned, making no move to release Nate from her grasp. "I rocked this man to sleep as an infant and bandaged his knees as a boy. Do you not remember me, little Nate?"

"I must disappoint you, madam," Nate said with an apologetic smile, despite the strange tinge of familiarity that had tugged at his chest the moment he'd entered the room. "I fear I remember very little of my childhood. I take it we were acquainted?"

"Acquainted!" Mrs. Dempierre scoffed, dropping her hands to her sides and taking a step back. "Why, your mother and I were as close as sisters. I knew you all the days of your life." She frowned, clearly displeased by the lack of recognition, and then lifted one pale shoulder, giving a little sigh. "You will remember in time. I am sure of it."

"I certainly hope so," Nate answered, his posture relaxed and his expression friendly, despite the cacophony of alarm sounding off within him. "In absence of my faulty memory, may I request introductions until such a time as my senses return to me?"

"Oh, of course, of course." She nodded, beckoning her daughter to her side. "I am Lady Therese Dempierre, erstwhile Comtesse and exile. This is my daughter, Giselle. We live on the other side of the white cliffs, at our English estate." Her face brightened, and her hands came clapping together. "Yes! You will surely remember it all once you've seen La Falaise. You loved to play there as a child!"

"I am certain you are correct," Nate said with a little bow. "I am, of course, Nathaniel Atlas, and this is my wife, Eleanor. I understand she became acquainted with Lady Giselle in the city yesterday?"

"It is a pleasure to make your acquaintance, Lady Dempierre," Nell said softly, stepping forward and giving a slight curtsy, which made her spectacles slide down again, caught by the upturned tip of her nose. "If we had known you were coming, we certainly would have prepared a finer reception."

"Oh, it is no matter! No matter at all! Gigi was telling me how delightful you were and when she said the name Atlas, I insisted we set out immediately and discover if Nathaniel had come home, at last."

"She did," Lady Giselle confirmed, her eyes still locked on Nell. "I wanted to ensure an ongoing acquaintance regardless, so I was rather pleased by her enthusiasm."

"You did?" Nell replied with obvious confusion.

It made Gigi Dempierre's lips curl up like a cat's. "Of course! If I am your friend, then perhaps you will sometimes lend me some of those fabulous gowns. You cannot fault my logic."

Her mother darted a quick, baffled glance over Eleanor's current clothing and pressed her lips tight together.

"We are in the process of opening up a house that has been closed tight for a decade," Nate said smoothly. "My wife and I have been making a morning of exploring, so, as you can see, we are not quite as presentable as you might otherwise find us."

"Nonsense, nonsense," Lady Dempierre insisted, waving her hand as though she could bat away ideas like summer flies. "You are perfect as you are. My daughter wishes to spend some time with your lovely bride. Perhaps you might indulge me in a tour of the house before it is reinvented? I have many fond memories here."

"It is hardly presentable for visitors, Lady Dempierre,"

Nathaniel said, suspicion beginning to weave its way through his thoughts.

"I do not mind, truly!" she insisted, stepping forward to take his arm as though the matter were already determined. "I have missed this house so very much."

He glanced at Nell, who gave an almost imperceptible nod, as though she wished him to accept the request. If she had something to gain by being left alone with the daughter, then perhaps it was worthwhile. He put on his gracious face and allowed the lady to take his arm. To his wife and Gigi Dempierre he said, "Please excuse us for a moment. I will return your mother to you shortly, though I cannot promise she will be free of dust."

"She's always a little dusty anyhow," Gigi replied with that feline smile, and Nate gave a short laugh rather than admit that he wasn't entirely sure what she meant.

Lady Dempierre heaved a sigh as they stepped back out into the foyer, clinging to his side as she gazed up and around the rooms.

"Is there any particular room you wish to see?" he asked politely,

"There is a portrait of your family somewhere here," she said, tilting her head up to meet his eyes. She looked remarkably like her daughter, still beautiful despite her age, and somehow wearing the slight wrinkles about her eyes like ornamental gems. She appeared very practiced at the art of batting her eyelashes to get things she wanted. "Do you remember sitting for it? It was right after Alice was born, about half a year before ..." She trailed off, blinking at her line of thought and releasing his arm to step away for a moment.

"Are you well?" Nate asked, though his heart was racing too.

She brushed her fingers under her eyes and along her cheeks, giving a tremulous laugh and shaking her head, making the silk petals in her hair tremble. "I am sorry. I haven't cried over what happened in so long, but being here again, it all feels so fresh. I should not come here and bring sad memories onto your head, nor should I let myself become so rattled on a social call. Forgive me."

"There is nothing to forgive," Nate assured her, though he was not yet sure that was strictly true. "I remember the portrait. My father gave me one of his medals to wear and I had to sit still for so very long."

She gave a sudden smile, those cheeks of hers rounding into perfect, pink apples. "Yes! Do you know where it is? I confess, after the house was abandoned, I have often thought of it, lost here in the dark, and wished I could have it for my own. Now that you are home, you must hang it proudly for all to see. I have so missed their faces, Nathaniel."

He was too stunned to reply, and perhaps it was for the best, for he was not sure what response would have been most tactful. He blinked at her for a moment, trying his hardest to find her in the rubble of his memories. There was something about her that was so familiar, but he could not grasp it.

"We haven't found it yet," he confessed. "When we do, I will certainly invite you to view it. Hopefully it has been covered all this while. I should like to see it as well."

"Yes, I hope so as well." She looked at him carefully, as though she was searching his face for some clue as to the portrait's whereabouts. When she spoke again, her voice was more level, cooler. "Have you yet opened the cellars?"

"No, not yet," Nate replied. "Do you think it is down there?"

"No. No, of course not. I simply remember that your parents kept several barrels of fine quality French vintage there, and was wondering if any yet survives. It would be wonderful to have a taste of home."

"I will send you a full barrel if we have any," he promised, keeping his expression pleasant but neutral as he led her into the dining room. "This is where we've made the most progress," he said, spreading his arms. "It seemed worthwhile to start with a single bedroom and a place to eat and then we will work outward. It is not finished, of course, but I have passed a round dozen meals here by now, and it is sufficient."

"Oh, these chairs." She sighed, brushing the coiling bevels carved into the wood. "It is funny how little things can spark the memory so. I can almost hear the ghosts of music in the walls."

"Speaking of music," Nate said, drawing her attention back to the present. "I have found some instruments in the ballroom, most notably a harp. They all require a fair deal of repair to be functional again. Might you have a recommendation? Mrs. Atlas is fond of playing the harp, and I would like to have that particular piece restored soon."

"Oh, certainly, certainly," she said with a nod. "I hope she will play for us someday. Oh, I hope our families will be dear friends again, Nathaniel, like they were in days past. I am just so happy to see you."

"I am certain we will become good friends," Nathaniel assured her. "Evidently, my wife and your daughter began that work quite on their own."

"Yes, I could scarcely believe it," she replied, though her eyes were fixed on the wall and she appeared far away.

"Perhaps once Meridian is back to rights, I could impose upon you to assist us in introductions around the county. I have spent much of my time in London and am at a loss of where to begin to build a social rapport." He tapped on his chin, as though deep in thought. "Perhaps as Yuletide draws near, there will be opportunities to fete nearby families? What do you think?"

"Oh, yes, yes." She nodded. "Winter can be most magical here on the coast. There are banquets and soirees abound, so long as you can make it through the snow to attend. Why not come to dinner at La Falaise? I am hosting a small gathering in a week's time and it would be no bother at all to include the Atlases. Indeed not, it would never be."

"That would be delightful. I cannot tell you how thankful I am that you stopped by. Are there any other rooms you'd like to see?"

"Oh, I could keep you all day and night exploring every nostalgic corner of this old house," she said with an apologetic laugh. "I shouldn't have imposed upon you. I was simply overwhelmed with news of your return, and knowing you are back here feels like all of the Atlases are at home again, in spirit."

Nate did not respond. He felt a niggle of guilt in his chest, digging at his intention to stay here for as little time as possible and abandon it yet again. He had been afraid that returning here would dredge up too many painful memories, and that around every corner he would find hurtful reminders of what he'd lost. Instead, everything here had been just as alien to him as Lady Dempierre, who evidently had known him from the day of his birth.

"Do you intend to restore the ceiling in here?" she asked, startling him out of his reverie.

"The ceiling?" he asked, glancing up at the mottled plaster above. "Was it painted?"

"Not painted. It was layered in silver leaf and created the most spectacular reflections of candlelight at dinner." She smiled, clearly caught up in another memory. "One winter, shortly after your parents married, your mother invited her dearest friends to pass a frigid February here. We came to keep her company while your father was away on business and she was still learning to be the lady of a grand estate. The five of us would sit in here every night and light as many candles as possible while we drank our tea and talked for hours and hours under the glow."

"That sounds like a beautiful memory," Nathaniel said, feeling the warmth of the memory as though it were a flame between them. He could barely recall his mother's face anymore, and here sat a woman who had known her intimately, who might be able to answer a great deal of questions. "I can only hope to create such warm memories here."

"It would be appropriate." She sighed, glancing up at the

ceiling once more with the past shining in her eyes. "It would honor her."

"Are these other ladies still in Kent?" he asked, wondering if perhaps a neutral party was preferable for questions about his mother, rather than the target of a secret assignation. "Perhaps I might make their acquaintance."

"I'm the only one in Kent, sadly," she said. "Though if you ever invited them, I would wager good coin that they would all return, just to have a night of memories in this room. It was silly, I know, five young girls huddled together under a sparkling ceiling, giggling ourselves silly in our cups, but it meant something to us. Do you know what those memories mean once you're old and the time is gone?"

"It's never really gone, if you remember it so clearly," he said, unable to suppress a flash of envy at her memories. He could not picture his parents in this room. He could not hear the echo of his mother's laugh. Still, hearing it recounted was a sort of proxy to memory, and she felt more real in this moment than she had when he sat in this room by himself.

When he glanced at the ceiling again, he noted a few flecks of silver that still clung to the plaster. Uncle Archie must have scraped it off and sold it to pay off one of his debts, he guessed. It explained a great many missing trinkets and smaller pieces that the house was missing since the last time he had been here.

Lady Dempierre continued talking, her voice wistful and far away. "For years after that winter, we kept a rotation of letters between us, the five girls who formed a sisterhood in a room with a sparkling ceiling. It is silly, of course, but we always meant to return here again, to repeat our ritual and recreate the magic. It never happened, of course. Marriage and life takes women on a merry ride of unpredictability that never slows or stops."

"Marriage is unpredictable for us all," he agreed. "Though it sounds like enduring bonds of friendship were forged here."

"Yes. We came up with a secret name for ourselves, convinced it would become a yearly tradition. It is sad, but the truth is that we were never all together again, not as a complete group."

"It is important, I suppose, to cherish special moments as they happen."

"Indeed, young man, indeed," she sniffed, dabbing at her eyes. "If we had known then that it would be the only time, perhaps we wouldn't have enjoyed ourselves so much and it would not have been as special. In the end, that February was the one and only convention of our little club, but all of us were forever changed that winter. I daresay even now, all these years later, each of us still considers herself a staunch member of our Silver Leaf Society."

CHAPTER 18

*B*y the time the Dempierres had been sent on their way, Nate felt like he'd run a marathon on an empty stomach. His wife, evidently, was feeling much the same. She maintained a bright smile as she waved them off, but as soon as they were out of view, she returned to the drawing room, tossed her spectacles onto the nearest surface, and slumped face-down onto one of the sofas like a sack of soiled linens.

"Have you ever met someone who is so energetic, it is as though the sheer force of their presence pulls all the energy you've got for yourself into their orbit, leaving you completely depleted?" she mumbled into the cushion.

"That bad, was it?" Nathaniel said, plopping down next to her and running a reassuring hand over her back. "And here I thought the two of you would be fast friends."

Nell groaned, shaking her head without raising it from her forearms. "Perhaps we were. It is difficult to say. She said I reminded her of one of her birds. A parakeet, I believe."

"Well, that's nonsense," Nate assured her. "You are quite clearly a starling."

It got a weak laugh out of her, but a laugh nonetheless. She heaved a little sigh and pulled herself up, turning to face him. "How did you find the mother?"

"Likely just as draining, but for different reasons," he said. "I need to reflect on what she said to me before we can move forward, but I did agree to a dinner invitation in a week's time. They wish to introduce us to the people worth knowing 'round Dover."

She gave a nod that could be described as accepting, if less than enthusiastic. He had the strangest urge to reach forward and tuck a wayward curl behind her ear, where it had escaped from her bun in a springy coil. "At least it isn't tonight."

She *was* birdlike in a way, he supposed. Delicate and poised and prone to being startled off, but certainly not a parakeet. Nell would never dress so garishly nor squawk so loudly.

At the sound of the front door being opened and shut again, they exchanged a look and sighed in unison. It was only Kit, however, and he strode into the drawing room, batting off a very flustered maid as he removed his own gloves and scarf.

"Sir!" the girl cried in distress, sparing a desperate glance at Nathaniel.

"It's all right," Nate assured her. "Kit never has been much for manners. You may return to your duties."

She shot Kit a look of disapproval, but did as she was told, bustling out as Kit tossed his things onto a nearby chair. He didn't acknowledge her at all, nor Nate's having to speak to her, and instead smiled genially at the two of them, as though their presence was an unexpected surprise.

"It's gotten cold today," he commented, heaving himself into the chair next to his things. "I predict snowfall in the next week or so."

Nell was doing her absolute best to stifle a yawn behind her dainty hands, though she was not fooling either of the gentlemen in attendance.

"This time of year makes me groggy too," Kit said sympathetically. "My mum swears by an afternoon nap to keep yourself going till the warmth comes back."

"Oh, a nap sounds just the thing," Nell agreed in a soft voice. "It must be well past midday by now, though I feel like I only just rolled out of bed."

"We had a number of surprises this morning," Nate said to his cousin. "It seems Mrs. Atlas is already attracting hopeful friends."

"It wasn't as grand as all that," she demurred, looking a bit embarrassed at the implication that such a thing were even possible. "Simply a local family wishing to say hello. I'm afraid I'm just not quite as exuberant as their daughter. Conversation with her has left me quite wrung out."

"You should indulge in that nap, my dear," Nate assured her, reaching over to give her hand a squeeze. "I promise to show you anything interesting we uncover while you're recovering. I imagine it will just be more dust and spiders."

"There was a family of squirrels in the lobby when we first got here," Kit told her cheerfully. "They seem to be settling into the oak outside nicely, even without the benefit of vaulted ceilings."

"We must invite them for Christmas," she said behind another yawn. She gave a sleepy smile to the two of them and pushed herself to her feet. "I am going to take your mother's advice. Perhaps the two of you might join us for dinner in a night or two? I am anxious to meet her."

"The feeling is mutual," Kit assured her, coming to his feet in a gesture of respect as she crossed the room. "Rest well, Mrs. Atlas."

"Thank you, Mr. Cooper," she said softly. To Nathaniel, she promised, "I won't sleep terribly long."

"Take as long as you need," he told her, the strangest feeling of contentment stirring within him at such a silly, simple exchange. When she closed the door behind her, he thought he might have sat there, staring at the spot where she'd been for quite a while, had his cousin not been present and so irritatingly perceptive.

"Who came to visit?" Kit asked, not bothering to return to his chair.

Nate sighed, rubbing his eyes in the hopes that it would give him a second wind. He hated having to recount events he hadn't properly parsed for himself yet, but Kit had always had the worst timing. "It was Lady Dempierre and the daughter," he said, ignoring the way Kit's eyes widened. "I think we need to go down to the cellars and investigate. Immediately."

"There are cellars?" Kit said in genuine bafflement.

"Evidently," Nate said with a shrug. He pushed himself to

his feet, noticing as he did that Nell had left her spectacles on the side table. He reached for them and tucked them carefully into his waistcoat to return to her later. When he looked back at his cousin, the quizzical expression was still painted over his face. "Shall we go?"

"I guess we shall," Kit answered, and without a second glance at his pile of discarded outerwear, he led the way out of the drawing room and in search of the cellars.

THEY WASTED about an hour asking the staff about any underground areas and making three full rotations of the property in search of the typical lean-to of a cellar entrance.

In the end, it was Kit who solved the puzzle.

"The drowning doors, remember?" he said, whipping around to grip Nathaniel by the shoulders, his eyes wide and blue. "We found those doors by the gazebo and your father said they covered an old well pit and that if we opened them, we'd fall in and drown. He put sod over them so we wouldn't find them again."

"Why would the entrance to a cellar be so far away from the house?" Nate asked skeptically. "It makes the most sense that it actually was a well."

"Well, the grounds are older than the house, aren't they? It's worth a look, anyhow. Come on!"

And he had been correct. After a bit of prodding around in the soft grasses beyond a rotting gazebo, they did indeed find hatch doors covered in a layer of earth.

"It's lucky we went looking for it now and not once the snow starts up," Nate pointed out as he helped his cousin dig away the layer of dirt and dry grass that covered the hinges. "Once the ground had frozen, we would have had to wait until spring to do anything."

"It's locked," Kit observed with a frown. "You reckon your father's spirit will swoop down and box my ears if I just shatter the padlock?"

"He might at that," Nate replied, rubbing at the back of his neck. "But I don't fancy going in search of some rusted old key that likely doesn't work anymore. Do you?"

By way of answer, Kit simply brought his spade down twice on the thinnest part of the lock until the rusty iron gave way beneath it. The two of them exchanged a look, both feeling like they were breaking a sacred rule by doing this, especially after having been explicitly warned against it. Twenty years is nothing when it comes to the fear of a father's wrath.

One of the hatch doors was so decomposed that it lifted clean away from its hinges with a pitiful splintering creak. If not for that stark reminder of the fragility of wood over time, they might not have bothered to return to the house for a new ladder—one that *hadn't* been sitting in a dank tunnel for half a lifetime. So, in his way, perhaps Walter Atlas was looking out for the boys after all.

"It doesn't smell half as bad as I anticipated," Kit commented, using the shaft of late-afternoon sunlight to spark a flame for the lanterns he'd brought down. "I expected an ungodly reek of mildew."

"I'm surprised there isn't a layer of water up to our knees, myself," Nate replied, leaping off the bottom rung of the ladder. "It's cold down here, but dry. What on earth?"

"Well, the French woman said there were vintages in barrels down here, didn't she? That'd make sense. They could be ignored for years at a time without fuss."

"She did," Nate confirmed, but something was still niggling at his brain. He took one of the lanterns and held it out, getting a view of the room around them. He couldn't see it all. It was significantly larger than a simple wine cellar.

He thought he could make out the shapes of a lighting system to illuminate this space as well as any room in the manor. There were indeed wine barrels here, stacked horizontally in a large trellis shelf against the wall, but that was hardly the only thing being stored in this enclave.

Long wooden boxes were stacked against one another from wall to wall, and there was a shelf with an assortment of strongboxes that weren't as accommodating to Kit's methods of brute force as the padlock without had been.

"Christ Almighty, how big is this place?" Kit marveled, sounding progressively farther away. "Look here, there's a tunnel passage."

Nate picked his way over to his cousin, careful with his footfalls to avoid anything that might break or burst or otherwise behave in an unpleasant manner. Kit was standing at the mouth of a long passageway, his lantern held out in front of him like some painting of a mystic, his golden hair in halo from the firelight.

"Well, then?" Nate asked, clapping his cousin on the shoulder. "Let's see how far it goes."

"Oh, is that what we're doing?" Kit mocked, his disbelief unable to override his sarcasm as Nathaniel swept past him. "What has gotten into you today? Stop walking so fast!"

Nate smirked to himself, pleased that for the first time since he'd been back, he was the one rattling the other. Kit's footsteps echoed against the stone walls as he chased after, coming up alongside his cousin with his breaths a little shallower than he was likely proud of.

"It is damned cold down here," Nate observed. "There could be a larder, I suppose. Cheeses and such would keep very well down here in the cooler months."

"I don't think a dairy locker has ever been quite this clandestine, Nathaniel," Kit replied dryly. "Whatever was going on down here, it was not a spot of brie to hold till spring."

"I'd like to assume it's harmless until we have proof to the contrary," Nate said, though he did not really mean it. Something had been going on here, clearly, something his father did not want them to discover.

"I can smell brine," Kit said, giving a theatrical sniff into the air. "Do you smell it?"

"Yes." Nate frowned, holding his lantern as far out in front of him as he could, though it was nothing but darkness for a long stretch ahead of them. "I would bet my last penny that this empties onto the shore somewhere."

"Ah. That'd explain the wine being French, wouldn't it, now?" Kit replied with a sigh. "You think it was your father?"

"It must have been both of them," Nate said slowly, nodding with his head that they should head back. "It would explain why they would travel to Calais in the early days of a war, I suppose."

"For black-market wine? I'm no sommelier, Nate, but I think that's a little unlikely, especially with Alice in arms."

They walked in silence after that, both likely attempting to unravel this new thread of information, which appeared to lead directly into a big, incomprehensible snarl. How would they even go about indexing the contraband stored down here without alerting the suspicions of the staff? It was obvious from the crates they'd seen that this was not just a matter of wine.

"Are you going to tell her?" Kit murmured, low enough to avoid the cave capturing his voice and throwing it back at him.

"Yes, and not because I'm some love-smitten fool, either," Nate snapped. "She's unseemly intelligent and has been involved with the Silver Leaf Society since she was fourteen. She might have some answers readily available that we'd otherwise spend months trying to work out for ourselves."

Kit made a noise somewhere between a scoff and a grunt. "She is a little bluestocking, isn't she? She wanted to ride over to Dover Castle and poke around inside!"

Nate laughed despite himself, absently touching her spectacles where they rested in the breast pocket of his waistcoat. "She quoted Francis Bacon at me this morning, casually, as though it were a thing she needn't even expend effort to summon."

"Well, you never have just done things the easy way," Kit

said cheerily. "I don't see why the endeavor of marriage should be any different. You are tripping up on all of your old pitfalls, though. Honestly, I'm surprised you take so long to learn."

"My marks were a great deal higher than yours, Christopher," Nate snapped, already shaking his head at the peal of laughter it won him. "Pray tell me, then, Professor. Where am I erring in my marriage? I am quite eager to hear the observations of a bachelor."

"I'm tempted not to say anything at all." He chuckled as they wove their way back through the crates and over to the ladder. "It's only a growing fondness of Eleanor that buys you my mercy."

"Growing fondness," Nate snorted. "You've known her a day. Careful, now, hand me the lantern."

Kit extinguished the lantern and handed it back to his cousin, waiting until both were secured on Nathaniel's belt before he began his ascent. "You always do this asinine division of your motives," he said between breaths as he heaved himself up. "I'm eating this apple because it is going to go bad soon, not because I like it. I'm joining this race because it will lead to valuable connections to further my career goals, not because I want to win. On and on you go, as though both things cannot be true at the same time. It's ridiculous."

Nate heaved himself out of the hatch and onto the grass, pondering over these words with no small amount of annoyance. "Get to the point," he muttered.

"That was the point," Kit said happily, dusting the debris from his trousers and reaching for the broken door to toss back over the hole in the earth. "I couldn't be any clearer if I did a song and dance."

"I agree. That is about where I'd rank your clarity," Nate replied. "If that's all, let's go have some tea and talk logistics. I'd rather be solving the problem under our feet than discussing the nuances of my marriage."

"There you go again," Kit said, throwing his hands up in exasperation.

Nate wasn't listening. Not really. Kit always was talking nonsense.

CHAPTER 19

*N*ell had always been reasonably talented at predicting the events ahead of her. She had become a keen observer on the sidelines of her finishing school and throughout her Seasons in London as a wallflower. However, she was quickly learning that this finely honed skill was useless at Meridian, and short of true psychic gifts, she had no means of foreseeing where any given moment might take her.

It wasn't that the surprises were unpleasant. No, quite the contrary. From the moment Nathaniel had burst in on her nap, ranting about a secret room in the ground and brandishing a stable boy's trousers at her, she had come to realize that her husband was a man far too complex to be predictable.

Further, he was considerate.

What other husband would think to find her a pair of trousers (a pair small enough to properly fit!) for her to wear to navigate an old cavern? What husband especially would consider such a thing on the understanding that she might wish to join him on an adventure most unsuitable for the average lady?

Of course, she knew a portion of that confidence in her nontraditional nature was due to the Silver Leaf Society rather than any particular quality she might have espoused in his presence, but all the same, it made her feel worthy. Stranger still, it made her feel visible, conspicuous even, for the first time in her life.

They had mostly been working at night to explore the cellars under the manor. Slipping out onto the doors hidden on the grounds under cover of dusk was prudent, as to not arouse too much curiosity from the staff. Without being certain just what they'd find in what could only be a smuggler's den, it was best not to draw attention to anything that might rain trouble down upon their heads.

Kit had been present for several of the visits into the cave, helping to repair and oil the lamps hanging on the walls so that they might have a clear view of their surroundings and the contraband therein, for contraband it most certainly was.

What they would ultimately do with all of it was a mystery. For now, the only thing to do was to create a list of everything they found, and (Nate insisted) to estimate its value.

Nell had spent the bulk of her life a member of a family that made the most of every spare pence. Seeing all of these things, discarded for decades, was bizarre. Further, so much of the gorgeous silks and satin and fur was eaten away by mold and age and rodents. It was almost enough to bring her to tears. What a horrible waste! What a tragic demise for something so fine, something someone might have treasured deeply! In the right hands, such things would have been heirlooms rather than rat's nests.

In truth, the only complaint she could muster from the last handful of days was that spending the night hours picking through a mysterious treasure trove left them both far too exhausted to use their bed for anything other than sleeping.

It was perhaps a small blessing, for the soreness that she'd experienced after their first encounter had now had time to fully resolve itself, and of course, it had given her time to contemplate how best to execute her next attempt at seduction.

It was not without progress in the matter of intimacy, though they had not yet made love again. Nathaniel no longer slept like a plank of wood, fit to roll right off his edge of the bed if a strong breeze happened in. She often fell asleep with the warmth of his leg against hers and the smell of his skin, always washed clean in fine sandalwood soap before slumber, lulling her to dreams.

On the day of the first snow, Nathaniel had sent a runner into Dover to retrieve several items for the both of them, including several more parcels from Madame Bisset's. To Nell's astonishment, it was not only the gowns and garments that arrived, but half a dozen pairs of brand new shoes, from embroidered slippers of jewel-toned silk to sturdy riding boots that gleamed with quality, all in boxes dusted with fine, frosted powder from the change of seasons outside.

"I feel a bit silly now, having ordered jewelry," Nate had commented over dinner. He had said it so casually, as though Nell were the sort of woman who was often gifted jewels. "With what we've found down below, I fear it is not only redundant, but rather paltry in comparison."

Nell had been unable to formulate a proper answer. How could she tell him that any gift from him, chosen for her, would be more precious to her than the full contents of their treasure hoard? How could she say such a thing without sounding absurd?

She had not yet worn any of her new gowns, instead limiting herself to the luxury of her nightgowns, some of the ribbons for her hair, and a particular pair of woolen stockings that were as soft against her skin as they were warm against the first frosty grip of early winter.

She knew Nate had taken note of her unchanged, boxy gowns, but he had not commented upon it. She hoped it was obvious that she did not wish to risk their perfection on mundane days of labor.

Perhaps when the house was finished and they settled into a normal state of affairs, she might wear some of her new things.

The idea of putting on those beautiful gowns for nothing more than a day about the manor gave her a queasy sort of nervousness, as though she were misbehaving by even considering such a thing. It seemed like such beautiful items should be reserved for special occasions, but there was so very much that Nathaniel had purchased, and she couldn't imagine that many special occasions arising for years.

She hadn't investigated the jewelry yet. It was in a wooden box on the vanity table in their bedroom, still secured with a ribbon and a tag bearing the jeweler's mark. She was saving the reveal for a moment when she could truly indulge in the joy of it, and examine every piece with as much indulgence as she wished. She did not wish to waste such a magical moment.

Of course, some things had to be opened right away, due to no one knowing exactly what was inside. For example, a curious little box had arrived alongside an order of toiletries, addressed to Mrs. Atlas. It was lined with stuffed satin and filled to the brim with creams and powders and pigments and pomades.

Sarah had been beside herself with excitement at this bizarre little box, fantasizing about how well she'd use the items to turn Nell into a ravishing beauty for the dinner party with the Dempierres.

It was a sweet sentiment, but Nell rather thought a few layers of rice powder would make precious little difference to any woman's appearance, lest it was caked on to the point of looking ghastly. Still, she didn't wish to dampen Sarah's fun, and perhaps, in practice, she might have some fun as well.

Running a household had always been an abstract concept for her, a thing studied in a classroom that she never thought she would need to employ. Of course, the restoration of a neglected manor is quite a bit different than day-to-day doings in a lady's townhouse, but Nell had taken to the task with true enthusiasm and enjoyment.

Watching the beauty of Meridian reveal itself, bit by bit, as the staff worked their magic on room after room was most gratifying. She thought it was rather like solving a puzzle, putting something that had gone into disarray back to rights.

She had designated the ballroom into three areas for all items on the ground floor that had been uncovered room to room. There was a corner for items to be restored, one for the things that might make for salvageable parts, and of course a pile of things that would eventually be disposed of. Mercifully, this final pile was the smallest of the three, though none of them were particularly large.

What was odd to her was the *lack* of general clutter that one ought to find in a home. It wasn't just knickknacks missing, but furniture, the occasional painting, and in several cases, the lighting fixtures. What sort of thief takes the time to remove a chandelier or roll up a rug? It was mysterious, to say the least.

Whatever had happened here was still a mystery to Nell, and one she felt she shouldn't question directly. She was reasonably certain that Nathaniel would answer her and be truthful if asked, but something terrible had obviously happened in this house, and her curiosity could not override her sense of compassion. It was terrible form to poke at another's pain without a bloody good reason, after all.

With the snowfall making access to the smuggler's cove less than convenient, Nathaniel decided to halt their investigation for the time being. This meant Kit was free to pursue his previous business without feeling obligated for daily stop-ins. Nell liked Kit, of course, but she had desperately wanted her husband all to herself during the last week, which was difficult to manage with Kit's cheerful, helpful presence always at hand.

Of course, on the very day that the prospect of a private evening as a pair finally became tenable, they were expected at La Falaise for a dinner party, which could not be missed, weather and willingness notwithstanding.

Nell had never much liked these types of soirees, where she was certain to either be bored senseless or deliberately seated next to an elderly person in the hopes that she could entertain them with intelligent conversation. She knew this socialization was an important step in their mission, but she dearly wished they could simply hole up inside throughout the winter and be bothered no more.

"Will you have to speak French all night, ma'am?" Sarah wondered as the two of them selected a gown from the array of new things made by Madame Bisset.

"I'm not certain," Nell replied thoughtfully. "It is possible. Nathaniel did say that the Dempierre family primarily keeps the company of their fellow exiled countrymen. It is no matter. There were entire days at Mrs. Arlington's where we were only permitted to speak French or Greek or Latin. It was an effective exercise to accomplish fluency, even if it was deeply irritating."

"I think the white and red suits you nicely," Sarah commented, holding up one gown and then another in Nell's direction. "Though it might not be as warm as the green. It shouldn't matter much if you go directly from house to carriage to house, though."

"Whatever you prefer," Nell said with a wave of her hand. "I am hopeless at such things. Simply instruct me in your grooming rituals and I will comply."

"Well, in that case, let's get your bath drawn. Readying a lady can be a time-consuming thing, ma'am."

Nell waited until she was alone in the bedroom, with fragrant floral steam curling out of the tub, and crossed the room to retrieve the jewelry box, still bound in its ribbon. If given the choice, she would have waited to indulge in this moment, but she knew Nathaniel would consider it very odd if she went to tonight's dinner without adornment.

She sat on the bed with her dressing gown pooled out around her bare legs and tugged the knot free from the ribbon, carefully curling it around her hand and setting it aside in a neat coil. She couldn't help but hold her breath as she unhooked the latch on the little wooden box and opened it for the first time.

She wasn't sure exactly what she had been expecting. Perhaps the dizzying wealth of what they'd been cataloging in the cellar had filled her mind with a gauche pirate's chest, filled to brimming with gold and gems.

Instead, the box was neatly arranged with elegant, understated pieces that very well suited her tastes. Pearl earrings, a strand of thin, braided gold to be worn about the wrist, an assortment of inlaid brooches, and so on.

In the center of the box was a delicate golden band, inlaid with smoky blue gemstones cut into faceted circles. This was the item she could not tear her eyes from. Something about it was special, amongst the other treasures before her, and she found herself taking great care in wedging it loose from its velvet crevice and holding it up to the light.

It sparkled, casting the tiniest of aquamarine prisms onto her fingers. If she hadn't held it up to inspect it so closely, she would have missed the engraving on the inner cusp, a simple calligraphy depicting two interlocking versions of the letter N.

Nathaniel and Nell.

This was her wedding ring.

She drew it onto her finger with only a slight trembling of her grasp, certain that before it could be arranged into place, this dream would be torn from her and cast into the harsh light of reality. Surely this wasn't truly happening, not to dowdy and invisible Eleanor Applegate!

And yet, there the ring sat, refusing to vanish in a puff of smoke or dissolve into the intangibility of dreams; proof of not only her marriage to a man she had admired from afar, but of his devotion to that marriage.

It might mean nothing to him, a mere symbol to keep up appearances. She would have been utterly convinced that's all it was, if not for that inscription, tucked into a place no one else could see.

She clasped her hand against her heart and gave a shaky sigh of wonder.

She could not bear to take it off for her bath, though she knew it was silly to wear jewels into the water. Truly, she thought she may never take it off again.

BEING that her husband was a man, Nell should have been unsurprised that he required barely any time at all to prepare for a dinner party. It was only that Nathaniel was not a man ever unconcerned with his presentation, and when one appeared in such exacting perfection on such a regular basis, it was easy to assume such beauty was the result of hours of work.

However, by the time he arrived in their rooms to change, Nell was already strapped into an assortment of overly luxurious underthings and had been victim to many serums and creams and powders upon her face, alongside a tiny smudge brush, dipped in what appeared to be soot, dabbed along her eyes.

She imagined she looked something like a grotesque porcelain doll and did not have the courage to confirm as such.

When her husband walked in, he was struck dumb for the slightest moment, hesitating at the doorway with his eyes locked on her, lips parted in surprise.

Sarah was completing the last of her hairstyle, which had required close to an hour of painstaking coiling with a heated wand. If not for the nearness of the heat, she might have fled her maid's attention straightaway, upon seeing his reaction.

Sarah was unperturbed, mumbling something of a good evening to her master between the hairpins in her teeth, her hands continuing to twist and fluff without interruption. Somehow her maid found such a task engaging, for Nell was entirely certain that she was utterly weary of it far faster than Sarah was, if indeed the girl tired at all of such things.

Nathaniel cleared his throat, giving one of his unreadable pleasant smiles and a slight bow as Nell felt her cheeks heating. He was polite to the end, wasn't he? She couldn't even think of a thing to say in greeting, instead just letting her eyes flicker shut as the last of her hair was wrested into its style.

The gown she would be wearing was spread out over their bed, though it had required neither the smoothing nor the mending Nell was accustomed to attending before a Society event. It was a creamy ivory with thin, bright red embroidery tracing images of large, abstract flowers throughout. It had a matching sash to be worn below the bust of that same vibrant crimson, and a second, smaller ribbon to be worn about the throat.

It was finer than things she'd seen worn by brides at the pulpit, and yet, compared to many of the other items now in her collection, she could not, with confidence, proclaim it the most beautiful thing she owned.

Nathaniel seemed well accustomed to dressing without the aid of a valet, and seemed unperturbed by Sarah's presence as he shrugged out of his jacket and tugged his cravat loose while a servant brought in a washbasin and necessities.

Surely he must know the way both women were watching him as he unbuttoned his waistcoat, the way their breath caught in tandem when he whipped his shirt up over his head. Still, he paid them no mind at all, instead intently focused on his task.

Sarah gave a firm tap to Nell's shoulder, indicating that she should stand, and motioned to the privacy screen that still sat in the corner of the room.

Well, it was a little silly to aim for modesty at this late juncture, but if it would prevent another woman from seeing her husband's full and considerable charms on display, she would not argue. Besides, it was an opportunity to check her appearance in the small hanging mirror in the corner, lest she realize she must scrub off the cosmetics immediately.

To her astonishment (and considerable relief), she did not immediately notice much of a difference in her appearance as she approached the aforementioned mirror. As she drew closer, she could see that her skin appeared more radiant than it usually looked, the color in her cheeks higher, and her lashes seemingly darker and more lustrous.

The fact that it was so very subtle was almost a disappointment, after all the layers of nonsense that it had taken to achieve. Still, it was not displeasing, and she found herself occupied with her reflection, listening to the splashing of Nathaniel's hands in the washbasin, until Sarah reappeared with her gown and selected jewelry, eager to complete her work.

The gown was laced tighter than she was accustomed to, melding closely to her figure, following every nuance of the enhanced hourglass provided by her stays. The red sash was long enough to fashion into a generous bow at the midpoint of her back, and when she looked down to admire the effect, she was alarmed at how conspicuous her bosom suddenly looked, pushed up and out of the gown's square neckline.

She instinctively moved to tug it up, hooking her thumbs under the seam.

"Oh, no you don't," Sarah hissed, slapping her hands away with such speed and commitment that Nell was too stunned to argue. "It fits as it's meant to."

"Does it?" Nell replied weakly, a nervous flutter skipping through her as the pearls were pinned to her ears and the red ribbon secured around her throat. "Are you certain?"

"Absolutely certain," Sarah huffed. "Now, let me see. Yes, ma'am, you look striking. Let's show your husband."

"Nathaniel!" Nell called out in a sudden flash of panic. "Are you ... quite decent?"

There was a pause as they awaited answer, and the voice that replied was clearly amused. "Most decent, dear wife."

Sarah smiled and stepped aside to allow for Nell to exit first, though she almost wished for the blockade of another human body.

She stepped out uncertainly, her eyes lowered and her bottom lip caught between her teeth. She held the heavy fabric of the skirt in her hands, stepping into the white slippers that were awaiting her next to the fireplace, and then turned to present herself to Nathaniel.

He was silent.

He was silent for so long that she had no choice but to raise her eyes to look at him. When she did, she found her gaze caught firmly within the intensity of those chameleon's eyes, sparkling like sunlight on the ocean, reflecting the firelight from the hearth so clearly that she felt warmth encasing her from all sides.

"Do you like it?" she asked, her voice coming out of her mouth so softly that she barely heard herself.

He blinked, that reassuring pleasantness sliding back over his face, his lips curving into his most charming smile. "Eleanor," he said in his honey-smooth voice, "you look lovely."

CHAPTER 20

As a rule, Nate usually enjoyed social events. It was a chance to flex his political muscles, to learn and study people, and of course to wear smart clothing and eat exceptional fare. In fact, he would wager his fortune that he had never in his life wished so desperately to forego *any* social obligation as much as he did the dinner at La Falaise tonight.

The last week had been trying enough, attempting to give his little wife the time and patience a woman required in the wake of her first intimate encounter. Nate had heard it mentioned once, between gentlemen ribbing a prospective groom one night at White's, that the way to a happy marital bed was to allow one's wife to initiate the second encounter, once she had recovered from a likely painful initiation. Attempting to stick to this nugget of wisdom was proving to be next to impossible.

If they hadn't been interrupted the morning after in the ballroom, things might have progressed immediately, but the appearance of Lady Dempierre and the subsequent discovery of the cellars had thrown everything askew. He'd had to bribe Kit with promises of his favorite meals and assistance in his work with the orchard deeds to get him to appear every day, serving as a buffer between the two of them should Nate lose his battle against his baser impulses.

This had proved equal parts effective and infuriating, especially with Kit's obvious ongoing amusement at the very concept of his marriage.

Tonight, though, it was as though the fatal blow had been dealt to his composure. He was under no illusion that he hadn't become extremely attracted to his wife, but he had not even considered, much less come to terms with, the prospect of every red-blooded man who saw her feeling the same. If she'd had gowns like this one and a maid so attentive during London, she'd have been swept up in her first Season, likely with a pack of suitors to choose from ravening at her heels.

He wasn't sure which was more tempting, the finished product or the vision she'd presented when he first walked in, corseted into her underthings with much flesh on display as her maid attended her hair, her lips glossy with rose oil and her cheeks warm and pink.

In the gown, her petite frame was lusciously curvaceous, emphasized by the dress he'd chosen at the whims of his own taste, without properly considering the consequences of seeing her in it. To his credit, it suited her very, very well. Too well. What had he been thinking, putting her in red?

Her coffee-brown hair was coiled over her shoulder, brushing the ribbon tied snugly about her slender, pale throat. Her breasts, which had always been effectively hidden from his view until that night they'd spent together, swelled temptingly over the lacy neckline, and when she turned her eyes up to meet his, that stormy, silvery blue was so striking that he'd felt his breath catch.

He wanted to do nothing else but drink in the vision of her in that dress almost as much as he wanted to remove it from her with extreme haste. Instead, he'd pressed his thumbnail into his palm and forced himself into his well-practiced charm and calm, assuring her that she looked well enough and that they must be off soon.

She had smiled in relief at his assurances, seemingly believing whatever he said at face value. She had crossed the room and retrieved a list of tasks for her maid, balancing her spectacles onto the upturned tip of her nose for a moment to review her own scribblings while he stood frozen in place, somehow even more enflamed by those silly, round frames appearing briefly on her face than he had been by the vision of her fit for portraiture.

He was the first to acknowledge that it was a strange thing to suddenly take issue with having an attractive wife, when he had been primed to marry a celebrated beauty with no concerns about the fact whatsoever. He couldn't make sense of it, nor did he particularly want to. He could keep control of his emotions, however irrational and overpowering they might be.

The drive through Dover was slower than it might otherwise have been, due to the foggy snowbank and iced slickness on the roads. Still, they made excellent time, and were fortunate enough to arrive at the doors of La Falaise amidst a retinue of other guests.

Nell clung to his side, her scent wafting up and coiling around him like a serpent as several passersby cast lengthy glances in her direction. She was gracious and pleasant, greeting everyone in impeccable French, her schoolgirl etiquette on bright display as they were led into a brightly lit antechamber, already dressed with garland for Yuletide.

When he reached up to pat her hand, he noted that she was wearing the wedding band he'd had made for her. He felt a twinge of regret that he had not remembered to wear the matching ring he'd commissioned for himself. A symbol signifying that they were a pair, belonging to one another, would have perhaps soothed some of his ruffled feathers at the prospect of others seeing her like this.

He did recognize the names of a few of the attendees, from their participation in the London Season and their stature amongst the *ton*. Two of the gentlemen in attendance had British wives, which at the very least did not leave them the only outliers in a very French affair.

The Dempierres waited until most of the party was assembled before making their appearances. They arrived just as their staff went about opening up the doors to a lavish dining room, descending down their grand staircase with regal bearing, assured that their entrance had been properly noted. The patriarch of the family was not nearly so pleasing to the eye as his wife and daughter, with modest bearing and very little hair on his head.

The daughter, Giselle, seemed to hone in on Eleanor immediately, her eyes sparkling with what appeared to be genuine excitement as she rushed over to greet them. She was dressed very lightly for winter, her hair coiled up and wrapped in a vibrant blue ribbon. She seemed completely uninterested in the several young men who attempted to greet her as she cut her path between the staircase and the Atlases.

"Oh, that gown was my favorite of the lot! I'm so pleased that you chose to wear it tonight!" she gushed by way of hello, taking Nell's free hand and grasping it between her own. "You clever thing, hiding what a beauty you are until the opportune moment. I can positively feel the buzz of envy already!"

"Envy?" Nell repeated with a genuine laugh. "I think not."

"Oh," Gigi said, her eyes going wide in astonishment as she lifted her gaze from Nell's to Nathaniel's. "She doesn't know."

"Hello, Lady Giselle," Nate replied, giving the girl a conspiratorial twist of the lips, which won him a brilliant smile.

"Just Giselle is fine, or Gigi, if you like! My parents cling to gentry, but I've never known it. Come, you will be seated near to me. I promise you've never had gooseberry cheese so divine in all your life!" She motioned for the two of them to follow her amongst the throng of others filing into the dining area, oblivious to the assembled hopefuls who had intended to speak with her before the meal.

"What don't I know?" Nell whispered, turning those lovely gray eyes up to him, blinking with those feathered lashes in earnest confusion.

He chuckled, wishing they were not in public just now, so that he might demonstrate to her the effect of her beauty tonight. Instead, he waited until they had taken their seats and leaned over to press a kiss into her cheek. Into her ear, he whispered softly that she might look at a certain gentleman to their left, who had been gaping at her for long enough that the woman seated to *his* left was now glaring.

She shivered, the fine hairs rising on her delectable little neck at the warmth of his breath. She turned her head toward his, close enough for their eyes to meet while they still might communicate in whispers. "I don't know that man at all," she insisted.

"No, of course you don't," he replied with amusement. "And he wishes to remedy that error post-haste in the most Biblical sense of the phrase."

Color flooded to her face, her eyes widening with understanding. "Oh, but I would never—!"

"I know that, my dear," he assured her. "Sadly for him and many of the other admirers you've already won tonight, you have already been claimed."

"By you?" she responded breathlessly, moistening her lips as a servant leaned over her shoulder to fill her glass of wine.

"By me," he replied, unable to mask the huskiness in his voice, "or don't you recall?"

She pressed her lips together, lowering her lashes and taking three very shallow little breaths. "I remember very well, Nathaniel," she breathed. "And often."

Heat spread within him, his eyes scraping over every delectable inch of her flesh in that gown. "And do you enjoy those memories, my dear?" he whispered. "Did you enjoy being claimed?"

She shivered, her voice little more than a whisper. "Nathaniel, I ..."

The sound of a fork ringing against crystal interrupted her thought, bringing both of their heads up with the sudden realization that they were in mixed company, and keenly observed besides. From across the table, Lady Dempierre was watching them with her eyebrows raised, while Gigi seemed both thrilled and entertained by the spectacle, resting her chin on her fingers with a feline smile on her lips.

He took a steadying breath, forcing his mask of placidity back into place as he turned his head to listen to Lord Dempierre's toast, which might have been the greatest oration ever given or as dull as brass for all he could focus upon it. Mercifully, regardless of the content, it was a short speech, immediately followed by the arrival of *amuse bouche* and the commencement of dinner conversation and the clattering of silverware.

"How go the renovations?" Lady Dempierre asked him politely, lifting her wine glass with a hand sporting a large ruby ring, which flashed in the candlelight. "It heartens me so to know Meridian is on the mend."

"We are making rapid progress," Nell replied on his behalf. "I have no doubt it will be a proper home again by spring."

"That's lovely, dear," Lady Dempierre said with a tight smile. "Nathaniel, did you happen to find that painting I mentioned? The portrait of your family? I have thought of it often since we last met and how dearly I should wish to see their faces again."

He considered her, careful to keep his thoughts masked

behind manners. "We have found a great deal of the artwork missing, sadly," he said, taking his time with delivering an answer. "Though I cannot imagine a thief taking a family portrait, for what value would it have to sell? I'm certain it will turn up eventually."

She returned his gaze with a shrewdness of her own, as though she were returning every impenetrable tactic to him in a gilt box. "I certainly hope it does."

"Oh, I did find the cellars, however," he added, lifting his fork to his mouth as her eyes widened upon him. He enjoyed taking his time chewing the morsel and reaching for his wine to complete the experience. "You were correct. They are very well stocked."

"With wine?" she asked thinly.

"Among things," Nell said pleasantly, making it clear that she was not ignorant of the machinations at play here. It won her a look of considerably more levity from the elder woman. "We brought you a bottle, of course, as requested."

"Yes," Nathaniel agreed with a little smile. "We hope it is a pleasing vintage."

"Perhaps we can share a glass soon," Nell added, smiling at Gigi rather than bothering to charm the mother. "It is so lovely to have made friends so quickly here in Kent. I hope that we will remain close through the winter."

"Oh, I hope so too!" Gigi replied, her eyes sparkling, though it was difficult to tell whether it was mischief or girlish enthusiasm lurking in them. "We must be regular intimates."

"That would be absolutely wonderful," Nell replied, falling into the rhythm of feminine bonding with the ease of a learned socialite. Nate wondered if she was channeling her dear friend Miss Blakely in this moment, for it certainly sounded that way.

"I so enjoy parties like this one, and I must have more chances to wear my new gowns! Your invitation was just the thing for this one," she continued, "though I was tempted to wear the green one with the feathers, do you recall it?"

"Oh, yes." Gigi nodded sagely, as though she'd never forget something so very important. "That one, I believe, would be better suited for a ball."

"Well, then we must hope someone throws one," Nell said happily, returning her attention to her plate, as though unaware of the sudden interest that Lady Dempierre had taken in this exchange.

"Indeed," Nate added. "Believe it or not, I have not yet had the chance to waltz with my bride."

"Oh, *maman*," Gigi squeaked, nigh bubbling over with excitement as she turned to touch her mother's arm. "We must have them at the winter masque!"

"Yes, Gigi," Lady Dempierre replied flatly. "It appears we must."

NATE FOUND the bulk of the event to be fairly standard and predictable.

Dinner was indeed exceptional, but if French exiles were accustomed to different post-dinner rituals than the English, they certainly hadn't retained them. The men and women separated for a time, which left him waving away cigar smoke and sipping a particularly robust brandy opposite the type of empty conversation one encounters at every social gathering.

He approached Lord Dempierre to thank him for the invitation, and got the distinct impression that the man had not the faintest clue who he was.

"I am very much looking forward to the winter masquerade," Nate had commented with polite enthusiasm. "It is, I understand, an exclusive affair."

"Oh," Lord Dempierre said, his focus seeming to wander to studying the wallpaper. "It is entirely my wife's doing. Women love such things, you know."

It was a relief when they were able to rejoin the women, for even if he hadn't been eager to gather his bride and return to Meridian, there was little of interest to be found amongst the men.

In her red and white dress, Nell was easy to spot in a crowd. She was among a trio of young ladies and had the flush of color on her cheeks that bode a cheery mood and much laughter. The gems in her wedding ring winked against the light as she raised her hand to brush away an errant strand of her hair and then reached forward to touch the gloved wrist of one of the other women, as though the other woman had just said something truly endearing.

She was such a curious creature. He leaned against a cocktail table, sipping his brandy, and simply watched her for a while as she endeared herself to an array of girls who were so very different from her.

In the autumn, when they'd been at Somerton together, Nell had kept the company of all of the young ladies in attendance. Despite her bookishness and unfashionable clothes, she seemed a treasured friend to the beauties of Society, to the prickly and independent Lady Heloise, and to the silly and frivolous daughters of Lord Benton.

Did she do it apurpose? Had she learned how to charm and win over all manner of other girls during her time at that finishing school? Or was it something that came naturally? From watching her, he would never have suspected calculation behind her motions, nor doubted the sincerity of her tinkling laugh.

He had never even bothered to take serious note of her until it was clear he was going to have to marry her, and even then, it was with little more than idle amusement. She was the perfect spy, he realized—utterly convincing and natural.

"Your wife is very beautiful," said a man with the faintest touch of an accent and a style about him of jaunty and deliberate disarray. "You are a lucky man."

"I agree," Nate replied, turning to the stranger with a little smile and an extension of his hand. "Pleasure to meet you. I am Nathaniel Atlas."

"Oh, I know," the man replied with a little chuckle, accepting the offer of a handshake. "We have heard of little else here at La Falaise for the last several weeks. Hark! The Atlas boy, at long last is returned and nobly restoring his ancestral manor. I did not know exactly what to expect of you from the fantastical descriptions. My mother is prone to exaggerate when excited."

"You are a Dempierre, then?" Now that he'd said it, it was

obvious. If his flaxen coloring hadn't given him away, the distinctively high cheekbones he shared with his mother and sister would have. His eyes were his father's, however, a light amber brown and (unlike his father's) engaged and focused upon Nate.

He gave a little bow, as though the honor of his name was a somewhat dubious one. "I am Mathias Dempierre, heir to the ghost of a title abroad and this precarious house on a rock. Pleasure to meet you."

"Likewise," Nathaniel responded. "Were you not seated with your family at dinner? I was across from the ladies and did not see you."

"Oh, I missed the dinner entirely," Mathias said with a careless shrug. "Mother will whinge, but I find these things intolerable. I must confess, however, to having my interest piqued for once at one of these gatherings. Your lovely bride caught my eye the instant I saw her."

Nathaniel smirked. "She would be flattered to hear it, but alas, she is no longer on the marriage mart."

"To everyone's utter devastation, of course." Mathias chuckled. "Tell me, Nathaniel, does your pretty bride know the meaning of wearing that red ribbon 'round her neck in French company?"

"Likely not," Nathaniel replied, glancing over his shoulder at Nell, who was still engaged in animated conversation, the bright red ribbon stark against her pale throat. "For if she did, she likely would have shared it with me."

Mathias grinned, his smile curling up at the corners of his lips in the same feline shape as his sister's. He clearly enjoyed having information that others did not. He ran an absent hand over his hair, mussing it further from any semblance of style, and leaned closer, to speak at a lower volume.

"My parents used to throw and attend many survivor's balls, remnants of their lost empire," he explained in a dramatic whisper. "These balls served as a balm for the tragedy, for what pain isn't cured by a graceful dance and a good glass of port, hm?"

"I am passingly familiar," Nathaniel said. "But I've never attended, nor heard tell of red necklaces."

"Well," Mathias continued, "these balls were exclusive, of course, to exiles of the elite. And like any good exclusion, there was a code of conduct. Anyone who had lost a family member to the guillotine wore a red ribbon around their throat, to signify, so others might know how much they'd lost and admire them most tragically."

Mathias let a beat of silence land and then leaned back, returning to his normal volume and flippancy. "From what I understand, it became rather fashionable to wear one, so many scrambled to find a family connection to someone who'd lost their head, just for the prestige of the ribbon."

"Ah," Nathaniel replied, inclining his head. "How delightfully morbid."

"*Mais c'est très français, non?*" Mathias replied, with a little wave of his hand. "I imagine her choice in adornment has caused some outraged clucking amongst the hens tonight. After all, they are the only ones old enough to remember such things. I personally enjoy both its unintended connotation and its effect on that lovely complexion."

"As do I," Nathaniel said pleasantly, sipping at his drink. The ease in his demeanor sent a clear message, in his estimation. He was not concerned about Nell being tempted away from him, especially by a man like Mathias Dempierre. She was his.

It seemed Dempierre was as delighted by Nathaniel's non-concern as he likely would have been by a jealous quip in reaction to his observation of Nell's allure. He clapped his hands together and laughed, utterly without care of raising eyebrows.

Nathaniel found his obvious disregard for the opinions of others intriguing if not somewhat enviable. He decided that he liked the man, all intrigue around his family aside, and found himself laughing along with Mathias, albeit in a more reserved manner.

The shared amusement sent a clear message. They understood one another. There was no animosity between them, simply an establishment of the verbal parrying and riposte that was the foundation of male friendship.

How very different it was to Nell's charm with the ladies.

"Ah!" Mathias exclaimed, glancing over Nate's shoulder. "The lady approaches us now."

Nathaniel didn't move, a light smile playing about his lips until Eleanor arrived at his arm, looping her hand through the crook of his elbow with a breezy familiarity that pleased him greatly.

"My dear," he said, turning his eyes down to meet hers, and allowing himself to linger over the little lurch of excitement in his belly at having her near again. "This is Mathias Dempierre, the eldest son of our hosts."

It took her a moment to register what he had said, and when she did, she let out a little gasp and turned to their new acquaintance, murmuring, "How do you do?"

"I am enchanted, Mrs. Atlas," Mathias said, sweeping into a courtly bow. "It is an honor to make your acquaintance."

"Likewise," Nell replied. "Gigi did not mention having siblings. Are there more young Dempierres milling about, or is it only the two of you?"

"Ah," he replied with a cryptic tilt of his head. "It often seems that everyone is family in some way or another. I see my dear sister has claimed you as her new favorite, in any event. I have not seen her so excited about a new acquaintance in some time. Gigi is only sporadically excitable."

"I like her very much as well," Nell said, squeezing Nathaniel's arm. "I assured her that we will see one another again soon. My husband and I regret that we cannot stay overly long, but we fear the snowfall will only get heavier as the night goes on."

"Nights like this one do have a habit of building intensity," Mathias replied, glancing between the two of them. He took a step back, folding his hands behind his back, and giving a casual bow. "Do not allow me to keep the newlyweds from their hearth. I trust we will cross paths again soon."

"I'm certain we will," Nathaniel replied. He would enjoy speaking more to Mathias Dempierre at some point in the future, but at the moment, he was more than willing to accommodate his wife's desire to be off, returned to the privacy of their own home. "It has been a pleasure."

"It has," the other man agreed, and gave a bow to the lady. "Mrs. Atlas."

"Lovely to meet you," Nell said sweetly, leaning into Nathaniel's body. "Truly, it has been a magical evening. Please pass our compliments along to your mother and father."

Nathaniel glanced down at her, flushed and happy and warm against his side, that intoxicating scent of hers, lavender and mint, floating up from the silky curls in her hair. It had indeed been an exceptional evening thus far.

He only hoped that the magic was not yet concluded.

CHAPTER 21

*N*ell was not certain if she was drunk on the wine or on the sheer pleasure of the evening. Whatever the cause, this may well have been the happiest night of her life.

Never in a thousand years did she expect to have Nathaniel Atlas, with all his elegant charm, whispering seductions into her ear and guiding her about a formal event with his hand resting possessively on the small of her back.

Never did she think she might experience what it is to feel beautiful and admired, the way her best friends from school had been at every ball in London. Not once did she think other ladies, beautiful ladies, would express admiration of her person rather than her mind or her steadfastness.

She felt like a girl in a fairy story, transported to a magical realm for one perfect night, clad in an impossibly beautiful gown and attending a party in a snow-dusted mansion on a cliff, with frosty waves from the sea crashing against the rocks down below. It was the stuff of fantasy, pure and indulgent.

Their coach came around so quickly that it too seemed affected by the perfection of the evening, arriving well before the transport of many other couples who had been waiting when they had arrived.

Nathaniel seemed to think nothing of it, as though he were accustomed to such privileges. He guided her through the flurries of white, never leaving her side. Before assisting her up into her seat, Nathaniel kissed her hand, as though they were still courting and he considered himself honored to be worthy of the task.

She flushed, delighted beyond words that all of the other people on the drive could see what he had done. They were strangers, every one, but those strangers had seen that Nathaniel Atlas, darling of Society and firebrand of Parliament, treated her, plain Miss Eleanor Applegate, as his treasured wife; a woman to be desired rather than an unwanted burden.

Her reverie over the thought rendered her somewhat distracted, so that she was not at all prepared for the arm that snaked around her waist as Nathaniel climbed in behind her, tugging her down onto his lap as he found his seat, much to the delight of the onlookers before, who were already buzzing amongst themselves as the carriage door swung shut.

She'd given a rather undignified squeak when he'd done it, and was blinking rapidly to process the strangeness of it, perched on his knee as the horses were urged into motion.

"There are snowflakes in your hair," he observed, stroking his long, elegant fingers over her curls.

"Nathaniel," she giggled, reaching up to stop his hand. "People saw you pull me onto your lap! I'm sure they are talking about it!"

"Oh, I certainly hope so," he replied, leaning forward to nuzzle at her neck. "I was ill prepared for all of those gentlemen sniffing after you. If there is gossip, now it will be only about how thoroughly you are mine."

"We have been so tired with the cellars that I had begun to wonder if I imagined that first night together," she confessed, sighing happily at the shivers that pulsed through her as he kissed and nibbled at the spot just beneath her ear. "Oh, that feels lovely."

"Why did you want to leave so early?" he murmured against her neck.

"Oh," she murmured, her head spinning from the attentions of his mouth, the warmth of his breath, and the way his hands had begun to slide over the sides of her waist. "I wished to return home before we were, once again, too tired to do aught but sleep once we retired."

He made a little sound of pleasure, kissing his way around to her throat. "And what," he growled softly, "did you wish to do instead?"

The truth was that she would have been completely satisfied simply having him alone and to herself for a few waking minutes. However, it was clear what he was insinuating. The assumption he had drawn was a far preferable outcome to that stolen time than any polite conversation she might have envisioned.

So, rather than be strictly honest, she stroked her fingernails through his hair and said, "I think you know."

He exhaled sharply, lifting his head and taking her chin between his fingers. His eyes were colorless in the dark, just another shade of disguise for a chameleon. They maintained their grip on her, their intensity, with or without color.

With his other hand wrapped tightly around her waist, he nudged his hips forward, pressing his arousal into her thighs, and watching her face so that he might enjoy the moment when she realized what she was feeling.

Her breath caught in her throat, the flash of heat that whipped through her effectively silencing any verbal reaction she might have had.

"Look what you've done to me," he whispered, still holding her by the chin, his gaze drinking up her own.

"Truly?" she breathed back, unable to resist leaning closer, brushing her nose against his, the proximity of him adding a heady wave to her already dizzied state. "Me?"

"Mm," he confirmed. "I have not ever been so tempted, by any woman."

"Oh," she whispered, unable to resist kissing his beautiful mouth, just lightly, testing how he might react. When he did not pull away or move to stop her, she pressed her lips more fully into his, wrapping her arms around his neck.

He released her chin, instead winding his fingers through

the curls cascading over her shoulder, his grip on her waist still tight. He allowed her to direct the intensity of the kiss, to decide when tongues might become involved and how deeply the intensity might dig.

She found that the more she kissed him, the more she *needed* to kiss him. Warmth was pooling in her center, that throbbing hardness against her thigh sending a primal urgency through her.

A sudden bump in the road jostled them with an abrupt loss of their bearings, almost sending Nell toppling to the floor. If Nathaniel hadn't been holding her so tightly, she certainly would have. Strangely, the initial startle seemed to fade into laughter for them both, perhaps in a bit of sheepishness at their own distraction.

She caught her lip in her teeth and eased her suddenly claw-like grip on her husband's shoulders.

"Ah," he said with a chuckle. "Perhaps we ought to await a more stationary venue to continue this activity."

"Perhaps so." She sighed and released her hold on him, slipping out of his grip on her waist as she leaned backward onto the opposite cushion. "Pity."

"If the journey were longer, I would absolutely take my chances," he said with an air of mischief. "Why, at the right moment, such a motion might have been a welcome enhancement."

"Nathaniel!" she gasped, almost immediately dissolving into scandalized giggles. She leaned against the side of the coach, overtaken by such a jest until she was short of breath.

The entire while, Nathaniel was watching her with that

same mysterious half smile he'd worn on their journey south from Scotland. Was he warmer now, or had she just become a bit more adept at finding the kindness in his face?

It hardly mattered. Just locking eyes with him in this way, silent and happy, sharing a moment of so many mixed feelings was lovely. Perhaps it was the wine. She'd had quite a bit of wine the last time they'd been intimate too. Maybe she would begin taking it with dinner if it had such a positive effect on her allure.

"Do you like your gown?" Nathaniel asked, eyes reflecting the light of the moon.

"Very much," she said earnestly. "I have never felt so beautiful."

He looked thoughtful, his hand propping up his chin as he leisurely appreciated the effect of her form in the red and white dress. "Your aunt is a wealthy woman," he said, after a moment. "Why did she leave you to wear those ill-fitting and unfashionable clothes?"

"Oh." Nell blinked, surprised. "I don't think she did any such thing on purpose. She simply never took much notice of me, and was already giving me so much. I would never complain about the things she had made for me. Aunt Zelda is a very busy woman."

"*She* had them made for you," he repeated, clearly surprised. "I assumed they had been the product of your parents' modest means. Eleanor, you must know she created them to hide your beauty as much as possible. Such a thing could only have been deliberate."

"Why on earth would she do something like that?" Nell

laughed, shaking her head. "She loves me."

"Yes, she loves you," he agreed. "But she believed the best path for your life would be to remain unmarried so that she might prime you as her little heiress."

"Nathaniel, I have always been a girl to whom spinsterhood has seemed a realistic proposition," she said, a little more soberly. "I was never an adept flirt or an exceptional beauty, and I have been told many times that I'm far too esoteric for my own good. She hardly needed to do anything to assist with my lack of appeal."

"She chose clothes that would hide your delicious little figure, keeping your feminine curves encased in rectangles of drab fabric. It was absolutely deliberate. It was sabotage that she likely believed was for your own good, or for her own good at the very least."

Nell was too stunned to reply. What he was saying was heinous, but it did have a ring of truth to it. Aunt Zelda always got what she wanted and was often pulling several strings at a time to ensure her desired outcome. And she had always besmirched the institution of marriage as a waste of a woman's abilities and something she considered beneath both herself and Nell. She had often looked down her nose at her sister—Nell's mother—for marrying so low and having a large brood of children.

Goodness.

She glanced out the carriage window, where little was visible other than the spattering of snow on the darkened window, lost in thought. It seemed only a breath later that they had arrived back home, with Meridian rising up grand and warm in front of them.

It was late, of course, and most of the household had retired. The butler offered to have Sarah rung up to assist Nell in undressing, but she quickly discouraged him from doing so. It likely seemed that she took pity on interrupting Sarah's rest, and perhaps she did, but in truth, she wanted to be alone in her bedchambers with her husband as quickly as possible.

He followed her up the stairs, opening the door to their room in front of her with a relieved sigh as he immediately began to remove his cuff links and loosen his cravat.

What a change this room had made since they'd arrived! The windows were now dressed with rich draperies, the wooden floor shone with polish, and an ornate rug unraveled over the gleaming slats in an arresting royal blue. The fire that crackled in the fireplace spread warmth over the space, casting a glow of welcome to this space that they had restored and made their own.

Nell crossed the room to her new vanity table and perched herself on the stool, making quick work of destroying the elaborate hairstyle that had taken so very long to achieve. She dropped hairpins by the cluster into a silver dish, relieved to free her scalp from their confines. It felt downright indulgent to shake her curls loose, even at the expense of ruining her miraculous transformation.

"I apologize," Nathaniel said softly from behind her, catching her eye in the vanity table's mirror. "I did not realize my observation earlier regarding your aunt might upset you, which was foolish and short-sighted of me. I do not doubt that you are well loved by your family, Eleanor."

"I am not upset," she replied, glancing over her shoulder as she continued to work her fingers through her tresses.

He was already shirtless, that light expanse of honey-brown hair glinting on his muscled chest in the firelight. She had kissed him tonight. And he had liked it. Perhaps she had been overthinking this seduction business, as she was prone to overthink all things.

An idea curled its way into her mind like a wisp of smoke from an extinguished candle. She decided she must act immediately, lest she convince herself she shouldn't. She gave him a sweet, reassuring smile and asked, "Will you help me with the gown?"

"I shall give it my best endeavor," he said with an apologetic laugh, crossing the room as she stood.

She was on the cusp of reaching for a ribbon to secure her hair for the night, but decided that no, it was far more effective as a weapon of sensuality unbound. She gathered it up and twisted it over her shoulder, turning her head in invitation as her husband approached her from behind. The warmth of his body was radiating off him, sending a delightful shiver through her own person, but she retained her bearing, disguising the flutter of nervousness that soared through her with the calm composure she had learned at school.

"Untie the sash first," she instructed, keenly aware of the nearness of his breath as he pulled the bow free from its knot, releasing the crimson band from around her rib cage. "There are small buttons along the back, if you would not mind undoing them."

He moved slowly, carefully releasing each little pearl from its eyelet with a brush of his fingertips on the exposed flesh along her spine, until to her disappointment, he reached the cusp of her underthings. He did seem to work faster once he had run out of bare skin to unveil, and after a short moment, the gown sagged enough for her to slip her arms out of the sleeves and let the entire affair pool at her feet.

She stepped out of the gown, leaving her slippers at the center of the puddle. Her stays had been fastened in the back, but rather than asking Nathaniel to remove this as well, she turned to face him, tugging loose the front end of the corseting, where the bow sat just between her breasts.

He seemed to swallow any impulse he might have had to move, his throat flexing as his eyes dropped to the workings of her hands, following her fingers as they tugged loose the strings, pulling each one free of its loop until only the last row remained and she could tug the corseting up over her head and toss it into the pile of her other things.

The shift hung lightly on her body, the fabric so fine and silken that it left very little to the imagination. She had his rapt attention, and did not wish to lose it, for in this moment she felt like she was casting the most wicked enchantment upon him. And of course, she reminded herself that she must act *before* thinking. It was going well so far.

She gathered it up from her thighs, bunching the skirt in her fists as the hem rose up to expose the tops of her stockings and the first hint of her thighs. She held her breath, banishing the instinct to be bashful as she worked the fabric up over her hips, revealing the dark triangle between her thighs and the curve of her waist.

She revealed parts of herself that she never thought a man might see. Her navel, the tiny cluster of freckles on her rib cage, and of course, her naked breasts. She pulled the shift off and sent it sailing into the established pile, leaving herself in nothing but her stockings, soft and ivory white, and her jewelry, the red satin choker stark against her slender throat.

"Will you help me with my stockings?" she asked, her voice only a touch thinner than it had been at the first request. She sat on the stool of the vanity table and lifted one leg toward him, with a pointed toe. Her heart was thudding against her chest, her skin prickling with the coolness of the air in the room. She could not account for what she was doing, but if he would keep looking at her that way forever, she might be capable of a great many surprising behaviors.

He caught her ankle in his hand, the heat of his skin melting through the fabric of her stockings. His eyes had gone dark, his pupils flared with only a thin line of that ever-changing hazel around them. The way he approached her was almost a challenge, the intensity on his face and the sureness of his posture making her pulse leap, the blood in her veins running hot and fast.

He kept his eyes locked on hers, despite the full display of her nudity as a visual temptation. He lowered himself to kneeling, propping her foot against his bare shoulder as his fingers began to slide up the length of the stocking, the tips of his manicured fingernails scraping lightly along the path of the fabric.

He plucked at the ribbon holding the first stocking in place, where she had secured it in a neat knot around the soft flesh of her thigh some hours prior. He defeated it with ease, the loose ribbon now allowing him to free her leg from the hold of the stocking and begin the process of rolling it down.

She shivered, the heat of his fingers against such a tender, forbidden area sending a flurry of unfamiliar and delicious sensations throughout her.

He leaned forward and replaced the top of the stocking with a soft kiss into her inner thigh. Her intake of breath at this kiss seemed to encourage him, for as he revealed more of her flesh, he continued to drop kisses on the freshly exposed skin, against her knee, the curve of her calf, her ankles. He took his time, and rather than tossing that first stocking into her haphazard pile, he folded it neatly next to him, as though it were precious.

He took hold of her naked ankle and lifted it from his shoulder, urging her knee to bend and her stance to widen as he guided her foot gently to the carpeted floor.

Nell realized she had stopped breathing, her last breath of air caught in her lungs like a rabbit in a snare. She was fascinated by his choices and stuck between the desire to hide herself from his view and a deep, rebellious thrill that was pushing against its cage in the darkest parts of her being. This wantonness had been dormant within her all along, stifled by her belief that she might never indulge in its whims.

He took a moment to appreciate the scandalous view he had created, her legs spread open with her most private part at eye level to his kneeling form. He glanced up at her, perhaps checking to make certain that he hadn't gone too far, and in answer she reached forward to stroke his hair, running her fingers through the silken mahogany strands, still arranged in stylish perfection from the party.

He released a heavy breath, his eyes flickering shut as he

leaned into her hand, seemingly melted into pleasure by the sensation. She had never imagined any man reacting so to her touch, least of all one so beautiful, one she had believed so utterly unattainable.

How often had she imagined him doing the smallest things to give her a thrill? She might have sustained herself for the rest of her days on a single memory of him kissing her hand or rewarding her with a smile meant only for her. And how often had she chided herself for such silly fantasies, believing such things impossible?

Last Season in London, during which he had seemed nothing less than a demigod to her, felt like a lifetime ago, blurred into the haze of this moment as his hands slid up the length of her last remaining article of clothing, handling the slender flesh of her thigh with a familiarity that bordered on ownership.

Did she belong to him now? She was his wife, after all.

She watched him gather the top of her remaining stocking in his hands and begin to pull it down, repeating his path of kisses, savoring this leg as much as the other. With her stance so wide now, she felt keenly aware of how close he hovered to the center of her desire, close enough that she could feel the softness of his breath slipping over parts of her she had never known existed or allowed herself to explore.

Did he belong to her too? Was matrimony an exchange of bodies behind the doors of a private bedroom?

He kissed the soft flesh behind her knee, the dimple just below it, the softness of her calf. When he had removed this final piece of clothing, he repeated what he had done before, and placed her leg out to the side, leaving her utterly exposed to him, legs spread wide on the little vanity stool.

He looked up at her through hooded eyes and a fringe of lashes as he slid his hands up along the smooth, exposed skin of her legs, inching ever closer to where they met.

"Nathaniel," she whispered, her body aflame with a deep and primal want, a demand she did not know how to answer.

"Hush," he replied softly, running his fingers ever so lightly over her sex. "You want this."

"I do," she managed, neither a question nor an agreement, before her words were scattered into oblivion, drowned in a gasp of surprise at the first contact of his mouth on her, kissing her *there*. Those gorgeous, sensual lips were brushing against what felt like the center of every feeling in her body, the key to utter bliss.

It was unbelievable how much sensation came of such a light touch, so much so that when his tongue appeared, lapping against her with slow and deliberate intention, she thought for a brief moment that she might faint.

There was nothing to hold on to to keep herself steady other than Nathaniel himself. Her hands fell to his shoulders, strong and solid and steady. This only seemed to inflame him, his arm coming up and wrapping around her backside, drawing her further forward on the stool.

The first night they had made love, Nell had attempted to restrain her many urges to vocalize, out of fear that she might sound ridiculous or off-putting. Tonight, she was unable to exert such self-control. While her voice had momentarily been snatched from her throat at that explosive first moment of contact, she now couldn't seem to restrain it.

Her cries seemed to encourage him, his attentions becoming stronger, deeper. He pushed his fingers into her as he continued to taste his fill.

She curled her toes into the plush fibers of the carpet beneath her bare feet, her eyes slipping shut as she gasped for breath. Her head spun, bursts of color seeming to erupt behind her eyelids as sensation overtook sense.

His fingers dug into the small of her back, holding her tight. He did not relent, despite the noises she made, his eyes turned up to watch her as her grip on herself slipped entirely away. She thought perhaps she said his name again, though she could not be certain. Everything was lost in the surge of crashing pleasure that broke over her body like waves from the sea breaking on the cliffs beneath them.

For a moment, it was as if she hovered outside of herself as all the tension in her limbs melted away into liquid submission. Whatever had just happened to her was an utterly divine if not an alarming thing to ponder some distant day in the future. For now, for once, her mind was silent. It had been rendered speechless.

By the time she fluttered her lashes, returning to the land of the living, Nathaniel was scooping her up off the stool, gathering her naked body against the warmth of his chest, and carrying her to the bed.

Rather than depositing her on the mattress, he somehow managed to climb into bed with her in tow, her naked body supine beneath him, weak with bliss and pliable.

"Don't move," he breathed into her ear, kissing her cheeks, her nose, her mouth, her chin. He disappeared for the briefest moment, despite her noise of protest, to rid himself of his trousers. It was shocking how cold she felt in that small moment without him.

When he returned, climbing back over her and sinking the weight of his body onto hers, she lifted her arms to pull him back to her, digging her fingers into his hair, gripping him tight to taste his lips as his hands began to roam over her, his touch firmer and more demanding as it slid along the sides of her frame and his hips dug into her own.

"Do it again," she whispered against his mouth, gasping for breath as he moved his kisses down the length of her throat, his finger sliding over the red ribbon she wore. "Please."

"Do what?" he mumbled, cupping her breast and dragging his thumb over her taut nipple as he kissed lower, capturing it in his mouth.

She gasped, arching her back, a fever seeming to rip through her as his tongue flicked against her. "Put yourself inside me. Nathaniel. Please."

He froze for a moment, lifting his head and rising to loom back over her. His hair was mussed from her hands and hung in its natural wave over his eyes. "What did you say?" he asked, rocking his hips forward so that she could feel the full power of his arousal against her stomach.

She huffed with impatience, squirming enough to free one of her legs from beneath his heavy thighs. She wrapped it around his waist, returning the motion of pushing her hips forward, the suggestive mime of what might follow. "Put yourself inside me," she repeated, a hint of desperation in her voice. "Nathaniel, I need it."

He groaned, as though the request had somehow dealt a blow to his person, and braced himself above her, reaching down to tease at her entrance with the head of his organ. "Like this?" he asked in a whisper.

"Deeper," she gasped, keeping her free leg tight around his middle. "Nathaniel, please."

"Sweet Christ," he muttered, abandoning his teasing in favor of satisfaction. He held her hips and pushed himself into her fully, their bodies utterly joined.

"Oh, yes," she breathed, running her fingers over his chest, testing the texture of that dusting of golden-brown hair beneath her fingers as she felt the weight of him within her. "Yes, just like that."

He lowered himself onto his elbows, beginning to push into her in long, slow thrusts. It felt different this time, less careful as he pumped his hips with the force of a man who was taking something he had long desired.

"You can have this anytime you want it," he whispered, his breath hot on her cheek. "You must know that."

"I didn't," she managed, closing her eyes and indulging in the sensation of it, the unbelievable intimacy of sharing her whole body with another person, of giving herself so fully to him and him to her.

She loved that he seemed to be equally in the thrall of pleasure, that her body was the answer to his satisfaction, that he seemed to lose a bit of his ever-present control, groaning in pleasure, picking up speed.

"I cannot get enough of you," he confessed, dropping his forehead onto hers, driving into her each time a little harder, a little more demanding. "Oh, God."

She wanted to respond, but the words turned to sparkling dust in her mind, her thoughts clouding over much the way they had a few moments prior, when she had been on the stool. It was all she could do to meet his motions, to invite him into her with unbridled welcome as his pace became more frenzied, his breathing shallower.

The second wave of pleasure that washed over her was not so strong nor so debilitating as the first, though it was glorious all the same. She held tight to him as he found his own climax, his body shaking with the force of it as he drove the last of his vigor into her body with a moan of sweet release.

They were both damp, covered in a thin sheen of sweat from their coupling. It made their skin glimmer in the fire-light, their limbs entangled over the rumpled silk sheets as they both struggled to catch their breath.

Nell almost protested when he slid off her, dropping onto his side and into the pillows. However, it seemed he did not intend to part from her so easily. He tugged her hand so that she would roll into him, face-to-face, so that he might study her in that way of his.

She could look into his eyes for eternity, she thought. There was a galaxy of color within, and just as much mystery as a sky full of stars. She thought she had never seen any work of art as beautiful as his eyes, and yet still, she could not stop her own from drooping shut, heavier and heavier, until there was nothing but his embrace in her dreams.

CHAPTER 22

*I*t took close to an hour before Nate felt the desire to make his way under the sheets. The fervor he had been worked into might as well have set him ablaze for a time. But, he supposed, returning to earth was a natural consequence of attaining a visit to heaven, and so he carefully rolled out of bed and considered the best way to work the coverlet out from under his sleeping wife without disturbing her.

He did his best, but in the end, she stirred anyway, her dark lashes blinking against her cheeks as she opened her eyes and smiled sleepily up at him.

"I'm just arranging the blankets," he explained in a gentle whisper. "Can I get you anything? Water?"

She nodded, reaching up to rub at her eyes with a broad yawn, that bright red ribbon still clinging to her neck.

"Might want to take your jewelry off," he suggested with a smile, turning to fetch the carafe of fresh water from the worktop near the fireplace. He poured two glasses and when he turned back, she was carefully setting the ribbon and her pearl earrings onto the nightstand, clutching the blanket up to her chest in some instinct of belated modesty.

"Not the ring?" he asked, noting the way it glinted in the firelight as he passed her the glass.

"No. I am not ready to part with it," she admitted, turning a bashful smile into the rim of her glass. "I wore it in the bath earlier."

"Did you?" he chuckled, delighted by the idea of it, if not the practicality. He turned and walked to the wardrobe, drawing out a night-rail for her and dressing gowns for them both, which he draped over the foot of the bed. He was in no particular hurry to clothe himself again. "I have a matching band myself. I was going to wait to begin wearing it until yours was finished. I'm pleased that I now can."

"Does it have the same engraving inside?" she asked softly, those wide gray eyes searching his so hopefully as he climbed back into the bed next to her.

"Of course," he said, reaching forward to stroke the side of her face. Never mind that it had been a whim to commission the engraving, something he had barely thought about at the time. He had ordered those rings weeks ago, back when his choices regarding Nell were made as more a matter of doing things the proper way rather than sentimentality.

None of that mattered. It meant something now.

She smiled, a blush spreading over the bridge of her nose, clearly very pleased to hear it. Making her smile like that was more gratifying by the day.

"I suppose I ought to write my aunt in the morning," she said, finishing her glass of water and turning her bare back to him for a moment to place it next to her jewelry on the nightstand. "I shall say that our invitation has been acquired, and damn you very much for buying me ugly gowns all my life."

Nate coughed on the unexpected burst of laughter that escaped him. "Perhaps something a bit more gentle," he suggested, unable to hide his amusement.

She turned back to him with a little smile, her hair in wild disarray around her, like some wild woman of the forest. "I would never," she assured him.

"It is my pleasure to be party to your blossoming, my dear," he said, leaning back onto the pillows and holding his arm out in an invitation for her to join him. When she did, curling into his side and laying her head on his chest, that spill of coffee-brown curls twining down her back, he felt for the briefest moment as though his heart ached.

"Nathaniel ..." she said softly, as though she was not sure if she should speak or not. "I want to know you. Physically, we have been intimate, but so much of you is still a mystery to me. I want to know the good and the bad, which I vowed to take in stride when we wed. I wish to truly be your wife."

"You *are* my wife," he responded immediately, then paused, considering her words. "What would you know of me?"

"Everything," she breathed, stroking her hand over the expanse of his chest. "Why did you become a politician? Why join the Silver Leaf? Why would you leave this beautiful home to decay? You are an enigma to me, even in the wake of our present intimacy, and I feel I am a simple and uninteresting thing next to you."

He considered this, weighing his options for a response in his head. "You are far from simple," he said first. "You may not have a tragic past and an air of mystery, but that is hardly a negative thing. You surprise me every day. The urge to know you completely is one I have felt as well. Perhaps we have been too consumed with the intrigue around us to converse as a husband and wife ought."

"It has been an unseemly amount of intrigue," she allowed. "You must know that I do not intend to surprise you."

"It would not be nearly so effective, were it deliberate," he said, dropping a kiss on the crown of her head. "The answers to your questions are all party to the same sad story, I'm afraid. Meridian reminds me of my family. Kent reminds me of the years after. Being reminded of what you have lost and all you have suffered is painful, and so I left it behind me."

"Your parents died," she said, half question, half statement. "Kit told me that you were raised as brothers."

"I was ten," he confirmed with a sigh. "My mother and father, along with my baby sister, Alice, drowned when their boat capsized on the Channel. It was a mysterious thing to happen on a calm and mild day. Suspicious, to say the least."

"You had a sister," she said, her voice tinged with unbearable pity.

"Barely. She was not yet even a year old," he told her. "Some years before tragedy struck, my mother's brother, Archibald, settled near to Meridian with his family. The Coopers are not from wealthy stock, but because my mother had the good fortune of marrying well above her station, she gifted my aunt and uncle a plot of orchards as a wedding gift, which provided them the opportunity to build their fortune and status. So, when I was orphaned, at least it was a simple thing to be sent to family living so near."

"Archibald is Kit's father?"

"Yes. You must understand that he was not of sound mind. Uncle Archie always had a touch of madness about him, but over the years a charming touch of eccentricity devolved into self-destruction. He was quick to believe in conspiracy and suspect others of working in secret to betray him. The older he got, the more tenuous his grasp on reality became. One was never certain if a conversation he recounted had happened with an actual human being or with the conjurings of his mind. He used to pull Kit and me out of bed and demand to know which of us was hiding in the walls, whispering to him."

He took a breath, remembering his uncle's panicked rage, his desperate hope for an explanation for the things he believed to be happening. As a child, it had made him angry. Now, it only made him sad.

"His fragile mind made him easy prey for unscrupulous men who profit from the gullibility of others. When it came to my parents, it was very difficult to know when to believe his stories and insight or disregard him entirely. It was difficult for me, because I craved anything he might divulge about the parents I had lost, both of whom I felt I had hardly known."

"Madness is always a tragedy," Nell said, without an affectation of sympathy or disgust. "My grandmother forgot who her children were, toward the end. She did not recognize the world around her anymore, and yet could not die until nature deemed the time appropriate. It terrifies me, Nathaniel. I cannot think of any illness more cruel than losing part of my mind."

Nate nodded, even though she could not see him. "Me too. He told me wild stories and I wanted to believe them all. He'd say that my parents had been involved in wartime espionage, that they had tangled with dangerous spies, betrayed people, sold secrets to the French, and so on. The stories varied, but his insistence that their deaths were no accident never did, and so I began to wonder if perhaps there was a nugget of truth amidst his delusions. I began to take serious note of the bits of his ramblings that were consistent."

"It must have been very difficult for a child, to be at the mercy of such a man."

"I daresay it was harder for Susan. Between Uncle Archie's unpredictable temper, often based on fabricated events for which we had no defense, and his tendency to enter into business dealings with money he did not have, he very quickly ended up both in debt and friendless in his time of need. I suspect that he entered Meridian House many times, looking for anything of value he might sell in a pinch."

"Was he violent?" she asked quietly.

"Not in the way you imagine," Nate replied. "He'd take the switch to us from time to time, but he never laid a hand on his wife. Some part of him knew that he was confused, and there would be these terrible moments of lucidity in which he would weep and apologize and promise never to lose himself again. It was a promise he could not keep, no matter how much he wished to."

She was quiet, her hand still moving on his chest, tracing shapes and swirls in a way he found strangely soothing.

"Rather than go to debtor's prison, he began to sell off the orchards, piece by piece, until nothing was left but a pair of cherry trees next to the house. The only thing left for him to lose was the house itself. Kit had enlisted in the army as soon as he'd finished school, and likely by deliberate design, was too far away to assist as things worsened."

"I do not blame him," Nell whispered. "Poor Kit. Poor Susan. Even your uncle was a victim to his own demons."

"By the time he had truly lost everything, I had already finished my education and begun my first term in the House of Commons. I had a singular, obsessive intention of rising as high as possible in Society, so that I might someday uncover the truth of what had befallen my parents. If indeed they were traitors, then they deserved the dignity of a trial and, if guilty, a humane execution. Alice should not have been harmed. I wanted answers. I wanted revenge."

She nodded, clinging to him in such a way that he thought they were silently comforting one another.

It did help, having her there. Her presence was more reassuring than any words she might have offered. He had recited some of these events once, when Kit had returned from the Continent, but it had still been so raw then, so unreal. Part of him felt as though he were piecing together the narrative of his own life for the first time, watching the events unfold in the dark as he spoke to another person in the anonymous safety of the witching hour.

"Susan found me in London one day, as I was leaving a pub. She had been crying and rushed toward me like I was the only thing that might save her from drowning in her own tears. She told me he'd been dragged off for his debts and that their home was being auctioned out from under her.

"It was an easy task for me to purchase the house. I restored the deed to Susan alone, so that once we got Uncle Archie back, he could not barter with it again. It turned out that saving my uncle was a far more complex matter than I had anticipated. In the days between his arrest and settling the business with their house, he had been tossed onto a boat due west, across the ocean, for a period of indenture against his latest slew of financial misfortune. He would be serving as a slave on a sugar plantation in Jamaica, in an aging body and a fragile mind."

He sighed, the memory of it conjuring forth the ghost of the weight he'd felt on his chest that day, the panic and resentment that had buried every facet of his humanity, fraying his emotions at the ends, until the only way to go on was in an armor of icy disposition.

"I knew that if I immediately took off to the other side of the world in search of him, I would lose everything I had worked for. It was difficult to be sensible about it, but I managed it. I spent two weeks soliciting every powerful contact I had, in the hopes that there was business in Jamaica that I might take on to justify departure while Parliament was in session.

"It took some doing, but I found a handful of tasks to legitimize my journey. In the end, colony tax defaults on British imports gave me a plausible issue to tackle, and some suspicions about the veracity of the current governor's dealings an additional incentive to set off under the appearance of state business."

"That was smart," she whispered.

He wondered if she was picturing it correctly. Could she conjure the image of his aunt in her tattered pink dress, sobbing on Oxford Street? Did she know the smell of brine and sodden wood at sea? She could not know Uncle Archie's face, which had become craggy with age by that point, and the terror he must have felt at being parceled off on a ship, surrounded by strangers.

"I was never certain if I hated my uncle more than I loved him," Nathaniel heard himself saying, as though his voice belonged to someone else. He paused in surprise at the statement, a twinge giving way in his chest. He had never said that to anyone before. He wasn't even certain he'd allowed himself to think it in such clear terms. It was the truth, however.

It was the truth.

There was a beat of silence, but she did not stop moving her hand, stroking it over the breadth of his chest in the most soothing way. She did not recoil or condemn him, nor did she murmur assurances that he surely didn't feel that way deep down. She was a woman who could comprehend the complexity of people and find a spark in the tangle to nurture. That was what he had seen tonight, when she had moved so easily amongst the party-goers, laughing with strangers as though they were old friends.

"What is Jamaica like?" she asked, nuzzling her cheek into the crook of his shoulder, sliding one of her legs over one of his in a gift of shared warmth.

He smiled, the feeling bittersweet. "If you had seen the beaches of Jamaica, you would never have stared so lovingly at the chilly English sea. It is a paradise of sun and golden sand. The water is pleasant rather than cold when it laps at your bare feet, and its color is vibrant turquoise. I wish I had been there with happier business to attend, for when I think about it now, it seems like a place one might spend a lifetime free of worries."

"No place is like that," she said, and he could feel the curve of a smile against his chest. "People are the same, rain or shine, and no matter how far you run, you can't escape yourself."

"True enough," he allowed. "But some problems are less daunting in paradise. It took me some time to track down exactly where my uncle was serving, and inquiries had to be made delicately so that I could resolve the situation without a scandal. It was too late, however, by the time I was given answers. Perhaps the sun drove him over the edge of his own sanity or perhaps his body could no longer tolerate the stress of his mind, but less than a week before I arrived, he had been found in his bed, cold and gone."

He sighed at the horrified gasp she gave, holding her tighter into his side. "It was the strangest thing," he told her. "Everyone at this plantation described him in glowing terms. The children of the African slaves called him 'grandfather,' and the women praised his gentleness with the little ones. The other white men, English and Irish indentured, described him as cheerful and warm. From all accounts, shackled to a life of slave labor, he was briefly at peace and then he departed the mortal coil. Perhaps for a moment, he was happy."

"Perhaps," Nell agreed. "It is hard to avoid happiness entirely, after all, just as it is hard to avoid sadness entirely."

"I brought him home in a casket and we buried him between the cherry trees," Nate continued. "He had forbidden us for years from going into Meridian House, insisting it was full of evil and regret. On some level, I must have agreed with him, because when I rode away from Kent after the burial, I thought I should never return again. Now, I can't help but wonder if he believed the house was cursed or if he simply didn't want us to discover how much he'd stolen over the years."

He gave a dry chuckle, though there was no humor in it. He felt suddenly uncertain about having launched into such a dark tirade, especially in the wake of such beautiful intimacy. "I suppose I should have begun with something lighter as an introduction into my private life," he said apologetically. "It is late, and I did not properly consider which story to tell."

"It is a story that answers many of my questions," she replied, tilting her head up to look at him in the dark. "I thank you for trusting me with it, Nathaniel."

"I find you unseemly trustworthy, Miss Applegate," he whispered, leaning down to capture her lips in a little kiss before he corrected himself to, "Nell."

For a time, he thought they might drift off to sleep like this, entwined under the coverlet, with some of the truth exposed between them. Her body, however, did not slacken into the surrender of rest. It was almost as though he could hear the whirring in her mind as she explored the story he told, assembling it, searching it, making sense of it.

It was no surprise when she spoke again.

"My aunt had the keys to Meridian," she recalled, "and you did not seem surprised by that, only irritated."

He sighed, knowing he had walked her directly into this realization. It was his own fault for not thinking it through. "They were friends," he decided to say, because it was true. "Lady Dempierre, my mother, your aunt, and two other ladies, evidently, were dear friends.

"I did not know until the day the Dempierre women surprised us with their visit. She told me a story about a winter they passed together in this house and how they would create the illusion of starlight by gathering in the dining room and lighting dozens of candles, which would refract the light off the silver gilt leafing on the ceiling. Nell, they called themselves the Silver Leaf Society. My mother was one of them."

"That makes sense," Nell replied, her tone suggesting a quick acceptance of this explosive revelation. She sounded as though this information was mundane and did not shock her to her core. "My aunt built her fortune and her independence through means no one has ever been quite clear on. She has also told me more than once that information is the most valuable contraband, and much easier to get past a customs officer than valuables."

"Your aunt is a smuggler?" he replied, aghast. The woman was a blackmailer and possibly a murderess, so naturally he should expect a longer list of crimes. Still, he had not expected it.

"Nathaniel," Nell said, lifting herself up so that she could look him in the eye. "What did you think the Silver Leaf Society was when you decided to join?"

He hesitated, caught in his own folly and surprise. "I assumed it was a branch of our parliamentary espionage operations," he admitted. "One of many active groups working in the shadows to impact the sway of the war."

She tilted her head, squinting at him in obvious befuddlement. "I am confused," she said slowly. "My aunt told me you had been asking questions about us, which led me to believe you knew exactly the nature of our business. I thought your inquiries were the reason I was tasked to deliver that invitation to you. If your mother was a founding member, and you knew that, why not go visit my aunt directly?"

"I did not know her identity," he said, thoroughly rid of any thought of sleep by the dull panic that had begun to scrape at his throat. "Her moniker was one of the things my uncle repeated many times over the years. Lady Silver did not play a coherent or consistent role in his ramblings, but he said her name enough that I felt compelled to investigate."

"And she sent us to meet the Dempierres," Nell added, dropping back down to his side. "When instead, she could have explained everything to us in half an hour over tea that day in London. Sometimes, I could strangle her. Please accept my apologies on her behalf."

Nathaniel would never say so, but the immense relief he felt in that moment, that her irritation was geared at Zelda

Smith and not him, was dizzying. She yawned, curling a hand against his heart, and murmured something of a good night, assuring him that they would talk more on the morrow.

He stared up at the ceiling, a great deal of questions buzzing in his mind that he had been ignoring with wondrous success for the last weeks. He had batted away the stirring of uncertainties about his goals of revenge and exposure. He had assured himself that Nell would understand, once the truth was revealed.

What did you think the Silver Leaf was?

Her question hovered over him. She hadn't confirmed nor denied his assumption about its purpose, but the way she had squinted at him made him wonder if he was missing a great deal of information. Considering how surprised he had been by Lady Dempierre's reminiscing, he likely was woefully underinformed.

It was, perhaps, apt that he had conjured the ghost of Uncle Archie tonight. For the first time in his life, he understood what it meant to doubt your own reality.

CHAPTER 23

*A*s the world continued to transform from autumn rust to winter blue, Nell began to use her new clothes in earnest. The things she had brought with her were simply no longer effective against the elements, especially with the prickly salt frost from the ocean blowing over the world in great sheets amidst the snow and ice.

She had written to everyone ahead of Christmas in the hopes that her letters could be delivered despite the snow. Family came first, of course. To her aunt, she sent news of their success in securing the invitation to the winter masquerade. To her family in Winchester, she compiled a lighthearted recollection of events since they had last seen her, making life sound magical and thrilling without raising any undue alarm. And, at last, to her brother Peter, she wrote a letter that she posted to Oxford University, in the hopes that he had returned there for the remainder of the year.

After that, the letters were somewhat more challenging. To Gloriana, first and foremost, she sent a long and heartfelt explanation for her choices, an apology for taking so long to write, and a sincere congratulations on the news of her own eminent nuptials to none other than Alex Somers, which she had spotted in the newspaper some days past. It was a relief, a substantial relief, to see that announcement and know that Glory had found her way to a more suitable match without too much time for heartbreak.

She had paused, her blood chilling in her veins at the thought of how close her husband had come to marrying one of her dearest friends. Would it have been the same, between the two of them? Would they have fallen into the habit of sleeping in each other's arms? Would they have made love so passionately and so frequently?

It was impossible to know the answer to that. Logically, she knew there was no reason Nathaniel couldn't have found happiness with her beautiful friend, but something tugged at the strings of her rationale and said *no, you are a different creature entirely.* Perhaps it was just pride, balking at the idea that her newfound happiness could have occurred with any other pairing but herself and Nathaniel.

Was she in love with him? Most assuredly. She was helplessly and utterly besotted in a way that felt richer and deeper than her infatuation with him had been, back when he was beyond reach. She could only hope that she was endearing herself to him as well, and that in time, he could come to feel for her as she felt for him.

Perhaps that had also influenced her to embrace her new finery and wear it daily. She knew she looked much more attractive in these things than in her old frocks, quite literally by design. She felt as though she walked taller and spoke more firmly when she was dressed in these things, when she had to pause upon passing a mirror to check that the reflection was indeed herself and not some other woman.

It also visibly pleased Gigi Dempierre, who had become a regular companion as the winter had set in.

After all, Nell had to fill her days with something after the ground had frozen too solid to allow any further capers beneath Meridian House, at least until spring. The staff had settled into their work restoring the house with such skill and speed that Nell was hardly needed for household management, aside from reviewing a few things every morning before breakfast and every evening after dinner.

With Gigi, every outing felt noteworthy. She had a way of noticing small details in the world, which, when pointed out, added such dimension to one's surroundings. Nell herself would never have noticed the man who was faking a limp until the woman he had been speaking to turned her back. She would have entirely missed the tiny clocks painted above the doorway of their favorite cafe. She never would have stopped to admire the painted parasol a woman was carrying to shield herself from the winter sun.

Perhaps most notably, Nell knew she would not have greeted Gigi's collection of songbirds at La Falaise with much more than a polite reception and nary a second thought, had the other woman not spent such much time and care introducing each for its unique personality and features. Now, Nell felt confident that she could accurately and confidently announce each of these birds at Britain's next royal reception, should they secure invitations.

To be frank, it had given her reservations about wearing her feathered dress to the upcoming masquerade.

"Don't be silly." Gigi laughed, collapsing onto one of Madame Bisset's sofas with a casual frivolousness that might only be found in the privacy of any other lady's bedchambers. "Songbirds didn't die to make that dress. I rather wager it was geese and a healthy dollop of black dye."

"Gigi!" Madame Bisset scolded, motioning for Gigi to take her shoes off the furniture. To Nell, she said, "It is best not to think overmuch about the origin of most things. That said, I do have many matching feathers left over to make a matching mask, and one for your husband, of course."

"And mine?" Gigi asked, flashing her dimples at the older woman. "Or shall I petition the local smith?"

"You will do no such thing!" the modiste huffed, dropping her hands onto her hips. "It will take some time, but you cannot trust that oaf with artistry! Imagine!"

"Madame Bisset rather fancies the smith," Gigi whispered theatrically to Nell. "He's got big, *strong* hands."

"Enough! *On y va. Allez!* I have work to do!" she said, flapping her hands at both women until they spilled back out onto the streets of Dover, unable to contain their giggles. Despite her tone, Madame Bisset was smiling as she shut the door on them, shaking her head with a fondness for Gigi's antics.

Gigi wasted no time gathering Nell's arm into a link with her own and starting off down the cobbled street. "Shall we go in search of mulled wine? Or perhaps a bite to eat, if you're hungry? I do not want to go back home yet. *Maman* is at her absolute worst when she's in the throes of Yuletide planning."

"My husband's cousin won't be retrieving me for another hour or two yet," Nell said, contemplating the height of the sun in the winter sky. "I was rather hoping we might explore some of the other shops in the town center. I still haven't found a Christmas gift for Nathaniel."

"Ah!" Gigi nodded with approval. "Even better, and we can get cups of hot cider from the stalls. What would you like to purchase for your handsome *beau*?"

"Is he a beau if I've already married him?" Nell asked with a laugh, allowing herself to be tugged down the first of a series of medieval streets toward a bustling holiday market in the square.

There had been something like this in Bath-Spa, during her days at finishing school. Mrs. Arlington always insisted their German counterparts did the best holiday markets in the world, but it had always been such fun to go browse the stalls before returning to Winchester for the holidays.

Her dear friend Tatiana had always insisted they go, dragging Gloriana and Nell toward the most eclectic vendors in search of gifts for their families. Without Tia, Nell was certain she'd never have found half so many unique things— arrangements of exotic insects pinned to careful displays under glass, tumbled crystals and gemstones, gleaming on bolts of velvet cloth, and handmade crafts made by the local wives rather than the artisans with storefronts. Many things were perhaps not suitable for Society, but quite pretty and charming in their own way.

None of those things sounded right for Nathaniel.

"I haven't the faintest idea," she confessed to her new friend, frowning. "Some weeks ago, I told him I wished to know everything there was about him, and though he's told me many stories of his life and experiences since then, I cannot think at all of what hobbies or leisurely pursuits might appeal to the man."

"Well, then," Gigi said, tilting her head with a mischievous gleam in her eye. "Shall we simply strip you naked and wrap you in a bow? I'm certain he'd enjoy the gesture."

Nell flushed, but did not balk at such a jest. "I'm afraid that would be rather redundant, at this point," she said instead, making the other girl the one who gasped with scandalized glee.

They bought cider from a vendor Gigi seemed to know, who smiled at her like an old friend as he passed over the steaming cups of liquid. Nell was beginning to realize that many men in the city of Dover were in love with Gigi Dempierre, and Gigi herself did not care a whit about it.

"It is only because I never leave Dover," she had explained, waving away the observation like a gnat. "If I vanished every spring like other young ladies, I would be no different from any of them. Familiarity breeds obsession, you know."

Nell laughed. "That is not how that expression goes, Gigi."

"Oh, it doesn't matter! *Alors*, does Nathaniel smoke a pipe?" she said briskly, gesturing to a display of wooden carvings, many elegant pipes among them.

Nell wrinkled her nose, sufficiently distracted. "No, and I shan't encourage him to consider the endeavor. My father does, though, and those do look very fine. Let's have a closer look."

By the time the sun had begun to set and it was time for Nell to return to Meridian, she had found gifts for both of her parents, her aunt, her twin brother, her youngest sister, and her grandfather, but was still none closer to even a glimmer of inspiration for what to get Nathaniel.

Once she had climbed into the carriage, opposite Kit, she posed the question to him. After all, if anyone would know her husband well enough to make a suggestion, it was Kit, but he only chuckled.

"That is the question, isn't it?" he said cheerily. "What does one get for the man who already has it all?"

"What are you getting him?" she asked, leaning forward curiously.

"I hadn't thought about it," he confessed. "In our youth, he only ever wanted books, and not the fun sort either."

"Machiavelli, Milton, and More," Nell recited, remembering the library in Marylebone. "I suppose that type of thing was practical, given his aspirations."

"Yes, but all the same, he was a boring youth."

Nell couldn't help but smile. She was certain her siblings would say very much the same, if asked how she was as a child. "I shall consider books, if nothing else comes to mind."

Kit considered her, shafts of purple twilight scattered through his fair hair as the carriage bounced along. "My mother kept a few things, over the years," he said, after a moment. "Things that she gathered from Meridian before anyone else could take them. Perhaps Nathaniel would enjoy having some of those things back."

"What sorts of things?" she asked, stopping short to stifle a yawn behind her gloved fingers. Winter always did this to her. Perhaps she might rest a while, before dinner, and then begin to parcel off these gifts to their rightful recipients.

Kit seemed unbothered by her rudeness, responding without so much as a pause. "She would know better than I. I believe it's some of his mother's jewelry, one of Alice's toys, a portrait of the family together, that sort of thing. My mother always hoped that Nathaniel would soften as he matured, and would one day want these things. Growing up, he openly reviled the very concept of sentiment."

"A portrait," Nell echoed. She found herself sitting immediately upright, all thoughts of rest and idle tasks dashed to dust with that one word. "Your mother has the portrait? Of the whole family together?"

Kit blinked back at her in surprise. "Yes. You don't mean to tell me Nathaniel has been searching for it?"

"Yes, he has!" she exclaimed, a surge of excitement bubbling up in her chest. "I can't believe we didn't think to ask you weeks ago! Oh, I would love to see that it is restored to Meridian, Christmas or no."

"How about we unveil it at dinner on Christmas Eve," Kit said, a fond little smile finding its way across his face at her bright-eyed enthusiasm. "Do not say anything to Nate. We will surprise him."

"All right," she replied, clasping her hands together. She knew she ought to consider the wisdom of withholding such information, but just now, with frost crackling at the carriage windows and gifts bursting from their packages at her side, she was far too excited by the days ahead of her to really consider how one might keep a secret from Nathaniel Atlas.

Besides, whether he had intended to or not, Kit had given her an idea.

CHAPTER 24

*N*athaniel had never much enjoyed Christmas.

Certainly, he enjoyed mince pie as much as the next man, and there was something calming about the solitude and silence of the winter, but as for yule logs and mistletoe and festive songs, he could not remember a time when they filled him with the sparkle of magic that others seemed to experience.

When he awoke on the morning of Christmas Eve to find dense, gray clouds sagging low in the sky over the ocean, he felt as though it were somehow his fault, like his inability to embrace the merry spirit of the season had chased away the bright sunlight that should always accompany such a time of joy.

He stood at the window, staring out at those clouds until the cold had crept from the glass pane, across the sill to his fingers, reminding him to get about the business of beginning his day. This was the third time in the last week that he had risen to find his wife already gone, likely entrenched in the business of preparing for tonight's dinner with the staff.

He smiled to himself, warmed more by the thought of her bubbling over with anticipation at hosting her first Christmas dinner than by the fire crackling nearby. The blue *Tales from the East* anthology had traveled from Nell's nightstand to his own, and in its place on her side was now a stack of three different books, which she had explained suited different moods she might have prior to slumber.

Her spectacles caught the faintest hint of sunlight which broke through those heavy clouds and sparkled as though they wished to be nowhere else aside from perhaps perched on their mistress's upturned nose.

He descended the stairs with Nell at the forefront of his thoughts. He expected to find her flipping through a recipe book for the dozenth time with the cook or perhaps at the writing desk in the study, scribbling yet more letters to her loved ones, thanking them for the parcels that had begun to arrive some days ago.

What he wasn't prepared for was finding her perched on the third-highest rung of a very elderly ladder, slinging the edge of an evergreen garland over a series of nails. Stuart, the footman, was standing at the base of the ladder, staring up at her with queasy discomfort as she chattered to him down below.

"I told her not to do it," came a voice from the banister. Nell's curly-haired lady's maid was watching it happen with a kind of rapt fascination that did not entirely disguise her disapproval with the goings-on. "She said we kept getting it wrong."

"It's essential for the arcs to be symmetrical, Sarah!" Nell called over her shoulder, beginning her descent on the ladder with a cacophony of alarming wooden squeaks.

Nathaniel stepped forward quickly and caught her about the waist, swinging her down to the ground before she could maneuver any further danger on that ladder. "Good God, Eleanor!" he muttered, for lack of any other words coming directly to mind.

She smiled brightly at him, her eyes sparkling like polished silver, and gestured above them to the work she'd done. "It's mistletoe," she said softly. "From the apple trees. I bought it in Dover, but Kit said we'll be able to gather our own next year. Isn't it beautiful?"

"It's a kissing bough, then?" Nathaniel responded with a raise of his brows, too taken by her happiness to maintain any outrage over her climbing ladders like a stable boy.

"It is," she confirmed, lifting her chin in invitation as he leaned down and pressed a warm, if chaste, kiss on her lips.

After all, they had an audience.

Next year.

He didn't dwell upon it, instead leading her into the dining room for a spot of tea and a small breakfast. The ceiling was finally dry and the chandelier rehung, restoring the room to some of its former splendor. It wasn't leafed with silver, but instead re-plastered with great swirls of powder blue, mimicking the lazy waves of an idyllic sea.

Had he really gone to all this trouble just to leave the house behind again, in the dust?

As they discussed their plans for tonight's dinner, sharing hot oats and honey with more of Aunt Susan's potted cherries, Nathaniel thought that this Meridian House was a far cry from the one that had haunted him.

Perhaps the floors that gleamed with a fresh coat of wax were the same planks of wood, and yes, the rooms had returned to the same lives they'd led before, but this place felt a world away from the crumbling manor on the cliff that he'd averted his eyes from, every time he'd passed it.

Next year.

It was worth considering. Tentatively.

He could not picture a kissing bough having quite the same charm in the echoing emptiness of Marylebone in the winter.

Kit arrived before luncheon, bringing with him the restored harp, freshly painted and tuned by the artisan Lady Dempierre had suggested. The piano had been repaired as well, and together the two men had managed to return both instruments to the ballroom without Nell's knowledge.

"Should we drape it with fabric?" Kit asked, straining his neck side to side as he considered the placement of the harp. Its sculpted embellishments had been painted, its wood polished, and brass settings restored to a gleam. "So that you can whip it away in a moment of great reveal?"

Nate chuckled, shaking his head. "I do not think I am capable of such a gesture without appearing utterly ridiculous."

"Yes, that was my hope," Kit agreed, clapping his cousin on the shoulder in good spirits. "Mother is beside herself with excitement for tonight. She has so missed being able to have a family around her in the holiday season."

He nodded, allowing Kit to depart for other business before dinner, and did his best to disregard the discomfort that had settled onto his shoulders at those words.

Kit had been in the army. Uncle Archie had vanished. Nate had tied himself to London. It had never occurred to him that his aunt had been alone and adrift on Christmas for all of those years. It was as though those holidays when he and Kit had been boys were nothing more than a fantasy, something he'd convinced himself had never been real, while she had likely mourned those lost days, alone at her hearth during the darkest and coldest times of the year.

It was unacceptable. He had behaved unacceptably.

Next year.

There was no point in pretending that his original plans still held any weight. He was no more likely to return to London full time than he was to tuck Nell away in some country cottage with her books. So why not consider the prospect of next year? Why not consider all the years thereafter?

It felt more alluring by the minute.

THE SNOW BEGAN to burst from those swollen clouds just before sunset, pouring from the sky in dizzy spirals of sparkling white.

Kit and Susan had been laughing like children as they ran from the carriage to the door of Meridian, snowflakes melting on their clothes and in their hair, and not at all detracting from their joy at the night ahead of them.

Nell was wearing forest green and silver, her brown curls caught up in a band of pearls and diamonds with dark tendrils of her hair springing out around the lines of her face.

Every time her wedding band caught the light and sparkled, he found himself thumbing his own ring. It had already become such second nature to wear it that he often forgot it was there. He liked the reminder of seeing its counterpart, flashing and glittering, as cheerful as his marriage had somehow become.

In the place of a traditional yule log, Nell had suggested that they begin their holiday tradition instead with a yule candle, which would require less tending and would create significantly less mess amidst the ongoing restoration of the house.

With the family all gathered around the table, ready to begin their Christmas feast, Nell revealed the thing—a thick stump of a candle with a long, twisting wick, which would burn from sunset to dawn.

"You must light it, Nathaniel," she said to him, her voice breathy with anticipation. "And at sunrise tomorrow, only you can extinguish it."

"What will happen if I don't?" he asked, teasing in his tone as he stood and gestured for the footman to bring him a lit taper.

"Ill fortune," Susan said immediately, "for the whole year."

"Death of a family member, according to my grandfather," Nell answered somberly. "It's all quite pagan, isn't it?"

"Now, now," Kit had responded. "Once we steal a tradition, it stays strictly Anglican for the remainder of eternity, my dear."

And so the first course had been served in the light of the flickering yule candle, which seemed to sweeten the wine and inspire the conversation that was held around it.

Nate found himself laughing from sincere amusement more than he could ever remember doing at a gathering of any sort, often catching his wife's eye across the table and holding it until she looked away with a blossoming of pink in her lovely cheeks.

He found himself wishing each course would come and go faster, anticipating the moment she would see the harp this evening. The servants had been told to gather in the ballroom for a special festivity, which would include sweets and wine for all, and perhaps, if anyone was moved to create it, music befitting the occasion.

If the food hadn't been so deliciously diverse, it might have been more difficult to remain patient. As it was, every temptation to hurry things along was soon silenced by the next flavor on offer from colorful plates of lovingly crafted fare.

It occurred to Nate that he had been missing this willingly, for many years. Smiling until his cheeks ached was a thing he could have had. He might have spent those cold holidays alone watching family across the table. The sight of the three of them, merry and familiar, laughing with one another, sharing stories from the past, was just as intoxicating as the wine. Just as potent.

"You cannot know how much I've missed this house," Susan said to him, as though she could hear his thoughts. "How much I've missed you, my darling boy."

He had reached across to squeeze her hand rather than attempt to find the words to respond. After all, how does one even begin to apologize for abandoning such a lovely, giving woman? How does one explain that he did not even consider what he'd done?

The only sincere apology was a lasting improvement, he believed, and so he silently committed to being a better nephew and perhaps, overall, a better man.

When the final bite of dessert had been consumed, and all insisted they could not bear another morsel, they all stood in tandem, playing yet again into those silly superstitions that had somehow survived the centuries.

He offered his wife his arm, and bade them all follow him to the ballroom, to join the staff for a spot of revelry before Christmas Day took each person to his or her private affairs.

"I have a surprise for you," he whispered softly into her ear, delighting in the way she squeezed his arm and stifled a little squeak of anticipation.

"I have one for you too," she said, biting down on her lip. "Well, two, really. I'll give you the other when we're alone."

"Oh?" he replied, intrigued.

The doors to the ballroom opened to reveal a glittering festivity, just on the cusp of beginning. Candles danced along the walls and the room gleamed like new, dressed in a dazzling glow of festive decor.

Nell gasped in delight, raising her fingers to her lips. She parted from Nathaniel to turn fully around, taking in every inch of the room, until her eyes fell on that harp. She turned back to him, beaming brighter than all the flames in the room combined, and threw herself into his arms for a tight embrace, which seemed to delight the servants assembled to join them.

"Shall I play?" she whispered, as though she could barely believe it. "I had forgotten that you intended to have it repaired."

"I would love to hear you play," he said, kissing her cheek softly. "We all would. Just give me one moment.

"I wanted to say a few words before we begin our celebration," he announced, leaving a hand on the small of Nell's back and using his politician's voice to project throughout the room. "So many of you here tonight followed your employer from a townhouse in London to a decaying manor by the sea. You took this adventure with me, and together we have restored this once grand house to its original beauty. I know you are far from home, and eventually, many of us will return to the city, but tonight, please share with me and mine the bounty of a year well lived. Happy Christmas!"

"Happy Christmas!" the room answered in a raucous cheer, laughter and excitement unleashed into the very oxygen with the glimmer of a long-anticipated night.

"One last thing!" Kit called, before everyone could dissolve into their own conversations and joys. "Mrs. Atlas and I have a final item to restore to this ballroom, in honor of those who danced here first, and called this place home."

Nate turned, curious and confused, to see his cousin motion to two of the footmen to carry in a large rectangle covered by a sheet.

"Since you declined a flamboyant reveal," Kit said, with a wink, "I will do the honors."

When he whipped back the covering, revealing the portrait, there was a beat of silence. Nate stood frozen, looking into the faces of the family he'd lost, at the child he had been.

They were posed in this very room, where his father thought the light was best. His mother wore a faint smile, holding a bundled baby close to her heart. His father stood with one hand on her shoulder and the other on young Nathaniel's. He looked like a serious child, clutching a wooden sailboat and standing responsibly upright with one of his father's military medals pinned to his chest. Of course, he remembered that his upright demeanor was the constant needling of the adults which had accomplished such an effect, rather than his own maturity at a young age.

His heart seemed to clench, painful, knotted, and then release as though twenty years of pain had pushed past the dam he'd built, sloshing over the top and pouring out into his chest.

He felt the tears on his cheeks before he registered producing them.

He wasn't the only one crying. Aunt Susan too had her fists at her mouth and sobs in her throat, but it was clear to anyone who looked that these were happy tears, for somehow she smiled through them, surrounded by the glow of her own happiness.

Nate knew he could not dissolve into a sobbing mess in front of his staff, much less his family, and so he strode across the room and pulled Kit into a tight embrace instead, relying on the movement and warmth of the gesture to mitigate his roiling emotions.

"It was your wife's idea," Kit whispered to Nate as they broke apart. "I would never have thought you wanted it."

"I didn't," Nate replied, dazed with his own emotion. "I would have declined. But now that I have it, I cannot imagine ever parting with it. What a gift!"

"Are you still talking about the painting?" Kit said with a nudge, nodding toward little Eleanor.

His wife was standing apart from the others, hope and uncertainty painted onto her face. She held her hands clasped in front of her, the wedding band caught in the ring of ballroom light.

She bit her lip, as she was wont to do when uncertain. The hope in her face, the eagerness to please him, could have broken his heart all over again.

He closed the space between them, and pulled her into his arms. He kissed her firmly and decisively, so that she would always know beyond a doubt that she was an Atlas now, and would never be so welcome anywhere as she was in his embrace.

CHAPTER 25

By the night of Epiphany, the ache in Nell's fingers had finally begun to subside.

It had been impossible to tear herself away from that harp. Its notes were clear and bright, the strings such a perfect balance of taut and supple, responding to every pluck of her fingers and every glide of her hand with the most deliciously beautiful music.

She hadn't ever been able to lose herself in her music like this before. At school, lessons were on a rigid schedule, and at home, there was no harp to play. At Meridian, she could create music until her fingers were too stiff to move and her calluses were pronounced enough to inspire a stern lecture from Sarah on the appropriate state of a lady's hands.

It had taken several rounds of argument before Sarah understood that the calluses must form, otherwise there would be blistering and bleeding anew every time she played her instrument again. It had been a hard-won battle, but won nonetheless.

After all, what did it matter this time of year, anyhow? Every venture out of doors required gloves, and tonight was no exception. Along with her face behind her feathered mask, her unladylike callouses were similarly disguised beneath elbow-length gloves of jade-colored silk.

"You have to put your mask on before we alight," she said to Nathaniel, who was openly admiring her from across the carriage, the ribbons at the edges of his glossy black mask twined around his fingers.

"You will have to assist me," he replied easily, beckoning her to join him on his bench. "I simply did not wish to have my vision obstructed for as long as you were mine alone to admire."

"Oh, stop it." She laughed, making her way over with a careful gathering of her feather-lined skirts and situating herself next to her husband. She slid the mask from his grip, the ribbons sliding over his fingers and into her lap as she allowed him to lean forward and capture her lips with his own; a kiss for their last moments of privacy for the evening.

"Are you certain there were no further instructions?" he asked, holding himself still as she slid the domino over his eyes, melding it against the line of his brow and the ridge of his nose. "It rather seems too fortunate to be possible."

"Yes, and I am relieved by it. Are you not? The last thing I want to do right now is engage in dishonesty and subterfuge. I have come to treasure Gigi as a friend, and the idea of betraying her trust sits ill within me."

"I understand," he said softly, as Nell's hands pulled neat knots in the ribbons securing his mask. "I am simply surprised that there was nothing in the letter beyond the instruction to 'attend and enjoy' this literal masquerade."

"Well, there was also the invoice," Nell said with a sheepish laugh, which was immediately met by one of genuine amusement from her husband.

She had purchased a print from Zelda's store as Nathaniel's Christmas gift, one she had run after their elopement, featuring a fairly accurate rendering of Nathaniel unveiling a bride with yet another veil on underneath. At the bottom, it sported the caption *MP Marries Mystery Maiden*.

It now sat propped against the mirror on the vanity table in their bedroom.

She colored a bit at her aunt's miserly behavior, and added, "Which, of course, I will pay of my own reserves. I assure you."

"Whatever the cost, it was well worth it," he assured her, turning before she could finish smoothing his hair over the ribbons and capturing her chin with his fingers. "Now, come kiss a strange man in a mask before your husband discovers us."

Her giggles were caught by the kiss, dissolving between them in a final, stolen moment before the carriage eased to a slick halt on the frosty cobbles outside of La Falaise.

Nathaniel looked like a seductive demon in his mask, hammered into a swirling design that ended in sharp points just beneath his eyes. It was too dark to tell what color they would appear to be when ringed by the dark leather, though Nell was finding that the longer she spent gazing into those eyes, the more constant they appeared to be, a color all their own that she was finding she enjoyed very much.

She leaned back and lifted her own mask by its handle over her eyes. "Do I look mysterious?" she asked somberly.

"I prefer you in your spectacles," he replied with a grin, "but you are fetching, as ever."

"Flatterer," she teased as the door was pulled open, momentarily blinding them both with the dazzle of torchlight arranged along the pathway leading into the manor.

It was not snowing tonight. Not yet, anyway.

The piles of sparkling crystalline white on either side of the drive bore testament to how frequent the snowfall had been this year, and how lasting the result of each storm was. Still, it was an otherworldly frame to their entrance, and Nell felt there was something rather magical about the combination of the fire and the ice, as her feather-lined dress brushed against the stone walkway while she clung to Nathaniel's arm.

The air was somehow electric, the charge of anticipation of being done, of completing a final night under her aunt's employ, crackling through the furs on her shoulders and spiraling down the bare arms she hid beneath.

They deposited their invitation on a gilded platter at the entrance and allowed masked footmen to relieve them of their coats.

In true masquerade style, there would be no announcements of guests tonight, on the assumption that they were well disguised in their finery. Nell rather thought the whole ruse a bit silly, especially for herself. After all, what good was a disguise when you were a head shorter than everyone else in the ballroom?

They were pointed down a candlelit corridor, covered in metallic sculptures imitating the winding of vines and leaves, coming together in a thicket overhead like a summer alcove in an enchanted garden.

Neither of them spoke, for it would have interrupted the effect of the decor, and perhaps might have lessened the impact of the moment they emerged into the ballroom, glittering in gold and white as dozens of couples spun in dance at the center of the floor.

Nell was entirely certain that she'd never seen anything half so striking, except, perhaps, when beholding the man next to her.

"Might I claim the first dance?" he asked, his voice low in her ear. "I fear we are quite tardy in having our first spin 'round the ballroom."

"I never dance before champagne," Nell said with a laugh. "You will not find me particularly graceful *en mouvement*."

"I appreciate the warning," he said with a smile as he gestured toward a table of glinting champagne flutes arranged before a half-circle of bottles. "I wouldn't love you half so well without your candor."

Nell was momentarily speechless, and very glad for the impending relief one finds in a sip of spirits. Had he just professed to love her? She thought so, but didn't dare ask, lest she was mistaken. In any event, they were intercepted by Gigi and Lady Dempierre en route to the table.

"Nell, my darling, there you are!" called Gigi, raising her

arm to wave them over. She was bedecked head to toe in periwinkle chiffon, hand-embroidered with a peacock and peahen in the midst of their mating dance. Of course, her mask was more peacock than peahen, but she had reasoned with Madame Bisset that "were the birds men and their ladies women, the standard of dress would be the other way around."

Evidently, the avian theme extended to the family, for Lady Dempierre was wrapped in white and wore a dove's face over her own.

Nathaniel gave a small, barely perceptible sigh of disappointment, which Nell met with a light jab of her elbow into his side. His distaste was not directed at Gigi. Indeed, he had been genuinely supportive of Nell nurturing a friendship here in Kent. Rather, he was exhausted of Lady Dempierre's unseemly enthusiasm toward his company and her unrelenting ability to monopolize it.

Nell could not entirely hide her amusement at his distress, for she never would have imagined Nathaniel Atlas so utterly exhausted by a middle-aged woman. Then again, she'd never have imagined he was ticklish either. Such were the discoveries of marriage.

"Oh, I am so pleased to see you!" Gigi exclaimed, stretching her hands out to tug Nell closer as the latter squeaked in alarm at nearly spilling her newly poured champagne. "*Maman* has been an utter bore, and Mathias keeps making bird puns. How did I arrive into such an insufferable family?"

"Every family is insufferable," Nell told her, sipping at her drink. "Were any of the puns particularly clever?"

"Of course not," Gigi sniffed. She glanced at her mother, who was having animated conversation with a tolerant Nathaniel, and lowered her voice. "I have been thinking about your proposal, that I join you in London this spring. I desperately want to, Eleanor, but I'm afraid my parents will be quite cross at even the suggestion of such a thing."

"Why are they so opposed?" Nell asked, unable to hide her exasperation with it. "You deserve to pursue a life of your own!"

"Do I?" Gigi sighed, taking a healthy swig of her own drink. "I suppose they can't stop me, if I set my mind to it. Are you certain I won't be a bother? I've never even visited London."

"You will be anything but a bother," Nell assured her. "Nathaniel will be much occupied once Parliament resumes, and it would be a great happiness for me to have a friend to pass the Season with. I can introduce you to my dear friend Tatiana. I think the two of you would get on famously."

Gigi pressed her lips together, attempting to contain her excitement. "I shall have to trust Mathias to care for my birds."

"You can bring a pair along, if you like," Nell said. "I know how dear they are to you, and I am fond of birdsong myself."

"What are the two of you conspiring?" Nathaniel asked pleasantly, appearing at Nell's side with a warm hand to the small of her back.

"Oh, all manner of criminal activity," Gigi replied easily, ignoring the irritated huff from her mother. "Sadly, your wife has nixed my dastardly plans."

"She has a habit of doing that," Nathaniel returned with a chuckle.

"Oh, you must excuse me," Gigi said, laying a hand on Nell's arm. "I promised this dance to that ridiculous Jean Catroux. Don't vanish on me! *A bientot!*"

The trio watched Gigi flounce away, the gathered blue of her skirt swaying prettily against the dance floor as she was received by a perfectly handsome-looking young man, preparing for the first chords of the quadrille. If her mother was aware of any unspoken social cue that she too ought to take her leave, she chose to disregard it, leaving them in a pause of awkward silence.

"Lady Dempierre, I find your ensemble tonight most striking," Nell said finally, and with genuine admiration. "You are positively glowing."

"Why, thank you, Mrs. Atlas!" Lady Dempierre smiled, though Nell got the impression that the elder woman still did not know quite what to make of her. "You are looking lovely yourself this evening. Did you have a pleasant New Year?"

"We did," Nell said, leaning slightly into the warmth of her husband's body at her side. "It was a perfect night to hide away from the snow and make merry inside. Oh! Did Nathaniel tell you? We found the portrait of his family! It is currently hanging in our sitting room."

At this news, Lady Dempierre's posture visibly changed, as though she'd drawn herself up to her full stature. It was difficult to read her face from behind her mask, but it was clear that her interest had been sharply piqued. "Is that so?"

she exclaimed breathlessly. "I am most happy to hear it! I should very much like to visit soon and see it myself. It would hearten me so to look upon Mary's face again."

"Do you think she'd feel the same?" came an icy voice from their left. "From what I recall, the two of you squabbled as often as not."

The hairs on Nell's arms rose, her skin prickling with cold disbelief. But, sure enough, she turned to find none other than her aunt Zelda, her features perfectly distinct despite the half-mask of red silk she wore. Her silver-white hair was gathered atop her head in its customary severe style, and her gown was a simple pattern of red and black.

Nathaniel's fingers curled around the curve of her waist, as though he were anchoring her in her moment of surprise.

"Zelda," Lady Dempierre said, her voice flat with her lack of enthusiasm. "As ever, I am surprised to see you. Nothing keeping you in London this year?"

"Oh, my darling Therese," Zelda said with a poisonous little smile. "You know I come every year, no matter the obstacle. I shall never miss it."

"Indeed?" Lady Dempierre replied with a little sigh. "And is our *darling* Harriet with you this evening? I have not seen her about on the dance floor, and the poor dear does have a tendency to stand out."

"Harriet had business to attend in London. Mrs. Goode is rather self-assured that way," Zelda said smoothly. "A woman to admire, wouldn't you agree? Especially without a husband to secure her ambitions."

The tension between the two women was nigh unbearable.

"I have often wondered," Lady Dempierre said with a lift of her chin. "At what point does a spinster change from a Miss to a Missus? It seems rather arbitrary."

"Oh, it certainly can be," Zelda replied easily, light glinting off her incisors. "I adjusted my own moniker upon opening my business. Harriet saw no reason to wait, and simply adapted the title as soon as she'd told her parents she did not intend to marry, ever. It is a badge of bravery, wouldn't you say, Nell?"

Nell started, so morbidly fascinated by the parlay happening before her that she'd almost forgotten her own presence amidst them. "I couldn't say, Aunt Zelda," she replied politely. "I secured my own title the traditional way."

"Ah, so you did," her aunt replied with a frown, which made Nathaniel bristle at Nell's side.

"Aunt!" Lady Dempierre exclaimed, utterly unconcerned with barbs that were neither directed at her nor delivered from her own lips. "You are Mrs. Atlas's aunt?!"

"Of course I am," Zelda replied with a humorless laugh. "You are losing your talent for information, Therese. It truly seems like a stroke of fate, wouldn't you say? That Mary's son and my favorite niece should fall in love and run off to Scotland together? The timing couldn't have been better."

"Fate, is it?" Nathaniel said, his voice dark and unnaturally calm. "Mrs. Smith, I do believe the time has come for an explanation. Evidently, you had no problem securing yourself an invitation to this ball, and yet, you schemed and contrived the first months of our marriage, seemingly for no reason at all."

"Oh, I'm the schemer, am I?" Zelda said, cutting her cool gaze to meet Nathaniel's. "Do you think I am ignorant to your true intentions, boy? Have you shared your suspicions with your wife, hm? I'd wager not. She might not be so pliable under your charms if she knew what you've been plotting all these years."

"Nathaniel and I are honest with one another," Nell said quickly, her heart lurching in her chest at this unpleasant turn of events. There would be time for an explanation later, in private. She knew very well how skilled her aunt was at inflammatory insinuations. The way her pulse had quickened was simply a reaction to her spouse being attacked, not fear. Not doubt. She trusted Nathaniel. She squared her shoulders. "And he is right. We are owed an explanation."

"Are you?" Zelda replied, turning that sharp look onto her niece that, without Nathaniel's support, might have sent Nell stumbling a few steps backward. "Honest with each other, I mean. So that is to say that you have confronted him about your suspicions, then? Regarding his murderous impulses?"

"I beg your pardon?" Nathaniel hissed, still holding tight to Nell's waist.

Lady Dempierre had crossed her arms over her chest, her posture rigid but unchanged throughout this development in the conversation. When Zelda turned to her, she appeared to have forgotten the enmity between them completely, and said to Zelda in a quick, businesslike tone, "They have found the cellars."

"Excellent," Zelda breathed. "Not a day too soon, either. Once we get a reply from Pauline, we will need to act quickly, lest we miss our window of opportunity."

"Yes," Therese Dempierre agreed with a sigh. "I suppose we have no choice."

"You may not have choices between the two of you," Nathaniel said, low and steady, "but my wife and I certainly do. No invitation has been extended to either of you regarding Meridian's cellars. You cannot seriously expect that we would entertain it at this point."

"Nathaniel," Nell whispered, setting a soft hand on his arm. "We ought to at least hear what is desired, shouldn't we? For the sake of the Silver Leaf."

He blinked down at her in stunned disbelief, something behind his eyes that sent a dart of pain directly into her heart.

"Pending, of course, an explanation," she added hurriedly. "For I am as confounded as you are by my aunt's presence here tonight and the unnecessary dance of futility she orchestrated."

"Oh, nonsense," Zelda snapped. "I gave you both exactly the amount of information you required, and the outcome has been ideal."

"Ideal?" echoed Nathaniel, a quaking aura of rage seeming to emanate from his collected composure. "Your manipulations of your own niece and, presumably, the son of your dead friend have been *ideal*?"

"So far," Zelda replied casually, shrugging her shoulders. "You no longer want to destroy me and my enterprise, damning countless souls to a fate worse than death, and I now have the means to reopen our access to the Channel, *if* you can get a grip on your temper. I'm certain that Therese and I can shine light on a great many questions you have, and perhaps a few that you would never have thought to ask."

Nell inhaled a shaky breath, her skin flushed with the desire to flee or perhaps simply to burst into tears. "Was it you?" she managed, her voice thin and cracking. "Were you involved in the death of the Atlas family?"

"Would it matter if I was?" Zelda asked, tilting her head curiously. "Apparently a few murders in one's history is no obstacle to your love and devotion, my darling girl."

That was the moment he released her. His hand dropped from her waist with a dead, listless weight that seemed far more defeated than any gesture of anger. It was as though all the life had slipped from his body from this abundance of horror and implication.

"I am going to return to Meridian," he said flatly, his eyes fixed on empty space rather than any of the three women. "Eleanor, you are welcome to return with me or to stay on to spend time with your aunt."

The implication was apparent. Nell was to make a choice. Immediately.

Zelda actually seemed amused by this test, as though she never would imagine herself the loser in a battle for Nell's affections.

Perhaps it was because of that, the wry and thin smile on the face of the woman she thought she'd really known, had trusted for her entire life, that Nell did not hesitate. She turned her back on her aunt, slipping her arm into her husband's, and said with the last dregs of her strength, "Let's go home."

CHAPTER 26

They hadn't spoken on the carriage ride home.

Nathaniel knew that this was his fault.

On the drive, her teeth chattering from the cold, Nell had begun to say something to him that had sounded much like an apology, and he had silenced her with a plea to wait until they were home. When they arrived back at Meridian, he had purposefully lingered downstairs while the maid helped Nell out of her beautiful gown, and the mask that had only been worn for under an hour at a ball they'd anticipated for months.

He thought perhaps he just needed some time to sit in silence before facing her. He had hidden the truth from her about his intentions. This much was true. But, considering what she thought him capable of and already hiding in his past, it seemed obvious now that he could have been completely open with her without driving her away.

She had chosen him tonight.

The thought of it made his throat constrict and his eyes burn. And so he poured himself a second glass of whiskey and closed those eyes against the press of reality upon his skin.

He knew she was waiting in their bed, likely rigid and anxious and full of so many words he was not yet ready to hear or respond to. The truth of the matter was that things had been so peaceful and idyllic, so completely unexpected, that he'd begun to think perhaps the mystery surrounding his parents was not as important as he'd believed it was.

He looked up at the portrait of his family, hanging over the fireplace in the sitting room, and frowned.

They were familiar to him and not, like a half-remembered dream.

His father looked approachable, kind even. They had the same eyes. Nathaniel's only memories of Walter were from a young boy's perspective, when a man grown appears impossibly large and strong. He had believed his father invincible, and the painting was a reminder that he had only been a man, in the end.

His mother was much as he remembered her, a faint smile of affection on her face as she held Alice bundled in her arms. Evidently she had not been the simple, maternal figure he had spent his life remembering. She had been far more mysterious than that. She had hidden treasures in the ground and nurtured friendships with the likes of Therese Dempierre and Zelda Smith.

There was no telling who Mary Atlas was at her core. Certainly not now.

He set his glass down, pushing himself to his feet and crossing the room to get a closer look at the thing. Lady Dempierre had been unusually fixated on it, hadn't she? It was suspicious, to say the least.

It took some maneuvering without a stepping stool or assistance, but after a moment, Nathaniel was able to wedge the thing off the wall and tip it forward to ease onto the ground without risking it being damaged by the flames in the hearth.

He set it face down, running his hands along the seam where the frame met the canvas. It would have been easy to miss, had he not been searching for something odd. If it had been more obvious, someone would have noticed it before now, but Aunt Susan had held on to this for years, and Kit had transported it with nary a raised eyebrow.

He was careful popping the frame loose, first spreading his jacket on the ground to cushion the painting beneath and then working bit by bit to separate wood from fabric. When he finally lifted it away, the small bulge he had felt was now visible, sitting against the rear of the frame, inside a small slot that had been split in the wrapping.

He reached inside, his heart hammering against his ribs, and closed his fingers around a small, leather-bound book, which he withdrew from inside the canvas frame with breath suspended in his lungs. It was black, wrapped in a strip of leather, and just a touch larger than a deck of cards.

The paper was warped and yellowed on the edges, and when he began to unwrap the leather holding the book closed, it was hard and brittle. Still, the book did open, and within it were pages and pages of his mother's tight, clean penmanship, arranged into the unmistakable columns of a business ledger.

His vision swam, his hands shaken by the tremor that ran through him. He recognized many of the items listed in a column named *Receipt and Exchange*. He recognized them because he'd indexed them himself, in a list very similar to this one.

What he didn't recognize were several sets of initialed codes listed, both as cargo and as goods. It was several pages later, under the large headline *Pending*, that he began to realize what he was looking at.

It was a list of names. A very long list of names, each with either an *F* or an *E* next to it. Many of them had been crossed out and annotated with a date.

Sure enough, when he flipped backward to check, the initials in the ledger matched with the names from the larger list. The Silver Leaf Society was smuggling, yes, but not riches and secrets. It was moving people between France and England at wartime, in both directions.

He didn't know what it meant. He couldn't think. He slapped the book closed and rubbed his eyes, resolving to immediately go to his wife and show her what he'd found. However, when he pushed himself to his feet, the book held tight in his hands, he found that he was not alone, and perhaps hadn't been for some time.

Zelda Smith was leaning against the door jamb, a familiar ring of keys dangling from her fingers. Her mask was gone, and she looked somehow older now than she had that day on Bond Street or even earlier tonight, in the ballroom at La Falaise.

"I let myself in," she said softly, answering the unasked question. She spoke without the taunting edge that had been in her voice just hours ago. It wasn't that she sounded apologetic. No, he rather thought she was incapable of apology. Instead, she simply looked tired and resigned.

She sighed, dropping the keys into her pocket, and crossed the room, pouring herself a glass of whiskey twice as full as his own. After tipping a portion of it into her mouth, she set the glass down, met his gaze, and said, "Nathaniel, I think it is time we talk."

NELL WIPED her eyes quickly at the sound of the doorknob turning, burrowing herself deeper under the blankets.

She hadn't been sure he would come to bed tonight, or ever again if truth be told. Her aunt had shattered whatever it was that had grown between them, as quickly and sharply as a snap of the fingers. Perhaps, if he were coming to their bed, all was not lost.

The glow of a handheld lantern shone in a shaft of light from the doorway to the foot of their bed, and for the briefest moment, Nell pondered whether or not she ought to feign sleep. That is, until she heard her aunt's voice in the dark.

"Nell? Are you asleep?"

She blinked hard, twice, just to ensure she wasn't in the midst of some cruel nightmare, but no, certain enough, her aunt was crossing the bedchamber, the heels of her dancing shoes clicking smartly against the wooden floor until she came to the corner of the rug.

"Aunt Zelda?" Nell murmured, her voice scratchy in her tear-strained throat. She pushed the blankets back and shoved herself up to sitting, blinking against the specter in front of her, haloed in light from the hall. "What are you doing here? Where is Nathaniel?"

"He's out," she said, dropping the lantern on the table and turning to face her niece with her arms crossed over her chest. She looked surprised, genuinely taken aback.

Nell thought that perhaps she'd been caught unawares by the beautiful nightgown or the sumptuous dressings of the room.

However, when she spoke, she said, "You've been crying."

"Of course I have," Nell replied, unable to stop a weak laugh at the absurdity of her aunt's shock over such an obvious reaction. "You know exactly what a rift you created tonight. How did you get into our house? Where did my husband go?"

"He went back to La Falaise, to retrieve Therese," Zelda replied, crossing the space between them to sit at the edge of the bed. She reached out a tremulous hand, touching Nell's cheek with the tips of her fingers and a frown. "He rather insisted I stay behind and use the time to apologize to you, and so here I am."

Nell raised her eyebrows, which caused her aunt's frown to deepen.

"I am sorry," she said, her voice hushed, either with shame

or distaste for her own words. "I did not realize my actions would cause you such distress."

"How could you not realize that!" Nell cried, flinching away from her aunt's touch. "He is my husband! We were happy!"

"Nell, he has been working for the last decade of his life to expose and destroy me. I thought he had trapped you into marriage by some convoluted scheme to hurt me, with no concern at all for you. I never imagined that ... well, that you were happy." Zelda grimaced, shaking her head. "I am not often such a poor judge of reality."

"I have always wanted to find love," Nell said, furrowing her brow. "I've told you that."

"Well, yes, you have," Zelda allowed. "I simply thought ... well, I thought you were like me, and you know very well that I have never held men in great esteem. I have always seen so much of myself in you, from such a young age, my love. It blinded me to our differences. Or, perhaps I did not want to see them."

"You dressed me poorly apurpose, didn't you?"

"I simply wished to spare you the annoyance of male persistence," she said with a sigh that bordered on irritation. "I've already said I was wrong. I see that I was. Am I to take it, then, that you have fallen in love with this husband of yours?"

"Yes, of course I have," Nell whispered, her fingers flying to her lips to stifle the sob that threatened to escape. "He is more than I could ever have hoped to find for myself."

"Nonsense. You are far too good for much better than the Atlas boy," Zelda sniffed. "Peter believes him a cold-blooded killer," she added, as though Nell could have forgotten her implication of just that not so long ago. "Has he told you he is not?"

"No." Nell frowned. "But I have not asked."

"Well, all will be clear soon," she said, her voice suddenly brisk and businesslike. She pushed herself from the bed and motioned for Nell to follow. "He will likely be back within the hour with Therese in tow. If you do not wish to receive her in your dressing gown, I suggest you put on some clothes."

Nell found herself putting her feet to the floor, her brow furrowed in confusion. "Why has he gone to get Lady Dempierre? It is rather late, and you obviously hate one another."

"I do not hate her! We have been friends our entire lives!"

Nell blinked at her aunt, true befuddlement writ on her face.

"Clothes, Nell," Zelda ordered before she could speak, "then you may ask all the questions you like."

CHAPTER 27

*I*t was all Nathaniel could do to not rush across the room the instant he returned and gather his wife in his arms.

She was seated on the sofa, the painting and its frame in a neat stack to her left, and she had chosen to read rather than spend time conversing with her aunt. The sight of her messy braid and the spectacles perched on her nose heartened him, for he had felt a true fear only moments ago that she had been lost to him forever.

Therese Dempierre had been waiting for him on the fringes of her party, which was still a bustling affair at this late hour. She had met him in the vine-covered corridor, as though she had sensed his arrival and intent. She had declined to converse on the drive over, which was well and fine for Nathaniel, as he'd already been given quite enough to process tonight. According to Zelda, however, there was a final piece of the puzzle which only Therese could provide, and so, it was necessary to retrieve her.

"Nathaniel," Nell said, a throaty emotion in her voice that seemed to mirror his own. She rose from her seat and crossed the room to him, stopping just short of making contact, uncertainty magnified in the round frames of her spectacles.

"Eleanor," he replied, reaching forward to take her hand. "All is well. Please, come sit beside me."

She nodded, gripping his hand tight enough that he could feel her wedding band, cool against the heat of his fingers. As often as he'd felt the warmth of their bond from the flash and glitter of the gems in that ring, it was in this moment that its symbolism felt most tangible to him.

They sat together on the settee, waiting for the other two women to find their places across from them. Lady Dempierre's eyes had fallen immediately to the dismantled portrait, and before she sat, she knelt before it, her eyes wet with emotion as she beheld the faces of the friends she had lost.

This surprised him. Deeply.

It was a certainty that she had known about the ledger hidden in the portrait, and as such, it had never occurred to him that her desire to see his mother's face again had also been sincere. She turned, brushing her fingers beneath her lashes, and sat down so close to Zelda Smith that no one would have guessed at the way they had been speaking to one another mere hours ago.

Nell squeezed his hand, looking over to him in curiosity. It seemed that whatever Mrs. Smith had used her alone time to convey, it had not been particularly explanatory.

"I found a ledger book tonight, concealed in the cavity of the family portrait," he said, speaking to his wife directly. "It was upon reviewing some of the entries in the ledger, and recognizing their correlation to what we found underground, that I made a startling discovery, one which you have certainly known all along. The Silver Leaf Society smuggles people between war zones."

"Not just anyone," Zelda said quickly, drawing the eyes of everyone in the room. "Prisoners of war, those separated from their families, and the odd special case. It is a service of humanity, not country. Your parents were not traitors, Nathaniel, but they were not patriots either, and in the end, this fact is what killed them. The Silver Leaf Society did not engineer their deaths, but we do feel responsible for what happened, and we always have."

He nodded, heaving a sigh as he turned back to his wife. "I am not a killer," he said in a properly sheepish fashion. "I suggested the murder of Alex Somers in an effort to determine whether or not he was in mortal danger for crossing what I believed to be a dangerous enforcer of the Crown. Had you or your brother agreed, I would have confirmed my suspicions about my family's demise and, of course, found a way to spirit Lord Alex to safety. In my self-involved hubris, I completely forgot about this deception and what it might have meant to you and your brother."

She blinked at him, and replied only with a faint, "Oh."

"Mary and Walter were forced to change the terms of a prisoner swap in Calais on the day that they died," Lady Dempierre said, twisting her hands in her lap. "The baby was never supposed to have gone along with them, but the poor darling had been down with colic and your mother couldn't bear to part from her. Mary was the linchpin in our entire operation, and she had no choice but to attend the exchange personally, so she brought Alice along. It was supposed to be a short, speedy affair, and one Mary could not miss lest she risk all that was at stake in our future."

"It should have been simple," Zelda added, exchanging a glance with Lady Dempierre. "It had always been simple before, but this was the first time that we were being paid with a British soldier, a prisoner of war, rather than simply valuables or a civilian caught on the wrong side of the conflict. We should have anticipated complications."

"As soon as they had their man, they turned on us," Therese said, tears brimming at her eyes. "They shot your father and our rescued soldier where they stood. It is impossible to know what might have happened if not for the Frenchman who'd made the passage with them. Mary turned to him and shoved Alice into his arms, and then charged the gunman, gripping a knife she had concealed in her skirts. She did succeed in killing your father's killer, but at the cost of her own life."

There was a heavy beat of silence. Nell's grip on Nathaniel's hand was pure steel, and felt, somehow, like protection from the horror hovering in the air.

"The baby lived," she said, her voice thin and hopeful. "Is that what you are saying? Alice Atlas lives?"

Nathaniel held his breath. It was surely too much to hope, too farfetched to believe, and yet, both women were nodding.

"Her name is now Isabelle, for by necessity, she could no

longer be an Atlas. She is quite safe, happy by all accounts, and lives in the Côte d'Azur, raised as a daughter by the man who saved her," Therese explained. "She doesn't know who she is. It would have been unsafe for her to know, and it would have been impossible to bring her home."

"Which isn't to say we didn't try," Zelda said pointedly. "We got a letter from the man, some months later, telling us in a roundabout way what had happened, but when we tried to return to the cove and plan a retrieval ... well ..."

"Your uncle tried to shoot us," Therese provided flatly. "He must have known the truth of Mary's doings at some point, but he had twisted them since her death, become confused. He told us if he ever saw either of us again, he would kill us like we had killed his sister."

"We never knew exactly where Alice had been taken. Neither of us even knew the prisoner's surname," Zelda said, motioning to the book in Nathaniel's hands, "until tonight."

"Isabelle's adoptive father obviously could not be explicit in his missives," Therese explained. "And he had every reason to believe I knew just as much as Mary would have, especially as I had no means to write him back. When we received a letter last spring alerting us to a rather extreme change in circumstances, we knew we had to act."

"Why in the name of God couldn't you just have told us this in London?" Nell demanded, echoing Nathaniel's exact reaction to the portion of this information that he had gotten from Zelda earlier. "We were all in the same room together months ago!"

She answered Nell the same way she had answered Nate.

"Your husband would not have believed me. He never trusted me to begin with, and if I had come out of the wings with wild stories and demands that you speak to Therese or find the portrait or grant me access to the cove, none of those things would ever have happened. I knew it would only take a short while at Meridian before you inevitably discovered much of this story on your own."

Nell did not immediately respond, her little body tense with anger as she glared at her aunt across the room. "We are not pawns for you to move across the chessboard."

"She isn't wrong," Nathaniel said begrudgingly. "I had quite a lot of misinformation, built on a hearty foundation of my own hubris. I would have reacted poorly to being directly confronted with any of this, especially prior to knowing you."

"We had hoped there would be more time," Zelda said, with as much of a tone of apology in her voice as she was capable of mustering beneath her customary crispness. "But events outside of our control forced us to move our plan up exponentially. I will say your surprise elopement did not help matters. The important thing is that I have many mechanisms in the works to retrieve your sister and reveal her identity to her, but we need access to the cove, and we need that ledger."

Nell did not answer on his behalf, instead turning her head up to search his face, her cheeks featuring two spots of bright pink where she wore her outrage.

"We could not simply tell you, dear," Zelda put in impatiently. "With all the other dishonesty at play, it seemed cruel to launch you into marriage with instructions of manipulation. Surely you can see the sense in that. You've always understood the importance of what we do."

It was clear now to Nathaniel in a way it never had been before, why someone like Nell would have become involved with her aunt's cause. She hadn't been motivated by funds nor hungry for prestige. The Silver Leaf Society was, somehow, amidst all the dark doings, ultimately a mission of compassion, not a game of cold espionage.

"Will my sister even wish to come back here?" he asked, breaking from his wife's intent gaze to turn back to the interlopers. "She has spent her whole life believing herself someone else."

"We can't know the answer to that, Mr. Atlas," Therese replied. "We simply believe that, in her place, we'd wish to know the truth."

"Precisely," Zelda agreed. "Which is why we must act now if we are going to act at all, before she can be married."

"Married?" Nell and Nathaniel repeated in a confused unison.

"Well, yes," Therese said with a strained smile. "That's the other matter we must discuss, if you are amenable to moving forward, that is."

Nathaniel sighed, glancing down at his wife for long enough to see her quick nod. Unspoken between them was the same thought: So much for tonight being their final mission with the Silver Leaf Society.

He tossed the ledger across the room, which was caught

deftly by Zelda Smith, whose expression had changed rapidly from weary confession to an anticipatory smile.

"All right, then," he relented. "What's next?"

~

THE SUN HAD ALREADY CRESTED the horizon by the time the Atlases sent their guests back to Dover.

Nell reasoned that they had expected to be awake all night in the first place, though the evening of dancing and laughter she had imagined was a far cry from the reality of what had unfolded around them. It was unquestionably a relief when they returned to their home, free of guests, and shut the door behind them.

They ascended the stairs in silence, their hands linked. If the maids attending the early-morning fires found anything amiss in this appearance of their employers, they did not express it, at least not so far as either could see.

The bedroom looked more welcoming than it ever had with slats of pink and orange dawn light floating through the break in the curtains, landing upon their bed like arrows pointing the way to rest, at long last. Nell removed her spectacles and began to work her way out of the simple dress she'd put on at her aunt's behest, listening to the thump of her husband's shoes hitting the floor and his sigh of relief as he dropped backward onto the pillows.

Nathaniel was as ruffled as she'd ever seen him, with blue smudges beneath his closed eyes and a slackness to his face that one might expect of a man who'd been to hell and back. How was it possible that he was still so beautiful, even like this? She couldn't help but smile, crossing the room to sink onto the bed next to him. She reached up to brush the unruly wave of his hair, which only escaped in these stolen hours, when the confines of careful styling could no longer tame it. She ran the silken tresses through her fingers, remembering the first time she had seen it in its natural state, that morning at the inn, and how impossible it had seemed at the time that she could ever touch him like this, of nothing but her own accord.

She thought perhaps he was asleep, but his lashes fluttered, his eyes opening to settle onto her as she touched him this way.

He turned his head and pressed a kiss into her palm, leaving them both adrift for a moment in this moment of silence and peace. He wrapped his arms around her, pulling her down to his side, and heaved a heavy sigh, knowing that they could never go back to the simplicity of their lives before tonight.

"Eleanor," he said after a moment, stroking his fingers down her back. "I am so, so sorry."

"Nathaniel—" she began, but he shook his head, unwilling to be silenced.

"Everything that has gone wrong has been due to my bull-headedness," he insisted. "I was so certain that I had the right of things and was too proud to admit to you when I began to wonder otherwise. I was afraid of losing you, if you ever found out what my intentions had been at the beginning. I swear to you, I was done with it. Kit will tell you. It was not worth the cost of the future to excavate the past."

"Kit knows?" she asked, tilting her head up to meet his eye.

"Kit knows what I believed to be true," Nate clarified. "He has never agreed with me that we ought to take accusations of espionage and intrigue from Uncle Archie as anything other than one of his many delusions. I suppose we were both wrong."

"He believed me complicit in this distortion of the Silver Leaf Society?" she asked, sounding small and far away, even to herself.

"No," he said immediately. "No. I told him only that I wished to ensure your protection, which led to our marriage, and he did not pry further. Of course, you required no protection at all, nor did you want it. You must have believed yourself at considerable risk, running off, alone with me."

"I could not believe you a killer," she replied, leaning forward into the warmth of his body, allowing the relief to prickle across her skin as he wrapped his arms around her. "But I did not ask, because I did not want to be wrong. I did not want to confront what it would mean to love you anyway, no matter what you had done."

"You never believed it?" he asked, a note of wry disbelief in his voice.

It made her smile, though perhaps it was not a thing most married pairs would consider humorous. "Perhaps at first. I told myself I was protecting Gloriana from you, that I was far more equipped to navigate matrimony with a dangerous man, but that was nonsense. Glory is more than strong and capable, and the truth of the matter was that I had been infatuated with you for months and I wanted you for my own."

"Did you?" he said, sounding utterly surprised, if not a smidgen scandalized. "I had no idea! You certainly never gave the slightest hint of any romantic interest."

"I don't know how one does give that manner of hint." She laughed, burying her blushing face in his chest.

"Do not fret," he said with clear amusement. "I would most certainly have mucked up the opportunity."

"Do you think less of me, now? Knowing I'm nothing more than a scheming debutante who trapped a bachelor into marriage?"

"A bachelor she loved?" Nathaniel prompted, something sheepish in his voice. "I do believe you used that word, just now."

"Did I?" she replied with a smile. "Surely it goes without saying."

"Perhaps, but I would very much enjoy hearing it. Here, I shall go first. I love you, Eleanor. I've been in love with you for quite some time now, without any intent or planning ahead, and it's been one damned surprise after another."

"And here I thought I was utterly predictable," she mused, shaking her head. "Very well, then. To begin with, I would categorize my fascination with you as a fantasy, a limerence. You cannot imagine my joy at discovering the reality to be so much more than what I had imagined. The idea that a future may have existed in which we did not marry is too chilling to rightly consider."

He was silent, smiling down at her with that half-cocked amusement that he'd worn across from her in a carriage, what seemed like a thousand years ago. His eyes glittered with gold and green and brown, a beautiful mirage of ever-changing nature.

"What!" she demanded, her brows drawing together in the beginnings of a pique. "Have I ruined it?"

"I daresay I am even more taken with you than I was a moment ago," he said with a chuckle, holding her tightly against him and dropping a firm kiss onto her head.

They lay like this for a while, quiet and entwined, with no masks nor artifice about them. They were simply Nell and Nathaniel, and that was enough.

"We have a damn gauntlet ahead of us, you know," he said, stroking her hair absently under the pads of his fingers.

"I do not even know where to begin," she confessed, lifting herself up to gaze down at him, her hair tumbling down over her shoulder. "What does one do first when there are so many things to achieve?"

"Well," he said with a half smile, "I rather thought our first order of business would be to hire a locksmith and have this house re-keyed."

She laughed, which made him laugh, and somehow in the next moment, they were kissing, tangled together and painted in sunrise-hued stripes from the light without.

"Do you think we are finished with surprises," she asked, brushing the tip of her nose against his, "at least for a little while?"

"Absolutely not," he chuckled, capturing another kiss as he rolled her onto her back. "I hope you surprise me for the rest of my life, Miss Applegate."

"Nell," she corrected, as she wrapped her arms around him.

EPILOGUE

My dearest brother,

I hope this missive reaches you in good health and positive spirits about the task ahead of you.

I can say with complete honesty that I am envious. You are on the cusp of a grand adventure and a heroic quest while I am contracting the movement of staff and the commission of furniture and all manner of boring nonsense.

Of course, I wouldn't have been able to come with you anyway, and I'm certain you do not want your bothersome sister along for such a thing anyhow. I'm certain the Season will bring its own set of excitements, especially for the wife of such an important man at such an important juncture in Parliamentary history.

I can't rightly travel in my condition anyway, can I? But I digress.

Everything is ready for you at Meridian House. As we left, the first blades of green, green grass had begun to explode through the layers of winter ice, and the fruit trees were soon to bud. Nathaniel has promised that we will one day enjoy all four seasons from our house on the cliff, but this year, I must make do with London.

And so I ask that you keep a little journal of all you see and experience during this mission. It would be a great gift to live through you vicariously, especially as I become more and more limited in my activities.

When you arrive in Kent, seek out Kit Cooper, my cousin through marriage. Kit will be on hand to assist you with everything you require and to tie up any final preparations before you set off across the Channel. I like Kit and am confident you will as well.

I must confess, I was rather amused to find out what Aunt Zelda actually meant when she said she required your sword arm, though I suppose you were less entertained by the deception. I will be sure to tease you for it quite thoroughly when next we meet.

There is much more I would like to say, but I know how you value brevity, so I will attempt to summarize my thoughts whilst they are limited to paper and ink.

I know this was not the future you imagined for me. It was not a future anyone could have predicted (except perhaps Tatiana Everstead). So, allow me to tell you from firsthand experience that life will never go quite as you planned, and it is all the more glorious for its detours. While it is painful to take a sabbatical from your studies, it may shape your life in ways you never could have anticipated.

I love you dearly, Peter, and I will be anxiously awaiting news of your return.

Be brave. Be bold. (But still prudent. Don't get carried away!)

There is no one I trust more with this task than you.

ALL MY LOVE,

Mrs. Eleanor Atlas

AUTHOR'S NOTE

Thank you so much for reading *Unmasking the Silver Heiress*! If you have a moment, please consider leaving me a review on Amazon, Bookbub, or Goodreads. Reviews mean the world to me and can make the all the difference in whether or not a book is successful.

The Silver Leaf Seductions has been a wild ride, so far! I hope you enjoyed watching Nathaniel and Nell fall in love. Keep an eye out in the coming months for the continuing story as Peter Applegate heads into the heart of France to retrieve the long-lost Isabelle.

Unveiling the Counterfeit Bride is coming in the summer of 2020. Stay tuned for updates!

I also love to hear from my readers! If you have feedback, questions, or ever just want to say hi, you can reach me at Ava@AvaDevlin.com

The Unread Letters of *Unmasking the Silver Heiress*

Nell and her network of friends and family exchanged quite a few letters during the events of this book. Check in with Gloriana Blakely, Tatiana Everstead, Heloise Somers, and more in these exclusive bonus letters!

Click Here to claim your FREE bonus

(Or head to AvaDevlin.com/Heiress)

Made in the USA
Middletown, DE
01 March 2023